Lockdown

Also by Sara Driscoll

Lockdown

SARA DRISCOLL

KENSINGTON
PUBLISHING CORP.

www.kensingtonbooks.com

Kensington Books are published by
Kensington Publishing Corp.
900 Third Avenue
New York, New York 10022

All Kensington titles, imprints, and distributed lines are available at special quantity discounts for bulk purchases for sales promotion, premiums, fund-raising, educational, or institutional use.

Special book excerpts or customized printings can also be created to fit specific needs. For details, write or phone the office of the Kensington Sales Manager: Kensington Publishing Corp., 900 Third Avenue, New York, NY 10022. Attn. Sales Department. Phone: 1-800-221-2647.

The K with book logo Reg US Pat. & TM Off.

First Electronic Edition: June 2024
ISBN: 978-1-4967-5187-4 (ebook)

First Kensington Trade Paperback Edition: June 2024
ISBN: 978-1-4967-5188-1

10 9 8 7 6 5 4 3 2 1

Printed in the United States of America

For Jordan

For all the times I "killed" you as my three-dimensional victim and for all the fight scene modeling where you stood in as my female protagonist, thank you for your good-natured role playing and support.

CHAPTER 1

A teenager darted off the sidewalk directly in front of Gemma Capello's car. She shot one hand out to grab the cake holder on the passenger seat a fraction of a second before she hammered the brakes, throwing her upper body sharply against the seat belt as she jammed her precious cargo against the chair back. Filling the air with colorful Italian commentary, she pushed her curly, shoulder-length brown hair away from where it had tumbled into her dark eyes, and then tracked the boy as he sprinted across the street to join the pack of kids waiting for him on the opposite sidewalk. They greeted him with hoots and back slaps before strolling off down the street, secure in their coolness.

Gemma narrowed her eyes on the group. "If you crushed my *cassata* because of your need to impress your friends, I'm *not* going to be happy." A horn blasted behind her, and she tossed up a hand gesture that would have made her brothers proud—angry Brooklynite meet irritated Sicilian—and hit the accelerator.

She glanced quickly at the container. After the long hours she spent putting it together, her cake had better be intact. Today was the twenty-fifth anniversary of her mother's murder, a day already bowing under the weight of grief, even all these years later. There was no need for the universe to add anything negative to it.

Knowing time didn't heal all wounds and today would be full of bad memories, she'd wanted to do something nice for her father, and through him for the rest of the family, because if she knew her brothers—and she did—all four of them would find a reason to drop by the family home today. So she'd spent the entire previous evening making a traditional Sicilian *cassata*, one of her father's favorite desserts.

Liqueur-soaked sponge cake, ricotta, and marzipan… what's not to love?

She'd certainly had a hard time keeping her youngest brother, Alex, out of it. They lived in the same Alphabet City apartment building on the Lower East Side, and he spent much of his free time in her larger and homier unit. The whole time she was baking, he'd been perched at her breakfast bar, chatting, playing with her cat, Mia, and stealing bits of sponge cake while he sipped her liqueur.

He didn't fool her for one moment. While Gemma was worried about her father and how the following day would impact him, Alex was worried about how it would impact her. Because twenty-five years ago, Maria Capello hadn't been the only one standing in line at the bank when everything went to hell; her ten-year-old daughter had been with her. When the robbery had gone wrong and suddenly become a hostage situation, they'd been trapped together. Until Maria had tried to talk the two gunmen into releasing the hostages, including her own daughter, and one of the men had silenced her with a bullet to the brain. Then Gemma, blood-splattered and terrified, had been alone.

It was a nightmare of a day for Gemma as well, but she was determined to stay occupied, which meant taking care of her father. He'd taken the day off knowing he'd be distracted—it was never a good situation when the NYPD Chief of Special Operations wasn't on his game. But spending the day alone was sure to sink him into a funk, so she'd also taken the day and was going to arrive on his doorstep first thing with the proposition of a spontaneous trip to his favorite hole-in-the-wall pub in a few hours for lunch. Later, there would be dinner and cake with the family as they gradually drifted home. It would mean a lot of cooking, but that would also help distract her today.

When the heart hurt, surrounding yourself with family was the best way to make it through.

Sometimes her family drove her crazy; today they would be her refuge.

The second youngest of five, Gemma was the only daughter. Like three of her four siblings and her father, she was an NYPD officer; only Matteo had broken with family tradition and had joined the FDNY. First response was hardwired into them, even if they hadn't all followed Tony Capello straight into the NYPD. Detective Gemma Capello had been on the force for fourteen years and was now one of the lead negotiators on the NYPD Hostage Negotiation Team.

Her early experience with hostage takers hadn't prescribed her career, but it had certainly contributed.

She braked to a stop at the intersection of Beverley Road and Coney Island Avenue and had a few seconds for a closer inspection of the cake carrier, only to relax when no smear of lemon frosting was visible against the side. The light changed, and she continued on her way toward Flatbush and the family homestead.

Tony still lived in the house in Brooklyn that had once held all seven of them. Though "rattling around" the family home might be a more apt description—since she and Alex had moved out years ago, Tony had lived alone in the big house. She'd once brought up the idea of selling and her father had been so definite he wouldn't leave Maria's home, she'd never suggested it again. In many ways, she understood. There were so many memories there, he couldn't bear to leave that tenuous connection to his beloved wife behind. And if Gemma was honest, she'd struggle with it, too. At some point, it would have to happen, but part of her was honestly relieved it was still some distance in the future. Maybe in three years, when her father took mandatory retirement, he'd consider it. Maybe, by then, she'd be ready, too.

Her phone rang through her car, and her gaze flicked to her dash screen. *Alex.* She pressed the button on her steering wheel to accept the call. "I'm not there yet. You know what Brooklyn traffic is like at this time of the morning. Give me another fifteen. Maybe twenty."

"That's not why I'm calling."

The whip-like quality of Alex's words and the intensity in his tone had the hair on the back of her neck rising in alarm. "What's wrong?"

"A school shooting was just reported. Gem, it's South Greenfield."

Fear slid sinuously like ice water through her veins. "That's Sam's school."

"Yes."

The oldest Capello sibling, Joe, had two boys, Sam and Gabriel. Gabe was still in middle school, but Sam was a freshman, only a few months into his high school experience, though this was *not* the experience anyone would have wished for. "*Gesù Cristo.*" Gemma's gaze found the street signs at the approaching intersection, and she calculated her position. "Do we know where he is? Has Joe talked to him?"

"No. It just started. They don't know anything yet."

She gauged the separation of traffic, signaled, and squeezed in between a delivery van and a sedan. The driver of the van audibly let her know in no uncertain terms what he thought of her driving. "I'm close."

"That's why you're my first call."

Alex knew her plans for the day, knew her timing. Knew that while she was off duty, nothing would stop her getting there when family was involved. The badge in her bag was all she needed.

She took a right onto Westminster. "Who reported it?"

"Nine-one-one is being flooded with calls from kids inside the school."

"Even if only a small percentage of students are allowed to have their handset with them during class, that's still a lot of active phones." She hit the gas and shot through the next intersection on the last fraction of a second of a yellow light. "Are they tracking social media?"

"I don't know. They will if they're smart."

"Kids with phones will use every communication strategy they have to get the word out."

"And to share their experience."

"That, too. I'm six or seven minutes out, max. Leave Dad off your call list."

"He's going to be furious to be kept in the dark."

"Then tell him those were my instructions and he can be furious at me. Hopefully he's left the TV off and is lying low today. He'll find out at some point, but hopefully by then we'll have Sam already in hand. I don't like what this would do to his head while it's ongoing."

"What about what it'll do to yours?"

"I walked out of the bank that day. He left something behind."

"So did you."

We all did. "I'll manage. I need to call Joe now and let him know I'll be on-site."

If Alex didn't like her dismissal of his concerns, he let it go. "Keep me in the loop."

"Always." She disconnected and then used voice commands to call Joe, allowing her to keep both hands on the wheel as she muscled through traffic.

Joe picked up as the first ring barely finished. "I can't talk now." His voice was ragged with stress.

"You can talk to me. I'm nearly at South Greenfield."

"What? How?"

"I was on my way to Dad's. Was going to surprise him and spend the day because…"

"Yeah."

"Alex called me and I redirected. I'll find him, Joe."

"You think they're going to let you get close?"

"Do you honestly think they're going to turn away a hostage negotiator after Platte Canyon and Marinette High Schools?" It didn't happen often, but those two shootings had turned into hostage situations taking hours to resolve. While both had ended with the death of the shooter, Gemma didn't mention the student at Platte Canyon High School who'd been gunned down by the hostage taker at the moment law enforcement stormed the room. Joe didn't need to know details, only that she had a place with law enforcement as they tackled this crisis. "They can try. I'll set them straight. You're on your way?"

"Yes. So's Alyssa."

Gemma hit Ditmas Avenue and made the turn to the southwest too fast, flying toward South Greenfield.

In the distance, sirens rose as a mournful wail.

"I may not be able to talk, but text me any details you learn. I'll call as soon as I have him."

"Gem." Joe's voice cracked on the single word, and Gemma's heart went out to him. Straight-shooting, serious Joe, the responsible older brother… the helplessness had to be overwhelming at a moment when he absolutely needed to keep his head. The moment his boy needed him most, and he was across town—might as well have been across planet—and it would likely be over, for better or for worse, before he was even halfway there.

Most school shootings only lasted approximately fifteen minutes. And five of those minutes had already ticked away.

"I can't…" Joe stumbled to a halt. "I need…"

"I know." Gemma understood the impossible mix of emotions he was trying to put into words. She wasn't a mother, but she was an aunt many times over and she loved her nieces and nephews as fiercely as if they were her own. More than that, as a fellow cop, she knew the kind of evil that could manifest in humankind, just as Joe did, and that had to terrify him as much as it did her. "I'll be there for him until you get there. He's ours, Joe." Her tone went to steel. "They can't have him."

"He's ours," he repeated, relief ever so slightly lightening his tone that his family was already closing ranks. "Just… hurry."

"Done. I'll get in touch when I can. Until then, know I'm fighting to get him out." She hung up, white-knuckled the steering wheel, and pressed down harder on the accelerator.

Get there.

CHAPTER 2

Detective Sean Logan swayed on the hard bench as the truck moved through midmorning traffic. The truck lurched abruptly—*another pothole*—and Logan bumped against Detective Scott, their helmets rapping together. Behind his safety glasses, Scott rolled his eyes at Logan before his attention wandered to where Lewis, Perez, and Sims were giving Wilson a hard time about the argument he had with his wife the previous night. Wilson, for his part, sat with his ballistic shield between his knees, his arms folded over the top, looking bored. He'd taken worse from these guys. Hell, he'd given worse.

Another harder jolt and the double benches of officers in the rear of the truck rolled with the motion, the equipment in the narrow open lockers behind them clanking with the sudden movement. Logan gripped the stock of the M4A1 carbine he wore on a single point sling cross-looped around his torso, and settled in for the ride.

It had been a quiet week for the NYPD Apprehension Tactical Team—better known as the A-Team—which, in law enforcement terms, was a good thing. No drug busts, no home invasions to interrupt, no calls for a sniper or an incursion team because some hothead decided if he couldn't have his wife, who'd announced she was taking the kids and leaving, no one could, and they all had to die. With the lull, the team was spending this week executing arrest warrants, and had just finished executing two in the same Brooklyn apartment on brothers who were a part of the local drug trade. The two men had put up only a minimal fight with their partners and children nearby, and were already contained and on their way to the 63rd Precinct.

Restlessness permeated the truck. It wasn't that A-Team officers went out of their way to find dangerous situations; rather, it had to do with the kind of men—and, less often, women—who made their way onto the team. A-Team officers had to be able to react to high stress, life-and-death situations with greater calm, logic, and a leveled-up skill higher than that required for most ordinary NYPD operations. The job often attracted adrenaline junkies, and Logan's teammates were jonesing for a fix. They were cross-trained with a wide variety of skills—including scuba diving, high-angle rope and rigging rescues, and hazardous materials containment. They were ready to meet whatever a situation dealt them.

Now all they needed was the situation.

His last true high-tension case had been the Rikers Island secure facility inmate riot four weeks before, an explosive situation that dragged on for five full days before hostage negotiations broke down and a full tactical response was required. Logan rolled his left shoulder, pleased when there wasn't even a twinge of residual pain from the knife wound he'd received during the incursion. The inmate who'd tried to gain control during the riot had attempted to make one last stand with a 3D-printed switchblade his girlfriend had sneaked in to him past the facility's metal detectors. It was sharp as hell and had caught Logan just at the edge of his Kevlar vest, but the plastic hilt had snapped off, leaving Logan with a painful trip to the ER to fish out the blade.

A sudden burst of static exploded from the radio in the cab, drawing his attention to where one of the team members, Detective McPherson, doubled as a driver and Sergeant Nilsson, the only officer in the truck not in body armor, sat in the passenger seat.

"Command to Truck 51."

Nilsson picked up the handset and raised it to his mouth. "Truck 51."

"Ten-thirty-four reported. Shots fired at South Greenfield High School. Redirect to Bay Parkway and East 2nd Street."

The banter in the rear of the truck instantly died and every head swiveled toward the cab.

McPherson hit the sirens and hammered the accelerator, liberally using his horn as they leapt forward. "Three minutes out," he reported, not taking his eyes off the road.

"Truck 51 responding, ETA three minutes. Command, can you confirm details?"

"Multiple 9-1-1 calls from students. Possible multiple shooters. Local units are responding."

Logan grabbed the end of the bench for stability as they whipped through traffic, his brain already snapped from relaxed to tactical mode.

This is the kind of job that'll get local units killed. We need to get there first.

Active shooter protocols specified that whoever arrived first should confront the gunman. And it wasn't that the patrol cops who'd arrive first weren't well-trained, competent officers. But they weren't trained specifically for this kind of crisis, and they certainly wouldn't be carrying and wearing the gear this kind of situation would likely need.

School shootings could be anything from a spurned kid with a grudge against a girl, to a gang shooting, to a Virginia Tech—like massacre with scores of casualties. But one thing was certain—if they arrived at an active shooter situation, they had one job: run directly toward the gunfire and take the shooter down or out.

This close, they'd hopefully be the first unit to respond, but the NYPD would be sending all available teams at their disposal.

He turned to his officers to find the jocularity of a few minutes ago gone. Instead, flat stares met his.

They were still armed and armored from the arrest warrant they'd just completed. Dressed entirely in black, each officer wore an equipment-packed Kevlar vest, helmet with video cam, radio headset, safety glasses, heavy boots, gloves, and tactical pants with pockets stuffed with anything they might need on the fly. Every officer wore a Glock 19 on his thigh in addition to a rifle on a sling strap.

He doubted any officer in the truck had ever had to deal with a school shooting. New York City had seen a few in its time, but none of the major headline-grabbing nightmares that places like Columbine, Parkland, and Blacksburg had weathered. Hopefully, they weren't walking into that kind of bloodbath, but they had to be prepared for an explosive situation. The worst part of their job was any situation involving kids, and a high school setup could involve up to thousands of teenagers.

They had to be mentally ready for what could be a high body count.

They were possibly about to walk into the worst situation any of them had ever seen, even in careers like his with nearly a decade and a half on the force. His guys had been restless and hoping for something more interesting than yet another arrest warrant, partly because they'd all experienced the high of a dangerous situation pulled off successfully. But success was never guaranteed. And what the NYPD might consider a success—stopping a shooter from killing any more kids from the moment they stepped on-site—didn't preclude the heartbreaking toll taken before they arrived. Or, more likely, the stuff of nightmares and PTSD.

Be careful what you wish for. You might just get it.

CHAPTER 3

East 2nd Street was one way, leading away from South Greenfield, so Gemma turned north off Avenue J. Street parking lined both sides of the road, so she pulled into a spot a half block up. She cut the engine, rooted through her bag to quickly grab her wallet and her badge, and jammed the bag under the passenger seat. In about five minutes, this entire area was going to be crawling with first responders; no one was going to break into her car to steal it. She tucked her wallet into the light, hooded jacket she'd put on that morning to ward off the November chill and clipped her badge onto the waistband of her dark wash jeans. One quick look in her rearview mirror revealed the flash of red and blue lights.

Hang on Sam, we're coming for you.

She thought briefly of texting him, but knew Joe would have already covered that—messages of love as well as a cop's advice on how to stay safe, stay alive. Her job was to join the law enforcement team outside.

She sprinted down the street toward the flashing lights. Beyond, the east wing of South Greenfield stood four stories tall against clear blue sky. As she approached, the rest of the school came into view. Built in the shape of an elongated, shallow *H* with short wings, red brick rose four stories tall, with wide windows running in straight lines across the edifice on every floor. A center walkway led to three sets of double doors spaced between four decorative columns that climbed to a roofline parapet with a turret clock.

Even from a distance, she could see a stream of students running from behind the school and a second pouring through the front doors. As she drew closer, both the deep *boom* of a shotgun and the rapid *crack crack* of a rifle ripped through the air. Students near the central doors screamed and scattered, some running back into the school, some falling to the ground.

Shooting escaping students? Or at cops to keep them away from the doors?

Two white and blue NYPD vehicles, an SUV and a cruiser, were pulled up even with the edge of the east wing. Answering gunfire came from behind the bulk of the SUV where the dark form of a police officer crouched.

Gemma's already rapid heart rate spiked higher. She understood returning fire, but what if the gunman had students with him for cover? Would they be able to see that?

As she neared the street corner, a pack of kids cleared the school property and sprinted farther down the street.

Get clear. Stay clear...

She hit Bay Parkway and brought her sprint down to a crouch, making herself as small a target as possible as she dove for cover behind the cruiser. The cop crouched by the hood of the SUV spun around, his Glock locked in a two-handed grip swinging toward her.

Gemma ripped off her badge and held it out. "Detective Gemma Capello, HNT."

The Glock snapped up to point at the sky. "Goddamn it, I could have killed you, thinking you were another gunman." Sweat beaded at his temples and his hands were visibly shaking. "Are you crazy?"

"Just on the run and trying not to be a target." Gemma glanced at the officer's nameplate—Officer Long. He was young, his blue eyes startled wide, and his lips parted around harsh breaths. He was holding, but she suspected this was the first time he'd come under direct fire and she could sense his fear mixed with dogged determination. "I couldn't afford to announce my presence loud enough that you could hear or else they"—she cocked her head toward the school—"might have also heard and tried to take me out."

"They're sending in HNT? Do we have hostages?"

"Not that I know of, but we could. Wouldn't be the first time in a situation like this, so I'm handy to have around." She clipped her badge back into place. "I'm off duty, but got word of the shooting and headed over because I was nearby." Another two shots and the car shuddered. *Both direct hits.*

The second officer scurried from around the rear of the SUV. It was a woman, likely ten years older than Officer Long, one with steady hands and a demeanor to match as her gaze dipped down to the badge visible at Gemma's waistband. "They're keeping us out."

"I thought I heard two weapons. Is that correct, Officer...?"

"Tessel. There's at least two. They're shooting from the third floor from more than one direction to keep us pinned down."

"If they've done any prep for this, they'll know active shooter protocol requires us to run toward any gunfire. They'll try to limit that," Gemma stated. "On the bright side, while they're pinning us down, they're not killing any students and may be giving them time to escape if they didn't shelter inside a locked classroom. I heard a shotgun and a rifle, both of which would easily cover this distance. And the shotgun would be useful if they have to shoot through barricaded doors." Gemma carefully eased up until she could peer through the window to the front walk. Her gaze skimmed over motionless bodies. "There are several people down and immobile in front of the school. A lot of kids ran back inside. There's a group of students and a teacher lined up against the outside wall. They know they're out of line of sight from the shooters above but are in full sight of us, so we can get to them when possible. They're safe for now." She scanned over the expanse of grass fronting the building, past one splayed body, and then snapped back as she registered a minute movement. "Wait! Someone's dragging themselves away from the school over the grass. They must be injured, but I can't tell how badly."

"How far away?" asked Long.

"About thirty feet. They're headed toward us because they can see the police presence, but if the shooters spot them, they're dead for sure. We can't just sit here and watch it happen." She glanced at the two officers. "Got a spare vest?"

"In the back of the SUV," said Tessel.

"Grab it for me. Then if you both lay down cover, I'll go for that student. I can get there and back inside of about twenty seconds. Thirty max. Try to keep the shooters busy that long."

"That's a lot of ground to cover. A lot of time to be an open target."

"I don't see any other choice. As a bonus, we're buying time for anyone inside."

Buying time for Sam.

Tessel went in through the rear door of the SUV and was out again with an extra Kevlar vest in seconds. She tossed it to Gemma, who shrugged it on and quickly secured it over her jacket.

Gemma crept to the front of the sedan, waiting just behind the tire. She looked back over her shoulder. "Ready when you are. Aim high in case the shooters are using hostages as shields."

"You got it."

As the first gun sounded behind her, Gemma burst from behind the hood of the car. She leapt over the curb and sprinted across the grass.

She shut everything else out—the noise of gunfire, the students pressed against the wall, the throb of her heart hammering—and narrowed her focus down to the form in the grass. She could see now it was a girl with an auburn ponytail, dressed in jeans, sneakers, and a bloodstained hoodie. Gemma knew to never move an injured victim until they could be assessed for spinal injuries, but there simply was no time. It was move her or lose her to a gunman's bullet.

Fifteen feet... ten feet... closing fast.

"Detective Gemma Capello, NYPD." Gemma's words shot out, rapid-fire. "I'm taking you to safety."

The green eyes that rose to hers were terrified, the girl's face deadly pale, but she immediately pushed off the ground and onto her hands and knees.

Gemma grabbed her by one arm and helped her as she staggered to her feet, a cry of agony ripping from her. Gemma pulled the girl's left arm over her shoulders, gripping it with her left hand, and wrapped her right arm around the girl's torso. The palm of her hand met with saturated cloth, but she gripped the girl as tight as she could and jogged her toward the cars.

Bullets screamed past, battering the school, but she didn't hear any return fire.

Driven to ground for now. Good.

With a gasp, the girl buckled, nearly going to her knees and taking Gemma with her. Gemma stumbled, bore down with a groan from deep in her chest, and dragged them both up. "A little farther," she ground out between clenched teeth as she more carried than led the injured girl. "Almost there…"

They cleared the hood of the car and then Gemma dropped down to her knees, bracing the girl between her body and the car. "Clear!" she called between gunshots, and both officers pulled back. Gemma turned her attention to the girl. No, not a girl, now that she had the time to really look. This was a young woman, possibly a senior. "Where are you hurt?"

For a moment, the young woman couldn't answer and simply hung on to Gemma, her fingers digging into Gemma's shoulders as she panted. Tremors vibrated through her body, broken occasionally by deep shudders that rung whimpers from her throat. "Hip." The word came out on a gasp. "Knocked me d-d-down. Didn't… didn't want to be a…" Another ragged breath trailed off into a half-moan. "Sitting duck." She looked up to Gemma, her eyes terrified and haunted. Pain dug harsh lines into her pale complexion, and a single tear rolled down her cheek.

"Let's get you on the ground." As gently as she could, taking as much of the student's weight as possible, Gemma helped the girl lower to the asphalt, her back against the cruiser. "Good… that's good. You're safe here, protected by the car." Gemma kept her hands on the girl's shoulders until she slumped, exhausted, her head bent and her breathing ragged. "EMTs are coming and will take care of you. I need to go help other students now."

The girl's head bobbed in understanding, but stayed bowed.

Gemma looked toward the two officers. So far, it was only the three of them. And active shooter protocol said that at least one of them needed to go in. Probably all of them. Now.

She looked down at the blood that covered her palm and soaked into the sleeve of her jacket. She shrugged and wiped her palm as clean as she could on the material of the side panel. She had a feeling she'd never want to wear the jacket after today anyway.

Her head whipped up at the sound of tires squealing as three more patrol cars converged on the site from the far end of the street. But it was the large, black, armored NYPD van, moving fast as it pulled onto Bay Parkway a few blocks away, that filled her with hope.

The A-Team.

Some days the force's tactical squad made her life beyond difficult.

Today was not going to be one of those days.

Help had arrived.

CHAPTER 4

Leaning forward on the bench with his boots braced as his body swayed with each bump, Logan took in as many details as he could. They were coming in hot, though silent, the sirens killed two blocks back to catch an edge of advantage by not announcing their presence to the shooters. Through the windshield, houses whipped by on both sides of the road, while farther ahead the red-brick, multistory bulk of a school grew larger. He tuned out the radio chatter between command and Nilsson; he'd already missed much of the communication while the siren wailed, and he knew his sergeant would distill the information down to what they needed to know in a matter of seconds. In the meantime, he concentrated on noting as much information about the site as he could to help form the offensive strategy.

Four stories. Brick construction. Single front walkway leading to a triple entryway on the north side. Double door entrance, east side. Two NYPD cruisers on scene. Officers sheltering behind. Possibly pinned down.

Lights flashed from the far end of the street as several cruisers roared toward them. More officers, but they were the only tactical unit so far.

Multiple teams meant the ability to breach in multiple locations simultaneously to surround and overwhelm the gunmen. More were on the way, but this unit wouldn't have the luxury of waiting for others to arrive. They would engage the shooters and hope for strength in numbers as soon as possible.

"Two officers on-site so far," Nilsson called, half-turned in his seat to keep one eye on their progress and one on his officers. "They're unable to enter. Multiple shooters on the upper floors keep them pinned down behind their cruisers. Several persons down on the front walk and grass, status unknown. Active shooters means we need to move. Two teams, Logan and Sims commanding. Use ballistic shields to get to the front door, one per team, then enter the school. Priority one is getting to the shooters. We'll help the students after, but we need to contain this now. Understood?"

"Yes, sir." It was a unison response from every officer.

A quick glance at the windshield showed them closing fast on the NYPD SUV. Movement by the school drew Logan's gaze, and, just before she was blocked by the side of the truck, he caught sight of a middle-aged woman running past a group of students pressed against the wall of the school. She ran toward the eastern wing, her eyes locked on their vehicle. *A teacher? Or principal? Circling around to them?*

Any intel they could receive before entering would increase their chances of success and would be worth a slight delay to avoid going in blind. It could, in fact, save them time in the end.

The van jerked to a stop and the two men at the rear of the team compartment threw open the doors. Officers jumped out in a continuous stream and formed their lines in the lee of the armored van, protected from any shooter's sight line. Logan jumped down to land on asphalt, one hand holding the pistol grip of his rifle to steady the weapon. He did a rapid check of his equipment—helmet level, chin strap tight, safety glasses snug, Glock 19 securely strapped to his right thigh, vest pulled down into place, extra magazines securely tucked into the front pocket. He adjusted the narrow boom mic that curved around his cheek to sit directly in front of his mouth for radio communications with the sergeant while deployed.

Ready.

His teammates were ready as well, with two detectives holding ballistic shields—long, rectangular steel panels with rounded corners and a clear strip of bulletproof glass for the user to see through. An active shooter situation, versus one with a passive shooter, meant they had to engage immediately to save lives. And that meant running directly into the line of fire. But, unlike the students currently facing a life-or-death situation, they had the training, equipment, and experience to come out of this type of situation alive.

For now, all was quiet, and no sounds of gunshots came from the school. Logan was confident it wouldn't last, but the sight of the A-Team van pulling up to the school may have given the shooters pause, as it became clear they were no longer the superior firepower.

Whatever the reason, the pause in the action gave him and his team a moment to prepare.

The only member of the team not already suited up for action, Nilsson jumped out of the truck dressed in his navy NYPD uniform, his pale blond hair catching the bright sunlight. He carried his Kevlar vest and helmet tucked under his arm. As the sergeant on an arrest warrant run, he stayed outside and coordinated while the teams went in; he would continue that role here as incident commander until a more senior officer arrived. "There's a lot of conflicting information coming in. I'll update on the fly, but we're looking at multiple shooters, possibly up to four or five. Possible additional snipers." As he talked, he donned his protective gear. "All calls report male shooters, white. Appearances vary—light hair and dark, different colored shirts, camo and black fatigues. Could be carrying a rifle or shotgun."

Logan absorbed the information but knew early situation reports were almost always chaotic. The hormones and neurotransmitters released during a terrifying incident actually impeded memory formation and, even immediately after an event, two people describing the same incident would have different recollections.

He hoped that was reality, because a situation with five shooters plus snipers was more than one team could manage.

The A-Team officers at the far end of the line shifted, and the sound of voices rose as uniformed cops pushed their way through—a man and a woman—followed by another woman wearing a Kevlar vest over dark jeans and a tan jacket, who was craning her neck to look behind her. Logan studied the last person coming through the group since they'd been told only two officers were on scene.

The woman turned to face forward, and recognition jolted.

Gem?

Logan had gone through the academy with Gemma Capello, and they had a history that ran the spectrum: from hot—that single night years ago in his bed he couldn't quite shake—to cold—when she froze him out after he killed the hostage taker she was trying to contain, because he didn't see any other way to save her brother's life—until the last case they'd worked together when they'd called a truce and met in the middle. He hadn't worked a case with her since the standoff at Rikers. With the exception of that moment a few weeks ago when he'd bumped into her at 1 Police Plaza, he hadn't had time to have a real conversation with her since that last early morning when she'd driven him home from the ER following his treatment for the stab wound he'd received during the inmate takedown. He'd been meaning to reach out, meaning to make sure the tentative connection they were rebuilding stayed vital, but time kept getting away from him.

Why is she here? Are there hostages we don't know about?

Sims clearly made the same connection. "Detective Capello? HNT's been called in?"

Gemma scanned the group of A-Team officers, giving Logan a short nod of acknowledgment before moving on. "Detective Sims. No, I was nearby when my brother Alex called me." Her gaze flicked back to Logan's. "Our nephew attends this school, so I came to help. I knew you'd be shorthanded at the beginning and I can help with student intel once we have a command center set up. And I'll be on-site in case the situation changes and you need HNT." She glanced toward the NYPD vehicles again as she rapidly outlined the situation. "We have one student with a gunshot wound sitting behind the cruiser. We pulled her off the front lawn." She held out her stained right hand, revealing her blood-soaked sleeve. "Hit in the hip, and needs medical care as soon as EMTs arrive, but she's stable on the short term."

"EMTs are on their way," Nilsson said.

"Who's that?"

Sims's question interrupting Nilsson had Logan following his gaze across the street at the far end of the building. The same woman he'd noticed a minute earlier was still on the move, sprinting as fast as the knee-high leather boots she wore paired with a navy shirt and white blouse would allow.

"I noticed her when we pulled up," said Logan. "Standing against the front wall of the school with a bunch of students, out of line of sight of an overhead shooter. As soon as she saw our truck, she ran along the wall toward the wing. I lost sight of her, but I think she's running a wide circle to get to us."

"Trying to stay out of the range of a bullet."

"Gutsy move. Stupid move, too, depending on which weapons we're looking at because she may still be in range." Nilsson tracked her progress, his gaze following her as she hit the intersection and pelted straight toward them.

"If she doesn't know guns, she may have no idea. She's moving fast." The school was blocked from Logan's view, but he could picture the geometry of the shot and the calculations required to hit a target in a dead run. "It's a shot any of us could make, but an amateur shooter high on adrenaline during a rampage? Doubtful." The woman was only thirty feet away now and closing fast. "Definitely gutsy." He stepped forward as the woman closed on them and held out his hands to catch her as she tried to brake from a sprint to a standstill in under five feet. She nearly slammed into him and he grasped her forearms to steady her.

Her face was sheet-white, except for two spots of color high on her cheekbones from her exertion. Her wide blue eyes darted from Logan to Sims to Nilsson to the men and women behind them. "Who's…" She had to pause to pant in a breath. "Who's in charge?"

"Me. I'm Sergeant Nilsson." He pulled her in closer to the truck to ensure she was shielded in case the shooting started again. "Tell us what you know."

The woman pulled in a ragged breath, but didn't pause. "Caroline Wallace. Was teaching one of my senior English classes when I heard music. We had one of the front windows cracked for some air and the last thing I expected to hear was Bon Jovi's 'Blaze of Glory.' When I looked out, there were two boys I didn't recognize coming up the front walk. Normally, fifteen minutes into class, the front of the school is pretty quiet, so it was unusual."

Logan exchanged a stony look with Sims. *I'm goin' down in a blaze of glory…* If that song was meant to be a message about a last stand, they were walking into a situation that was beyond dangerous.

"And the dusters also caught my attention," the teacher continued.

"Dusters?" Nilsson asked.

"Dusters. Trench coats. They both wore them. Long and black."

Logan swore quietly under his breath, a sentiment echoed by several other A-Team members.

Every tactical officer knew the details of Columbine: how in 1999, two boys had planned to bomb their high school cafeteria, hoping to kill hundreds, and then stand at right angles to each other out in the parking lot with a rifle and shotgun to mow down any students who tried to escape the bomb and subsequent fire. Many people knew about Columbine, but fewer knew the attack was actually a failed bombing and not a successful mass shooting. When the bombs didn't go off, the boys moved to plan B, entered the school wearing trench coats, and started shooting students and teachers. Twelve innocent students and one teacher died that day.

Two boys had entered the school today wearing trench coats.

That day in 1999, officers from Jefferson County had set up a perimeter around the school, not actually entering the building until after the two shooters had taken their own lives. In fact, the boys had been dead for over three hours before their bodies were discovered. The failure at Columbine was the catalyst for the development of modern active shooter protocols. But it was notorious in more ways than one, and, horrifically, a group of people who called themselves "Columbiners" revered the two boys, considering them outcasts who rose up to take on their oppressors. Their methods were studied and used as a template by those planning a similar assault.

If the music was bad, the trench coats were worse.

"Can you give us anything else on the boys?" Nilsson pressed.

Caroline closed her eyes as if willing an image of the boys to appear. She kept her eyes closed as she talked. "One had dark hair, one light. They looked tall, not basketball player tall, but senior tall. I doubt they were freshmen. The breeze blew one of their coats open and I thought I saw something long and black under the coat. But it was so fast and he was wearing dark pants, so I doubted what I saw until about twenty seconds later, when we heard the first shots. Then I knew, even before the announcement came over the PA system, that we were in hard lockdown."

Hard lockdown—Department of Education speak for students in imminent danger. A situation where every adult and student knew to get to a classroom and shelter in place.

"You never saw clearly exposed weapons?"

She opened her eyes. "No. Just that single hint, which didn't mean anything to me at the time." She shrugged. "I'm not a gun person."

"It's still useful intel. The trench coats are bad symbolically, but could also be good news," Logan said.

Caroline stared at him in horror. "Good news?"

"It's all relative. There are reports of four or five gunmen. But clothing changes can create an additional reported gunman. One gunman is described wearing a coat; a second doesn't have one. It could be the same guy, just missing the coat." Logan looked at Nilsson. "My take—they needed the coats to hide their weapons, then ditched them for freedom of movement as soon as they got inside. We have positive confirmation of two suspects; that may be it."

"We may have multiple entry points," said Turner. The only woman on this unit, Casey Turner made a point of contributing to every conversation, as if reinforcing her place on the team. Some guys might doubt it, but Logan didn't. Turner had proved herself time and again in his eyes. "In which case, there may really be four or five gunmen."

"Everything is on the table until we know otherwise," Nilsson said. "Anything else you can tell us?"

"They entered the school through the front foyer." Caroline's voice was steadier now as she settled into her story and caught her breath. "That's where they started shooting. We heard running and screaming, so I closed the door and had the kids go into lockdown mode. We turned off the lights and pushed my desk and a filing cabinet in front of the door and hunkered down."

"How did you get out?"

"While we were barricading the door, a couple of the boys got the bright idea to see if they could kick the air conditioning unit out of the window. Our windows are security-sealed with metal mesh, except for that one spot. They pulled desks over, lay back on them, and horse-kicked the unit until it toppled out onto the grass below. That gave us a single window section to squeeze through." She ran her hands over her hips. "I probably had the hardest time getting through, but every one of us made it. As soon as we were all out and about to make a run for it, they started shooting from above us, so we huddled against the wall until I saw you drive up."

"One other thing will help us—what's the population of the school?"

"More than four thousand students, which is why I didn't think much of two boys who were unfamiliar to me. There are so many kids. And one hundred fifty-seven teachers on top of that. Usually another five or six admin staff in the office."

Nilsson turned to his officers. "You're ready?"

"Affirmative," Sims said.

"Affirmative," Logan echoed.

As if to twist the knife a little further, shots sounded from deep inside the school.

Shotgun.

"Time to move. We'll lay down cover to get you to the front door in case they're still at the windows." Nilsson rounded on Gemma. "You carrying?"

Gemma shook her head. "I'm officially off duty."

"Wilson, get Detective Capello a Glock."

"Yes, sir." Wilson skirted the group and climbed into the van.

"I want you moving in thirty seconds. Comms check."

Logan adjusted his headphones more securely into place and nodded. "Nilsson to Unit 1."

Nilsson's words came in loud and clear through Logan's headset. "Unit 1, check."

"Nilsson to Unit 2."

"Unit 2, check," Sims replied.

Wilson jumped out of the van and handed Gemma a Glock 19 in a thigh holster like the A-Team officers wore and three extra magazines. He jogged back into place as she strapped on the holster and slid the magazines into her jacket pocket below the line of her vest.

Logan and Sims fell into place directly behind an officer holding a ballistic shield in one hand and his Glock in the other. Except for that first man in each unit, all other officers held their rifles at the ready.

"Capello, you and your officers space yourselves out behind both the cruiser and SUV so we can spread out the coverage," Nilsson commanded. "I'll stay down at this end."

"Yes, sir. Long, Tessel, with me." The officers followed Gemma as she wound through the two lines of A-Team members. They slipped quickly between the van and the SUV and then spread out between the SUV and the cruiser. Gemma crouched next to a red-haired girl with bloody clothes. She pulled the Glock from its holster, gripping it in both hands, her right index finger lying along the trigger guard, looked back, and nodded. They were ready.

Nilsson took up a position near the right passenger door of the van. He gave his officers one last check before turning toward the school. "Go, go, go!"

Nilsson, Long, Tessel, and Gemma fired toward the school, their gunshots a simultaneous explosion of sound.

The A-Team units ran for the front walk.

CHAPTER 5

Logan jogged up the front walk in a half crouch, the stock of his M4A1 carbine pressed tight to his right shoulder, his gloved hands locked around the barrel and pistol grip, with his ungloved index finger lying along the trigger guard, ready to move instantly to an active shooting position. The teams ran in a modified snake formation behind Redding and Wilson and their ballistic shields. Each front man had two gunners who ran side by side behind them, their rifles just outside the ballistic shield so both could set up a shot if needed and could also take cover. The remaining three officers on each team ran behind them in a line.

Logan took the Unit 1 right gunner position behind Redding with Lewis—conveniently a left-handed shooter—beside him. If needed, Logan could shoot left-handed to fill that role, but even with extensive practice, being right-eye dominant, he would always shoot better right-handed. Turner, Lin, and Perez filled out the rest of his team.

Crack! Crack, crack! The covering gunfire ricocheted off the outer wall, accompanying the snap of brick crumbling around the force of penetrating bullets. They wouldn't pierce through to the other side, but it would be enough to keep any shooter from appearing in the windows to return fire.

They moved fast, but even so, Logan took in the building as they approached, knowing sometimes little details could make the difference between life and death.

Red and blue lights flashing off the front windows dull on the first and second floors. Reflects off third and fourth floors. All the lower floor windows are meshed for security. If kids are going to jump, it'll only be from above. Anyone on the first and second floor is trapped in their room unless they figure out the workaround those kids did. Older building, limited entrances. Only three sets of double doors on the street side.

As they jogged toward the front steps, Logan gave the still form lying at the edge of the pavement a single rapid glance, taking in everything he needed to see in that fraction of a second. *Teenage boy. Headshot.* The tactical officer clinically noted the spreading puddle of blood and the catastrophic damage the bullet had caused, while the man couldn't keep himself from registering the marks of the teenager he'd once been himself—the sprinkle of acne, the concert T-shirt from a band that spoke to him personally, and the shoes costing him two weeks' pay he'd willingly laid down to impress the girl two rows over in chemistry class. An investment that would now never come to fruition.

Logan turned away, bearing down on the fury that rose in a red mist to cloud his judgment like bullet spray. *Not now.*

There was no help for the boy, and he had to stay focused to keep other students from also becoming victims. There'd be time for rage afterward.

The two teams separated at the front doors, Logan's team taking the left set of doors, Sims's team taking the middle. Each officer with a shield halted far enough away to allow the right-hand door to swing open. Behind Logan, Turner ran forward, grasping the door handle as Logan and Lewis aimed their rifles at the entryway in case anyone stood on the other side once the door was open.

"On my mark!" Logan called. "One, two, *mark!*"

Turner wrenched the door open while, in the next doorway over, Douglas did the same. Keeping both eyes open to maintain an extended field of view, Logan stared down the sight, his attention locked on the red laser dot of his target as the space beyond the door was revealed. Screams met them as a group of about twenty-five students froze, ducked, or bolted backward at the sight of weapons pointed at them. The terror was clear in their eyes—trapped in place by gunshots inside the school, more out front driving them back in, and now facing a dozen weapons.

"NYPD!" Logan called. "Coming in."

"You're clear." A male voice rose from behind the students huddled near the door. A man in a navy suit jacket with a navy and charcoal patterned tie pushed through the kids. He was tall and slender, his sandy hair thinning, his face pale, and his hands bloody. "They passed through here and went up the steps to the second floor. I could hear them from the office. I'm Principal Baker. They…" For the first time, he stumbled, then he gathered himself and bore down. "They killed Officer Kail. He was the only person in the foyer when they came in because classes were underway."

As if following an unspoken order, the students behind him moved aside to reveal a man sprawled on the ground in the middle of the foyer. Even from this distance, Logan recognized the patch sewn onto the shoulder of his French blue, long-sleeved uniform shirt. It was identical to the patch he wore himself, with the exception that above *Police Department, City of New York* were the words *School Safety.* It was the school resource officer, the man tasked with protecting the students inside South Greenfield High School.

The shooters had taken him out first to allow them free access to the building and its occupants.

The A-Team officers were standing in a large open foyer. Directly in front of them, a staircase easily twenty feet wide rose to the second floor. To the right of the stairway was a wooden door with *OFFICE* stenciled in large black letters on the frosted glass window. Twin opposing hallways stretched left and right from the center of the foyer.

Sims's gaze flicked from the downed man to Baker. "You're sure he's gone?"

"Yes."

Sims nodded and turned away. Though it might seem cold to outside eyes, the A-Team was familiar with the concept of a battlefield mentality: save as many as you can, then return for the injured and the dead.

This one was already lost.

Logan stepped forward, rapidly scanning the body. The man lay face up, three gunshot wounds tearing open ferocious injuries, drenching his shirt with blood. He wore a heavy utility belt, still weighed down with multiple pouches and components, except the holster at his hip was empty. Near the body, at the bottom of the stairs, lay a tangled pile of black fabric. "Trench coats are here. SRO's handgun is gone. Another weapon's in play."

"Added it to their arsenal," Sims said. "The coats are confirmation the multiple shooters could be the same two boys with and without their coats."

Logan could see how they'd made their entrance, striding up the front walk, blasting their bravado for all the world to hear. They'd taken out the school resource officer as they'd come through the door, blowing him backward off his feet, killing him instantly. Those had been the shots that drove Caroline Wallace and her class into lockdown. Then they'd ditched their coats and continued up the stairs.

More muffled gunshots echoed through the hallways. Not on this floor, but how far up?

They had to move now—every second wasted could be someone gone—but getting their bearings now could save minutes and lives later. Tension crawling up the back of his neck as body and brain battled over the need to strategize versus the need to act, Logan turned to Baker. "We need the layout of the school. Exits. Stairwells. Student areas. *Quickly.*"

"The school is a long *H* with a block around the main entrance front and back." Baker's words matched Logan's rushed cadence. "Center staircase to second floor. From there up, two central staircases on either side of the main block on the back side to the third and fourth floor. In the middle of each end wing on the far side, there's a central staircase leading to the ground floor and double external doors. Ground floor doors here, two sets through the gym directly behind us, two more through the cafeteria beside that. Doors from the gym and cafeteria lead directly outside."

Older construction, grandfathered, not up to current code. Not enough staircases. Not enough exits. Steel mesh on the first and second floor to keep vandals out, but traps students in.

"We're driving the shooters away from the front windows, but we can't chance they aren't there and out of sight. As long as there's no shooting, stay here. Officers will assist you shortly. If you have to go outside, stay against the school and under the windows until we know where they are." Logan met Baker's eyes. "We can't spare any officers to assist you."

"We'll be fine. I have this bunch."

Logan turned to Sims. "Center staircase together. Then we'll decide from there if we split up." He activated his mic. "Unit 1 to Nilsson. We have Principal Baker and approximately twenty-five students in the foyer inside the main doors. They require assistance to exit the building. Officer Kail, the school resource officer, is deceased by GSW. His service weapon is missing. We're going upstairs to intercept active shooters. Send in subsequent units for floor-by-floor sweep starting on the ground floor."

"Copy Unit 1. Newest reports indicate shooters on three and four. Shooter on three, white male, dark hair, green fatigues, black T-shirt. Carrying a semiautomatic rifle. Magazines to reload in cargo pockets of the fatigues. Shooter on four, white male, light hair, black jeans, black hoodie, wearing a waist pouch at his hip. That one has a shotgun."

"We'll split up and cover floors three and four. Ten-four." Logan tapped his mic off.

"Good luck, officers. Be safe." Extending both arms, Baker crowded students back a pace as Redding and Wilson led the two lines forward at a jog, across the foyer and up the wide central staircase.

Logan sent a brief look beyond the staircase to two sets of closed doors marked *GYMNASIUM* and a sign beside the leftmost doors with an arrow marked *CAFETERIA* pointing farther east. Two large rooms that at certain times of the day held masses of students and could have led to a high kill count. Yet the shooters had walked right past without checking, likely because of multiple escape routes in those locations. Instead, they'd headed for the upper floors, where there was limited access to staircases and a possibly deadly drop from any open window.

Not an impetuous rage killing. These boys have this planned out.

Rifles braced and sweeping the outer boundaries, the two teams ran up the outer edges of the staircase. At the top, Redding and Wilson eased out, peering through the narrow window at the top of the shield.

"East hallway, two down," Redding said. "A large blood smear outside of the second doorway on the right. Looks like someone went down in the doorway and got pulled in."

"West hallway, one student down," Wilson reported. "Otherwise empty."

More shots echoed, closer this time, but not with the clarity that said the shooters were on this floor.

"Unit 2, take the third floor," Logan ordered. "We'll take the fourth."

Sims nodded. "Unit 2, southwest staircase."

The two teams moved simultaneously, splitting away from each other to jog toward a staircase visible through the wired-glass door and the floor-to-ceiling window beside it. Now on flat ground, the last officer in each unit turned backward, watching the team's six as they moved across the floor. Just because the shots came from above didn't mean there wasn't another shooter looking to come up behind them. They needed to be ready for anything.

Logan glanced at the bodies as they moved past. Two girls lay facedown, shot in the back.

Trying to escape. Weren't a threat.

He turned away. He already knew what they were dealing with; he didn't need to torture himself with more kids he couldn't help. He needed to stay focused on those he could.

The glass entryway of the staircase at least showed their path was clear. Redding waited while Lewis pushed the door open for him, then went through and up. More gunfire, but now the sounds echoed differently.

Shots fired on both the third and fourth floors.

They ran up the stairs, pausing as they rounded the landing leading to the third floor, but the hallway beyond the glass was empty. They jogged past the third floor—the hallway empty opposite the stairwell—and headed for the fourth.

Nilsson's words came back to Logan: *Shooter on four, white male, light hair, black jeans, black hoodie, wearing a waist pouch at his hip. That one has a shotgun.*

He could give up, or they'd be forced to take him out. Either way, they were going to stop this.

Now.

CHAPTER 6

"Hold!"

Gemma pulled back from where she peeked over the top of the hood of the cruiser, lowering the Glock she gripped in both hands. Under cover, she looked toward the rear of the A-Team van where Nilsson was now visible. "They're clear?" she called.

"Affirmative. Come back."

Sirens in the distance, growing in volume and direction, told of yet more incoming forces.

Gemma scurried along the cruiser and SUV to the van and was joined by the other officers as three more cruisers pulled up. "What's next?"

"I need to stay in contact with my teams, but Detective Marlo has a suggestion. See if you can make it work." Nilsson turned away as he raised his radio to his lips. "Nilsson to Unit 1. Update."

Gemma turned to Marlo, who must have arrived in one of the incoming waves of officers. The detective carried the air of a senior investigator who'd seen it all—or thought he had until he came to work today. Tall and leaning toward portliness, he wore a green-speckled tie with the NYPD standard dark suit and white shirt. "I'm Detective Capello. What's your idea?"

Marlo pointed toward the school, his index finger drawing a lateral line as he talked. "There are kids along the front wall of the school we need to get to safety. And reports of more in the foyer with no protection, but who don't dare leave the building for fear of sniping. We need to get them out of there."

"Agreed. What do you have in mind?"

Marlo dropped his hand to the floor of the van. "We could use the armored van for cover. Drive it up to the school, get as close as possible and load the kids in and drive them out. Any of you driven a vehicle of this size?"

Gemma shook her head as did Long and Tessel.

"Me neither. And now's not the time to learn."

Another A-Team van roared down East 3rd Street and pulled to the side of the road. The rear doors slammed open and officers poured out.

"Hang on. That may be our ticket." Marlo jogged across the road, meeting the van commander, and the two of them stepped behind the cover of the van. They were too far away to be targets except by the most expert of marksmen in a controlled environment, but defensive thinking was second nature from their training.

Assume everyone and everything was a risk. Definitely the mindset for today.

More sirens, more lights. NYPD vehicles were flooding in from all sides. No one bothered to keep their approach quiet at this point, now that the shooters knew the NYPD was on-site.

Gemma glanced at her watch. Logan, Sims, and their teams had been in for a full four minutes by now, and the faint echo of gunfire could still be heard. But was it from the A-Team or the shooters?

"Capello!"

Gemma spotted Marlo waving her over. She ran across the road to find him standing with another A-Team officer, a man whose height and ramrod stiff posture she instantly recognized, even with his military haircut hidden from sight under his helmet—Lieutenant Sanders. For once Gemma was happy to see Sanders, who had the reputation as a bit of a shoot-first-ask-questions-later kind of guy. During a hostage situation, that went against everything Gemma was trying to accomplish. Right now, while her nephew was possibly trapped inside the school with a gunman and there was no hostage taker to reason with, Gemma could appreciate Sanders's typical level of aggression. "Do we have a plan?"

"Yes." Sanders answered before Marlo even opened his mouth to respond. "We'll load up again with all of us in the back, including you and Marlo. Kerns will drive us up to the front door since Sims and Logan reported it's a safe site. We'll unload at the steps out of the sight line of any shooter above or to either side. You and Marlo will load the students. Me and my team will head upstairs to back up whichever team is facing the more active shooter. Two more teams of my guys are nearly here. One can head upstairs while the other can clear the ground floor, checking for shooters and evacuating students. We don't know if we've contained all the shooters at this point, but we need to determine a safe exit route to evacuate students quickly and safely. We'll make sure that path exists or we'll pin down any shooter we encounter. Let's move!"

While Sanders returned to the passenger seat beside Detective Kerns, Gemma and Marlo climbed into the back with the A-Team officers. Gemma stood between the seated men, holding on to one of the steel railings installed along the roof of the van, peering out through the windshield. Kerns deftly took them in front of the school, turned in the street until they were almost perpendicular in the road, then reversed, popping them over the curb and up the sidewalk to stop just short of the front steps. Gemma noticed Kerns kept to the west side of the front walk, carefully avoiding the body on the east side.

They pushed open the doors as soon as the van braked and officers jumped out, the bunker team immediately forming up with the rest of the men behind them.

Ahead of them, one of the front doors opened, and a middle-aged man in a jacket and tie leaned out. "The front foyer is clear. It's safe to come in."

"Go!" Sanders commanded, jumping out, and the A-Team officers flowed through the door as students jostled out of their way.

Gemma jumped out and lowered the step for the van before running for the front doors. She yanked the door open to find herself face-to-face with the same man. "Get the kids into the van. We're going to get you out of here safely."

The man turned to the students. "Guys, the NYPD wants you in the van. No panicking. Do it fast and orderly." He turned back to Gemma. "Principal Baker. Thank you for coming for us."

"Detective Capello. You too, sir. In you go."

"Not as long as there are kids still here. I go last."

Gemma recognized the rock-solid determination and the sense of responsibility. These were his kids and he wasn't going to abandon any of them to save himself, and she'd only waste her time trying to convince him.

Marlo stood by the steps, ushering kids in, while Kerns packed them in as tight as he could from inside.

Gemma scanned each student's face as they ran past, watching for that familiar mop of dark brown curls, and the warm brown eyes so much like his father's. So much like her own. And even though she knew the chances of finding Sam here at the front door were close to zero, some of the hope she held on to so tightly cracked.

When the truck was full, Marlo slammed the doors and Kerns pulled away with a promise to return as fast as possible. Then Marlo darted out of sight along the front wall of the school and Gemma could hear the low tone of his voice.

Calling over the kids trapped on the front wall.

Gemma was left standing inside the foyer, the air heavy with the sulfurous odor of spent gunpowder, with Baker, four students, a dead school resource officer, and a pile of what she was sure was the shooters' discarded trench coats.

From upstairs came a muted double *boom* of gunfire. With each sound, the students flinched. One girl was curled in a corner by the door, sobbing into arms crossed over her bent knees. "Let's get them out into the front," she said to Baker. "Up against the wall. I'll take this one."

"Kids, outside. Up against the brick wall. You'll be safe there. Go! I'm right behind you."

As Baker herded the kids outside, Gemma knelt down next to the girl and laid her hand on her arm. The girl flinched, whimpered, and pulled in closer, away from Gemma's touch.

"Honey, I'm Detective Capello from the NYPD. I'm here to take you to safety."

The girl made a sound like a wounded animal.

"Let me help you out of here."

Frantic head shakes accompanied a mumble.

"Say it again, honey."

"They killed Adrian." The words were nearly inaudible. "We were running to safety and they shot him. Can't go out there."

Gemma scanned the girl, cold horror washing over her as she realized the teen's right sleeve was splattered with blood and brain matter. *The body on the front walk.*

"You only have to get to the van at the bottom of the steps. You don't have to run down the front walk." Gemma leaned over to look out the door. To her relief, Kerns was just about to back up to the school again. *That was fast.* "What's your name?"

"Carla."

"Carla, the van is pulling up now. I need you to come with me."

The girl just shook her head again, so frozen with fear she couldn't stand, even if it would save her life.

From the sound coming through the doors, the van had arrived and Marlo was loading everyone in.

Gemma wasn't leaving this girl behind, even if she had to carry her out. She stood, grasped Carla's upper arms, and hauled her upright, catching her with one arm around her waist when she staggered. Carla's face, now exposed, was deadly pale, her eyes blank. *In shock.* "We're not going without you, Carla. Help me if you can."

The girl seemed truly out of it, and, while she stayed on her feet, Gemma had to lead her forward, supporting most of her weight through the double doors and down the steps.

Gemma looked up to find Baker still standing on the bottom step. He looked unsure, as if he didn't feel he could leave the school while even one student was still inside. "Mr. Baker, Carla's in shock. Can you climb in and we'll pass her to you?"

"Of course." Baker scrambled up the steps and then turned and held out both his hands.

Marlo and Gemma helped her up and Baker led her to an open spot on the bench seat.

Gemma looked around before meeting Marlo's eyes. "Is that everyone?"

"Yes. Good job there. I wasn't sure Baker was going to leave willingly. Up you go."

Gemma climbed in and Marlo followed, slamming the doors behind them. The van lurched forward and Gemma grabbed for the overhead bar, swaying as the van bumped over the sidewalk and then down the street. Kerns turned left down East 3rd Street and pulled over. Marlo opened the door, jumped out, and then helped students down and directed them along Bay Parkway, away from the school. Students ran, some holding hands, some holding each other, some flat-out sprinting, putting as much distance as possible between themselves and the horror they'd just experienced. Another girl had her arm around Carla, leading her slowly away from the van. Baker brought up the rear, ensuring there were no stragglers.

Gemma hopped down and watched the students moving away as Detective Kerns joined her. "Don't we need to keep track of who we're pulling out of the school? We can't just let them run off."

"They're not. While we've been busy, more first responders have been arriving," reported Kerns. "We have a medical triage area set up one block northeast at Bay and East 4th. Everyone gets checked out, critical injuries are taken away immediately, and everyone is logged before loading them onto school buses. We're pulling out anyone who witnessed the shooter for questioning here so we get that information faster. Word's gone out to parents to meet their kids at the Barclays Center. It's about five miles away, but it's the only building big enough to house the number of people we're looking at. Once the kids get there, they'll be re-logged, and anyone who saw the shooters and hasn't already been questioned will be interviewed before going in to meet their parents."

"Good setup. Hard to capture all the witnesses at once, especially when you have kids in shock, but that two-fisted approach gives them their best chance at it."

A low rumble caught Gemma's attention, even over the calls of students and the incoming wail of sirens. A long boxy white and blue NYPD truck pulled up on Bay Parkway on the wrong side of the street—not a problem, as the road was completely blocked off at this point. Across the rear panel, large block letters read SPECIAL OPERATIONS DIVISION TACTICAL OPERATIONS COMMAND. It had the dimensions of an FDNY ladder truck, but instead of carrying firefighting equipment, it carried all the communications and computer equipment required to run an op of this size instead of running incident command from a number of vehicles and strictly via handheld radios. Now they'd be able to mount the kind of concerted, coordinated effort this situation required.

Time to go introduce herself to the incident commander and find out how she could best help the effort.

Gemma's phone buzzed in her back pocket, and she pulled it out to check on the caller. *Joe.* "Any news?"

"No." Stress ran like a lava flow behind Joe's single word. "He hasn't called or texted. He hasn't responded to calls or messages from Alyssa or me. You haven't seen him? You're there?"

"I'm here. Some kids got out before we got here, and we have more out, but I haven't seen him yet. Most of the kids are locked down. That's the safest place for them to be."

"Reports say it's more than one shooter."

She knew what the reports said, what Caroline Wallace had seen, and what she'd witnessed herself, but she tried to ease her brother as best she could. "You know what early reports are like. Five reports about the same suspect can all be different. And it's chaos in there."

"But from what you're seeing, could there be more than one?"

There was safeguarding her brother, and then there was straight-out lying. She couldn't—wouldn't—lie to his direct question. "Yes."

"Dio ci aiuti."

Joe was trying to hide it, but because she knew him so well, she could hear the raw fear, partly because she felt it herself. "Take a breath, Joe." Only silence met her. "I'll wait." She could practically see him grinding his teeth, but heard his inhale and heavy exhale. "I know it's hard not to think like a father right now"—his harsh laugh cut her off, but she pressed on—"but you need to think like a cop. That mindset is in our bones. Lean on it. Think rationally. There are lots of reasons why we haven't heard from him." He started to speak, but she steamrolled over him. "Not that reason. Lots of teachers don't allow cell phones in class. Didn't you tell me one of them had a basket on her desk and everyone had to drop their phone in it at the beginning of class?"

"Yeah."

"Or other teachers want them to keep their phones on silent and in their bags. He may have had to abandon it when the shooting started. He's a smart kid, and he knows the three rules of an active shooter. I've been there when you've drilled him on it."

"Run, hide, fight." Joe's response was automatic, ingrained from years as a father and even more as a cop.

"He knows what to do. Hell, Joe, he's a Capello. It's in his bones, too. Trust him to do everything he can to keep himself safe. Then trust us to find him."

"Are officers in the school?"

"Yes. The first A-Team truck pulled up just after I got here. Shooters were picking off students on the front grass, so we gave them cover to get inside."

"Who?"

"Nilsson's team. Logan, Sims, Lewis, Perez, Turner. Wilson and Redding. And more. They're good officers and they know how to handle this. Let them do their job. Are you going to the Barclays Center?"

"Alyssa is. I'm coming to you. There have to be some perks of being NYPD."

"And a Capello. When will you be here?"

"Twenty minutes. Maybe twenty-five. If this goddamned traffic"— his voice rose, anger and frustration overflowing—"will get out of my way."

"There's a good chance we'll be wrapped before you get here and you'll get to see him. Hang on, and I'll see you when you get here."

"Yeah." The breath he sucked in whistled slightly through his teeth. "Thanks."

"You know there's no thanks required. Now get your ass down here." She cut the connection and let her head droop. She could argue the logic of her point so quickly because it was the same argument she was constantly having with herself.

Come on, Sam. Let us know you're okay.

A slideshow of images spun in her mind.

Tony, standing in the hospital room, cradling the tiny swaddled baby with a blue cap in his arms, talking to his long-dead wife. "Do you see him, Maria? He has your eyes." A determined ten-month-old pulling himself up on the couch and learning how to walk on his own. A young boy with a bat nearly as tall as him playing T-ball. An eight-year-old already skating circles around his aunt as they circled the rink at Rockefeller Center beneath a glorious Christmas tree. A middle schooler proudly showing off his track and field ribbons after a meet. An excited freshman getting ready for his first day of high school, nervous that after being a senior at middle school, he was now the newbie.

Hang on, Sam. I'm here, and more help is coming. You're not alone.

She looked down at the phone still in her hand for a moment and then speed dialed a familiar number.

"Garcia." The deep voice of Lieutenant Tomás Garcia carried down the line.

"Sir, it's Capello."

"What do you need, Capello?" He sounded harried. "Wait. Aren't you off today?"

"Officially, yes. And I was on my way to my dad's when my brother Alex called to tell me about the South Greenfield situation. I was only a few blocks away so I came down."

"No one's requested HNT."

"I know, sir. And they don't need it so far. But my nephew is in there, so I couldn't just drive by, not when I could help. Laying down cover for the A-Team entrance, pulling out students. Now I'm going to go help debrief them. I wanted to let you know."

"What's your take on it?"

"Two boys were seen walking into the school about fifteen minutes after class started, by which point all the stragglers would have already been in their classes. Came in blasting Bon Jovi's 'Blaze of Glory.'"

"Christ."

"Exactly. By all reports, it's bad in there." When Garcia stayed quiet, she asked, "What are you thinking?"

"I think I'm going to see who's nearby and send them over. No one's requested it, but if it's two kids, maybe we'll be able to get them to a place where they can be talked down. The A-Team guys aren't going to want to kill a kid. They will, if given no choice, but maybe they won't have to. Yeah, let me see who's nearby in case we need to put together a team, even just one more detective. Anyone out of the area won't be able to get there soon enough. Keep me in the loop via text, Capello. I'll come down, too, if needed."

"Yes, sir. Thank you, sir." She hung up.

Pocketing her phone, she jogged in the direction of the new command center where officers were setting up—pushing out the tip-out sections of the truck to expand the internal space, and dropping steps into place. She stopped as another truck drove through the next intersection. This one, smaller than the command center truck, was emblazoned with TRUCK SIX NYPD POLICE and carried any extra rescue and tactical equipment they might need.

She sent up a plea to the universe. *Keep Dad away from his phone and his TV. Even if just for another half hour.* That would likely be all they'd need. Surely the A-Team would have the situation contained by then.

She'd need it contained by then. And she'd need to have Sam with her to buffer the fury she knew was coming.

Because once Tony Capello found out she was keeping him in the dark when his eldest grandchild was in harm's way, there'd be hell to pay.

CHAPTER 7

Logan's team jogged up the unnaturally deserted staircase.

Logan could picture what it would look like at class change with kids bolting up and down the stairs, lapping anyone walking instead of running, and jostling for position to be the first to make it to the next door. Now, it was eerily subdued except for their own footsteps, the *boom* of shotgun fire that echoed down the stairwell, and their rapid breathing—they might be used to the inherent danger in this kind of scenario, but they weren't stupid enough to not be on high alert.

The desertion made sense and filled Logan with hope. These were kids who had grown up with lockdown drills at least twice a year. At the first announcement of trouble, they'd have known exactly what to do: gather in any stragglers from the hallway, close and lock the door, turn off the light, close the blinds, move away from the doorway, and stay silent and out of sight. The announcement would have made it clear this was not a drill, but, even through the terror of the current situation, the constant repetition of previous drills hopefully made it a rote response. That was the point of the drills, after all.

Although in this case, Logan couldn't help thinking the repetition of the drills must have also informed the shooters in their planning. They would know the expected protocol and would try to circumvent it to cause the most damage.

When they got to the fourth floor, Redding paused long enough to scan the hallway on the other side of the security glass through the window in the ballistic shield. "Clear!"

Redding stepped through into the hallway, shield raised, followed by Logan, with Lewis immediately behind him and then forming up to his left. The rest of the team fell into place.

A shotgun blast came from down a hallway followed by a muffled shout that carried an edge of snarl. "It's up to me if you live or die!" Another blast. "And I say you don't deserve to live!"

What caught Logan's attention was the lack of screaming that followed the blast. Were the kids terrified into silence? He didn't think so.

Wanting the advantage of surprise, and not wanting to push the shooter into a last-ditch attempt to take as many lives as possible before confronting officers, Logan conveyed his orders via hand signal, and they jogged quietly down the hallway, their rubber-soled boots almost silent on the hallway floor under the *boom* of the gunshots.

Surprise wasn't Logan's sole strategy. They were using the ballistic shield for cover, and while it would protect them from a handgun or shotgun, it would offer no protection from a rifle or a .50-caliber bullet. And right now, while Logan knew this shooter was using a shotgun and hadn't been reported with a rifle, he couldn't know for sure that there wasn't one present. Also, with only one shield, he couldn't guarantee the protection of the entire team, so it was key not to make themselves targets. As the only team on-site, they couldn't help these kids in these crucial early minutes if they were wounded or dead.

They moved quickly, Lin bringing up the rear.

"You wanted to leave me out of things, you wanted to make fun of me. Not making fun of me now, are you? I'm going to be fucking remembered now! But not by you, because you're going to die!" The mania in the voice at the end of the hall, followed by laughter, sent a chill down Logan's spine.

Tension flayed the ends of Logan's nerves. This whole situation unsettled him. He was used to high-stress incidents, but never had there been stakes this high. Sure, there had been innocents involved, but never children by the thousands. And there was no separation this time, no distance from a sniper's nest stories above, no physical—and moral?—separation through a prison's security doors. Only a matter of feet, and if the wrong person abruptly popped into view, the potential of the wrong life lost. A mistake made, never to be rectified.

The pressure of the lack of room for error was suffocating. This wasn't a situation where they could go in, guns blazing. There were simply too many innocents to be caught in the crossfire.

They traveled down the hallway, passing pairs of closed doors, all with no light coming from the long narrow window that ran down one side of the door. A quick glance inside any uncovered windows showed a deserted space.

Everyone is hiding.

But Logan noted there were large, ragged holes in the ceiling tiles overhead, about every twenty feet.

Walked down the hallway, big man in charge. Shooting off the shotgun every few doorways into the ceiling to terrify those inside.

Because shotguns are loud, it would have worked like a charm. The kids inside must have thought they were going to die.

It was a waste of ammunition in a weapon that could only carry somewhere between two and thirteen shells at one time, depending on if it was a break-action model or a pump-action design with a magazine tube installed. But the waist pouch he'd been spotted in gave Logan a clue as to his strategy. Depending on the pouch, it could be jammed with loose shells or have stacks of open boxes of shells, possibly different types, all easily at hand for tactical reloading—which is when a shooter reloads on the fly, before his firearm is empty, ensuring he constantly has a full load ready to go. It would explain the gap in the holes in the ceiling tiles as he traversed the hallway. A practiced shooter could load a shell in seconds while on the move.

At this distance, it was impossible to tell what ammunition the gunman was shooting—slugs or buckshot. Contrary to popular belief, buckshot didn't fly apart the moment it left the barrel, but would travel twenty feet or more as a cluster before spreading out. In the mere handful of feet between the shotgun muzzle and the ceiling, there would be no difference between buckshot and a single slug. Each single jagged hole told him nothing about what they were up against except the catastrophic damage of the weapon up close.

Logan's money was on the largest of buckshot—double or triple aught. These kids had clearly planned the attack. A single shot would kill limited people. Buckshot, even close up, would kill the first target, and then would spray out the back, diverted by the body of the first victim to kill countless others behind in a potentially wide arc. Cruel and horrific, but he'd seen nothing so far to make him think there wasn't cold logic behind the attack.

Unit 1 moved forward. This close to the action, the air was smoky with sulfurous gunpowder so thick it was gritty between Logan's clenched teeth.

The taunting from the end of the hallway was getting louder. The egotistical words were no longer important; the rage and power were all that mattered to Logan, as he knew there would be no reasoning with anyone who hated the world and everyone in it. Each shot was preceded by the mechanical *clack clack* of the shotgun fore-end as the shooter racked the next shell into the chamber.

Pump-action. Greater capacity of shells.

Redding slowed as they came to an open doorway on their right, glancing back at Logan for direction. Logan signaled the team to the wall at the edge of the doorway, and then to stop as only he and Redding moved toward the class. Redding inched forward, leaning to the left to give Logan a view through the shield's ballistic glass.

The broken glass window in the half-open door was the first clue of the horror that lay around the corner. Logan stared through the gap in the shattered glass, but all he could see was a row of large square desks, some with their surfaces angled like a drafting table and holding a large piece of paper filled with a colorful drawing, with stools haphazardly pushed into the aisles. But there was no sign of students or the teacher.

Forced his way into an empty classroom? Then kept going on to the next room when there was no one here?

He couldn't take that chance. Even with shots fired down the hallway, there was no guarantee they weren't moving in pairs and there wasn't a shooter still in this room who could come up behind them if they neglected to check. Moving forward with Redding, he used the muzzle of his rifle to push the door open as they stepped into the classroom. The almost musical shiver of shotgun shell casings pushed by the door to roll across the floor told him they were already too late.

Fourteen years on the force and he thought he'd become desensitized. Jaded, even. As his stomach lurched into his throat, he realized he couldn't have been more wrong.

The classroom hadn't been deserted. But following procedures, the teacher and students had sought shelter away from the door where they couldn't be seen from the hallway. They'd gathered in the far corner against the hallway wall, next to a run of cupboards and drying racks. It was smart positioning. The only way they'd be targets was if the shooter shot out the window, reached in, opened the door, and stepped into the room. Then they'd be sitting ducks.

And were.

It was hard to tell in the crumple of bloodied bodies where one ended and the next began. Blood splashed over cupboards and splattered artwork hanging on the walls. It ran in rivulets across the floor and soaked into clothing. The rear wall was pockmarked with clusters of holes in a pattern he instantaneously recognized.

Buckshot.

In a break in the shouting, he could hear the low thread of a moan.

Not all dead.

But a quick glance around the room full of art tables but without a teacher's desk said that unless a shooter was hiding inside a cupboard—and every place of concealment in the school was considered a hot zone and would be searched—the room was clear and they had to move on. They'd return for anyone still alive, but they had to keep more students from this fate. Also, backup was incoming. They'd help find and extract the living.

Logan swallowed hard, trying to compartmentalize the tangled jumble of fury, shock, and sorrow roiling through him. They had to stop the shooter with a goal not to exact revenge for young lives cut down before they had a chance to experience the joys and sorrows of life, but to allow the criminal justice system to do its job. And that meant taking the shooter alive, if possible.

Though he had to admit the need for revenge was building in him. It was never something he'd act on—his training and instincts were too on point for that—but the very human emotion burned red hot.

Put it away. Get the job done.

He and Redding stepped into the hallway and gave the hand signal to move forward.

The words coming from the classroom were clearer now as they approached.

"You don't think that door is seriously going to keep me out, do you? *Me?*" A moment of silence passed. "Let me show you what I think about that."

Boom boom boom boom boom.

Logan's headset was electronically modified to dampen the sound of gunshots while still allowing spoken words to be heard, and he could still hear the *click* pause *click* pause *click* that followed it.

Reloading.

Time to move, while the shooter was still prepping to go through the door.

They were just short of the classroom when his radio gave a short burst of static. "Unit 1, Unit 2." Nilsson's voice was tight. "We've been informed the shooters are actively live streaming."

Logan snapped up a hand to his team to freeze, whispering "Hold" to Redding in front of him.

"I repeat," Nilsson continued, "the shooters are live streaming to Facebook. I haven't seen it myself, but I'm trying to get access so we can use it to our advantage. We're also getting in contact with Facebook's Law Enforcement Response Team, but for now it's live. That means you're taking these shooters down in public. I don't know how many eyes are on it, but it could be plenty. Until we get that feed turned off, the world is watching. Contain and apprehend. And get those feeds off."

Logan keyed his mic twice, the code for an acknowledged message when he couldn't actually talk. He heard two more clicks—Sims had also received the message.

Social media streaming. Which meant the shooter had a GoPro or an equivalent live streaming camera somewhere on him to capture all the blood, gore, and terror. A vision of the classroom they'd just left filled his mind.

They'd known anyone who could do this was nothing short of evil, but to get an extra thrill out of broadcasting the kills to the world was next level.

Time to stop him before he could get through whatever door was keeping him out.

They could storm the room and take down the shooter, but they had to try for surrender first. Clearly there was a separation between shooter and students at this time, which bought them the opportunity to not simply go in actively firing. But the moment he started shooting again, Logan's hands were tied. There was a risk, of course, the shooter would return fire. A shotgun blast could carry an immense amount of power, and rounds aimed directly at a painted cinder-block wall from only feet away could pierce clean through with either buckshot or slugs.

He glanced at his team and gave them the hand signal to get down. They had helmets and body armor, but if something came through the wall at them, it might be game over. A shooter would likely aim for center mass, so they needed to get below that, yet still stay close enough to go through the door if a single student was in imminent danger.

The team dropped to a crouch from which they could spring at a moment's notice and Redding turned the ballistic shield sideways to cover as much of the team as possible.

They were ready.

"NYPD! Put your weapon down and get your hands in the air!" Logan's bellow echoed through the hallway, which worked for him. He hoped the sound carried to the locked down classrooms around them.

Hang on a little longer. Help is here.

A second of silence dragged on to two seconds. Then five.

Maybe they had a chance to end this without more bloodshed. Because surely there had been enough of that already.

That hope was shattered by the sharp *click clack* of the fore-end of a pump-action shotgun.

Logan had just enough time to yell "Stay down!" to his team as he curled in tight over his rifle.

Repetitive, explosive rounds shattered the wall beside them, spraying them with shards of cement.

CHAPTER 8

Gemma was almost at the command center when an unmarked, charcoal SUV took the corner onto Bay Parkway at high speed and pulled up on the wrong side of the road behind the command center. The driver's door opened and a tall, dark-haired man climbed out and headed in the direction of the command center with a purposeful stride. Gemma immediately recognized both the man and the meaning behind the unmarked vehicle. The officer, dressed in a white shirt and navy tie under a navy windbreaker, was Lieutenant Noah Morin, and he was here today as one of the NYPD citywide patrol supervisors—ESU command officers who stayed in motion during their shifts in different city districts, immediately available in times of crisis.

The incident commander had arrived.

Gemma was grateful it was Morin on duty that day. She'd worked with him as he'd come up through the A-Team until he'd been promoted to lieutenant and had taken a sideways transfer into crisis command. He was smart, steady, and logical. She couldn't have asked for anyone better.

By the time she ran up to the command center, a group was already forming around Morin, who was questioning those around him, clearly getting the lay of the land.

"Nilsson, you're still managing your teams?"

"Yes, sir."

"And current intel is shooters on three and four?"

"Yes, sir."

"Have we been able to sweep the school?"

"We're making progress a floor at a time. Teams are still incoming. But there have been no other reports of gunfire."

"We need to be sure. Do we have enough teams inside on three and four?"

"I have one unit on three west and one on four east. Sanders just went in with his team and is headed upstairs to assist Unit 2 on the third floor. When the new teams arrive, we'll evaluate if we need more upstairs; if not, we'll start the sweeps of one and two. We need to ensure it's only two shooters. Initial intel reported multiple shooters, but there have been no recent reports except from the third and fourth floor."

"Agreed. Who's leading the existing teams?"

"Sims is leading Unit 2 on three," said Nilsson. "Logan has Unit 1 on four."

"Stay in touch with your officers and keep me updated." Morin turned toward Gemma as Nilsson jogged to his truck. "Capello, HNT has been called in?"

"No, sir. I'm not officially on duty today. But I was only blocks away when the shooting happened and I came down to lend a hand. Sir, my nephew is in there. If I can help get students to safety, then at least I'm being proactive in saving someone, even if it's not him." She looked past Morin's shoulder to the cluster of officers and EMTs a block down the street around a line of ambulances. "I was going to go talk to some of the students who've evacuated to help build the information database. With your permission, sir."

"Approved. I don't know who's spearheading that yet, so I'll come over as soon as I can once the new tactical teams are deployed."

"Thank you, sir."

Gemma threaded her way through the pack of NYPD personnel and broke through to open sidewalk. She took the block at a jog, dropping to a walk as she approached the rear of the last ambulance in the line. The doors were thrown open and a glassy-eyed boy sat on the rear bumper, holding a stack of gauze pads to a bleeding head wound as a paramedic shone a light into his pupils. Ahead of the ambulance, a thirty-something, auburn-haired detective in a dark suit and color-matched tie was speaking to a group of students, separating them out into groups and assigning officers to talk to them.

The detective looked up as Gemma approached and flashed her badge. "Detective Capello, HNT. Lieutenant Morin cleared me to come down and give you a hand talking to students."

"Detective Holt. Appreciate that. We're still figuring out who our shooters are." Holt turned to survey the students sitting and standing on the grass on the far side of the sidewalk, some alone, some in groups, some already talking to officers. Many looked dazed, several were crying, one boy paced back and forth over a ten-foot stretch of grass, seemingly unable to hold still, laden with grief and rage. "These kids are lucky to be alive. A lot of them thought they were hearing fireworks, or saw kids drop after being shot, but didn't understand what was going on until they didn't get up again. They're terrified and they're traumatized." Holt gestured to a cluster of three girls sitting about fifteen feet away. "Can you take that group? They're badly shaken and I think they might do better with a woman's lighter touch. They got caught on the second floor when the shooters came up the main staircase. Only one of the three of them is able to coherently communicate currently. The other two are showing greater signs of shock. Start with the one and it might draw the others out. They've had a little time to settle, so they may be calmer and ready to talk now."

"Leave it with me." Gemma reflexively reached for her left blazer pocket and the compact pad of paper and the pen she normally kept there in case she needed to make notes, but her fingers touched nylon instead, the NYPD windbreaker she'd borrowed after discarding her blood-soaked jacket, not wanting her own presence to further scar already traumatized kids. It was a reminder that her on-duty accouterments were at home. "Sorry, I came in when I was off duty. Do you have a notepad I can borrow?"

"Take this." A patrol officer to Holt's left extended a clipboard and pen. "More supplies are incoming."

"Thanks." Gemma accepted the clipboard and pen and crossed the sidewalk toward the group of girls.

She took in details as she approached: The three girls showed the diversity of Brooklyn, with skin tones from deep umber, to medium mocha, to sheet-white with shock. Two of the three looked young, possibly freshmen, while the third girl looked older. The younger two wore black yoga pants, one paired with a long sweater and the other a sweatshirt, while the older girl wore torn jeans, a white scoop-neck

T-shirt, and a khaki drill jacket. Only the girl in the sweater—her arm around the student in the sweatshirt who hunched in on herself—watched Gemma's approach. The third girl sat, her eyes huge in her unnaturally pale face and fixed on the sidewalk, her arms wrapped around her bent knees, rocking rhythmically back and forth. As she got closer, Gemma could see someone had wrapped a blanket around her shoulders, but it had slipped out of her lax fingers to pool on the grass behind her.

"Let me help you with that." Gemma set the clipboard down on the ground and bent to pick up the blanket, draping it over the girl's stooped shoulders. "Can you hold this?" She wrapped one of the girl's ice-cold hands around the edge of the blanket, but as soon as she let go, the hand drooped to fall into her lap. Without missing a beat, Gemma pulled the blanket more securely around the girl's shoulders, twisted the ends together, and set them in her lap.

Individuals suffering from shock following a fight-or-flight fear reaction, where the surge of adrenaline drew all the blood to the center of the body to protect the vital organs, were often left feeling chilled. The blanket helped warm, but it also helped comfort, and, clearly, this girl needed both treatment aspects, especially when Gemma needed her to talk.

Gemma sat down on the grass beside the students, crossing her legs and making eye contact with the only student who was watching her. "I'm Detective Capello, but you can call me Gemma. I'd like to talk to you about what happened inside the school today. Is that all right?" Sweater girl nodded and Gemma picked up the clipboard and held the pen poised. "Can I get your names?"

"Letisha Coleman." The girl's voice came out slightly raspy, and she gave Gemma a smile that wobbled badly, but she pushed on. "Everyone calls me Tish." She looked down at the girl curled beside her. "This is Diya Khatun." She glanced at the third girl and shrugged. Evidently, they were strangers who had come together in the crisis.

Gemma waited a few beats for the third girl to offer her name, but was met by silence. Knowing it was a possibility the girl might need one-on-one privacy to come out of her personal hellscape, Gemma opted to give it a few minutes before applying gentle pressure. "Thank you. First, I want to say that I'm so sorry about what you just went through.

But you can help us stop the shooters. If we know who they are, learn about them, we can use it to stop them and take them into custody."

Diya's head snapped up. Her eyes were bloodshot and her cheeks were damp. "You're not going to kill them?" Behind the shock and sorrow was a thread of fury Gemma couldn't blame her for.

"That's never our first choice. And it's not our job. It's up to the judiciary to decide their fate."

Tish made a derogatory grunt in the back of her throat. "Of course they won't. You saw them. They're white. They'll go easy on them."

"Untrue." Gemma didn't want to begin the discussion with an argument, but she wanted to make sure these students didn't shut down on her because they thought their experiences weren't useful or important. "Anyone responsible for this violence will be prosecuted to the full extent of the law if they're taken into custody. And if they try to harm anyone else, leaving our officers with no choice but lethal force, that's what they'll use. In an active shooter scenario, the safety of the victims is the most important aspect. They'll do what's needed." She met the girl's eyes. "They'll be contained. How the situation turns out depends entirely on them."

The girl simply stared for a slow count of three, then nodded.

"I'd like to hear about your experience. Can you tell me what you saw?"

A fat tear broke free to roll down Diya's cheek. "They... they killed Tonya." The last word broke on a half-gasp.

"I'm so sorry."

But the girl steamrolled over Gemma's words of condolence, the cork coming out of the bottle, driven by rage. "We were going to the greenhouse. Mr. Tompkins—" Her breath caught and another tear slid free. "Mr. Tompkins was taking us down to look at our botany project." As she spoke, her hands dug into the grass on either side of her hips, curling around the blades in a white-knuckled grip as if she needed to hold on to something solid. "But then we walked right into them on the main staircase."

A vision of the main foyer filled Gemma's mind. "They were coming up the staircase when you were going down?" Gemma asked.

"We never went down. We came to the top of the stairs and saw them. And we ran." She closed her eyes, her upper body swaying slightly, grass tearing under the force of her grasp.

"I got this." Tish ran her hand up and down Diya's back. The eyes that met Gemma's were dry and steady, though she worried her lower lip. "There were two of them, blasting some oldies tune as they climbed the stairs. They both had guns. I don't know much about guns—I hate them—but I think one was a shotgun and the other was a rifle. I don't know anything more specific than that."

Gemma couldn't help but be impressed by Tish's presence of mind. She was clearly stressed—her shaking hands gave away her reaction to the incident in a way her overtly calm demeanor did not—but she had the strength to keep it together and to fight to help in any way she could. That kind of courage under fire was hardwired into some people. "That's helpful. Did you recognize them?"

"No. There are thousands of us at Greenfield. No way to know them all."

"Russ Shea." A pause. "Hank Richter."

Gemma froze at the quiet, toneless words spoken by the third girl. Identifying the shooters was huge. If they could positively ID them this early, law enforcement might be able to understand their motive and find a way to talk them down.

The girl's eyes were still fixed sightlessly on the sidewalk and she continued her rhythmic rocking, but she'd obviously been following the conversation. Gemma lay her hand on the girl's arm, feeling a ripple run through her body. "Can you tell me your name?"

The pause lasted so long, Gemma thought the girl hadn't heard her. But then she slowly stopped rocking, like a pendulum coming to rest. "Olivia Aldrich."

"Thank you, Olivia. You said two names."

"Russ Shea. Hank Richter."

Gemma noted the two names on the clipboard. "They're the shooters? You're sure?"

"Yes."

CHAPTER 9

Haunted blue eyes finally rose to meet Gemma's. "I mean, I th-think so." Olivia closed her eyes and gave her head a shake. "No. They were."

"These are boys who go to the school? You know them?"

"Know of. They're seniors like me. I had them both in classes over the years."

"This is important, Olivia, so we have to be sure. Russ Shea and Hank Richter. Those were the boys you saw. The ones who entered the school with firearms and started shooting."

Tears filled the girl's eyes, and her lips compressed into a thin white line, but she nodded.

Gemma rubbed her arm. "You're doing great. I need to report this, but then I'll be back and I'd like you to walk me through what you saw." She pushed to her feet and speed-walked past kids talking to cops to where Holt stood with Morin, talking to a pair of officers. "Sir!" She waited until Morin looked in her direction. "I have two potential suspect names."

Morin stepped toward her to meet her in the middle of the sidewalk. "Who identified them?"

Gemma pulled the pad off the clipboard, ripped off the top sheet, and extended it. "Olivia Aldrich, one of the three girls I'm interviewing. She's a senior, and says she recognized both from being in classes with them in the past. I wanted to get these names to you right away. Any other leads?"

Holt studied the names on the paper in Morin's hand. "Not so far. We'll get started on these names and will work on consensus identification from the students. No adult who knows them has come close enough to ID them and been able to exit the building."

"Those are exactly the kind of adults they might have targeted."

"Unfortunately, there's a good chance you're correct," Morin agreed. "Good work, Detective."

"It's not me; it's them. I'll let you know if I get anything else significant and you'll get my full notes." Gemma jogged back to the trio, who still sat silent and motionless on the grass. She dropped down beside them and met all three pairs of eyes. "You hanging in?" She waited for nods of assent and then pushed on. "I need you to tell me everything you can about what happened earlier to help me understand what's happening inside right now." She turned to Tish and Diya. "You were both in the same class and were both headed to the greenhouse?"

"Yes."

"And you ran into the shooters on the main staircase. Did you get a good look at them?"

Tish shrugged. "Sort of, it's mostly just a jumble. One guy, the leader, he had light hair. The other guy had dark hair. One wore a light shirt, one wore dark." She frowned, her face crumpling. "I don't remember which was which."

Gemma latched onto the personality descriptor rather than the physical. "The one with light hair was the leader? What makes you say that?"

"As soon as they saw us, he raised his shotgun, but he didn't pull the trigger. He told the other one to take us out. Egged him on. Specifically singled out Tonya." She shuddered, pulling in a jagged breath that jerked her shoulders. "And the other guy took the shot. It happened so fast, we were frozen in shock. Until she went down. Then we ran."

"Which was the right thing to do. You went back the way you came?"

"Yes. But it wasn't just us. The whole class was coming out and we tried to get back toward our classroom. He shot…" Tish had to stop as her words wavered. She swallowed hard and sucked in a breath. "He shot Brielle in the back and she went down."

"Who shot her?"

"Hank." Olivia's voice was low and shaky. "I saw it."

"We didn't stop for her. Or Tonya." Diya's words were a tortured whisper, her eyes fixed on her lap. "We're cowards."

"Because you didn't stop for those girls?" Gemma asked gently.

"They both went down, and we didn't help them or anything." Tear-flooded eyes rose to Gemma's. "Maybe we could have saved one of them. Or both."

Gemma kept her voice calm but firm, knowing these girls would forever carry her words as they attempted to navigate the guilt. "You could have died making the attempt. Were you in the path of the shooters so if you'd stopped to help her, you'd have been an even greater target?"

"I guess."

Gemma had to strain to hear Diya's words. "You had to take care of yourself. Going back would have been a death sentence. You weren't being a coward—you made a calculation about your chances of survival and knew you couldn't help them." She covered one of Diya's hands with her own. "I understand. I've had to make the same calculation."

"But you probably went back."

"That's not a fair comparison. I have academy training and years of experience. And even with that, I've sometimes had to leave someone behind to save myself so I can fight again another day. Now you'll fight again another day."

Diya nodded silently, but some of the strain eased from her expression.

Gemma turned to Tish. "What happened after that?"

"We went to run back to our classroom. There was no announcement yet, but we knew this was exactly what we'd drilled for. And then…" Tish stopped, raising her eyes skyward, blinking furiously as she fought tears. "Mr. Tompkins stepped out of the classroom and started pulling students inside. And… and… they shot him." She lost the battle, a tear finally breaking free to trickle down her cheek. "Not just once. The light-haired guy with the shotgun shot Mr. Tompkins a bunch of times in the chest. He fell facedown in the doorway, but you could tell he was dead from the blood on the back of his shirt. With him in the doorway, we wouldn't be able to get the door shut quickly, so we ran as fast as we could for the end of the hall and the exit that took us down to the ground floor."

Gemma turned to Olivia. "You weren't with this class?"

"No. I had a spare. I came in early to talk to Ms. Symanski about my independent English project and I was on my way down to the caf to grab a snack and spread out at a table to do my functions homework.

I walked right into the middle of it. When I got to the top of the stairs, they were about halfway up and I booked it for the door." Once Olivia was talking, it poured out of her as she slid a sideways glance at the other two girls. "I ran past them and just kept going." Her shoulders slumped and she curled inward. "I tried to warn them, but I don't think they understood."

"It was all so fast, I didn't understand what was happening." Diya's words came out on a whisper. "I heard what you said, but it didn't make sense at first. Then it made awful sense and we knew we were going to die. So we ran."

"Which was exactly the right thing to do. You didn't see what the boys did after you ran for the far doors?"

Tish started to speak, then stopped, her lips frozen around an unspoken word and her brows folded together. "They didn't kill us." She worried the hem of her sweater, rubbing it between index finger and thumb. "They didn't even shoot at us." She looked up. "I don't think they stayed on that floor."

"We know there's a shooter on the third floor and one on the fourth. If you saw the only two shooters, they might be those same boys. We're trying to determine if there are any more based on description. I'd like you all to describe the boys you saw."

"I told you who they were," Olivia protested.

"I know, honey, but I need this for my notes. I don't doubt your identification, but this is part of building the case." Gemma would never spell it out for the girls, but one suggestion of names didn't make a positive identification. It would help build a case, but a person could try to muddy the waters, strike out at someone who they viewed as having done them wrong, or could simply have made an error under extreme stress. "One at a time, tell me what you saw. Tish, let's begin with you. Close your eyes and concentrate. Describe them for me."

Tish's eyes slid shut, her lids sporadically clenching, driven by terrible memories. "They were older than me. Juniors or maybe seniors. I'd never seen either of them before as far as I know. One was blond, one had dark hair. The one with the dark hair was carrying the shotgun."

"No," Diya cut in. "He had the rifle." The corners of her lips curved down. "He's the one who killed Tonya. Though I don't think he enjoyed it the way the other one did."

That caught Gemma's attention. "What do you mean?"

"The blond boy, he was grinning the whole time. Laughing. Especially as he killed Mr. Tompkins."

Gemma continued making notes on her clipboard, but her mind was two blocks down the street, inside the school. Whichever A-Team was confronting that shooter needed to be extremely careful, because that kind of glee was indicative of a dangerous power trip. Perhaps for the first time, the boy was a man exercising control over life and death and reveling in it. "What about the dark-haired shooter?"

"He looked more... resigned. Like maybe the attack wasn't going the way he thought it would."

Gemma's pen kept scratching on the paper. *Blond—dominant. Brunette—submissive.* In a paired attack versus those carried out by a lone-wolf gunman, usually one of the two shooters was the dominant player, bringing along a submissive individual who would take part, as much to please the dominant shooter as himself. But that description gave her hope. In the case of a situation like Columbine, because the shooters stayed together, they committed suicide together. But Gemma knew the prevailing theory of the boys' interactions said that if they'd split up, the submissive shooter might have been talked down, talked into surrender.

These boys had also split up. Some careful handling might win the day yet.

Gemma remembered Sanders was inside now. Hotheaded Sanders might not be the right commander for this incident after all. Luckily, while Morin held the same rank as Sanders, Morin would call the shots as incident commander, so perhaps there was still a path to ending the incident with as little loss of life as possible.

"What were they wearing?" Gemma asked.

This time it was Olivia who closed her eyes. "Russ is the one with dark hair. He had on green pants, you know the kind commandos wear? A dark shirt. Might have been navy? Maybe black. Hank was dressed in dark clothes."

"No," Diya interrupted. "He was wearing khaki green."

"Pants or shirt?" Gemma asked.

Diya paused to think. "Jacket."

"No, he wasn't," Tish said. "Neither were wearing coats."

The shooters had entered the school wearing black trench coats; Gemma had seen those same coats tossed carelessly in the foyer.

According to Diya's account, Hank would have layered one coat over another, which didn't make sense, as the layers would only hamper his movements at a time when he needed the most mobility possible. Her gaze traveled to Olivia and the puzzle pieces clicked into place.

As an officer and negotiator, Gemma knew the tricks stress could play on both the mind and memories. She'd seen it in the past. Two people could experience the same event and they'd remember it differently. It wasn't that one of them was lying—it had to do with biochemistry and how memories were formed and subtly altered under stress. Instead of recording an event like it was a full-length movie, the mind recorded snapshots and then tried to sew them into a seamless story, sometimes by merging those snapshots or reordering them. For the victim recounting their experience, this altered memory was now how, in their recollection, the event had transpired. It was also documented that the higher the stress, the less someone remembered. Someone spotting the shooters from the safety of a distant window would actually present a more reliable description than someone who had come face-to-face with them, separated by twenty feet of hallway as they stared down the barrel of a firearm. Add in the death of the student standing beside them, and memory formation would be further degraded.

Often in a situation like this, consensus descriptions won the day. Put enough people together and a more accurate description would start to take form. In this case, two of the three girls remembered one thing and the other remembered something totally different. It was her truth, even if it was wrong.

"Diya, when you ran down the hallway and out of the building, was anyone in front of you?"

"A few kids. We were all running for our lives."

"Of course you were. Was Olivia in front of you?"

Diya turned to look at Olivia. "Maybe?"

"Yes, she was," Tish said. "She was about fifteen feet in front of us on the steps down."

"That's what I thought. Look at what Olivia is wearing." Gemma waited while Diya's gaze traveled from her shoes to her jacket. "Is it possible you're remembering her khaki jacket?"

"Why would I remember her jacket on one of the shooters?"

"Because the mind can play tricks on us at times of high stress. Memories get jumbled and you think you're telling it how it happened, but it's how your mind has put the scene together. It's okay, we know it happens. It's why we talk to so many people." She gave Diya a gentle smile. "You're not doing anything wrong. Tell us everything you can, and we'll work out the rest." She looked from one girl, to the next, to the next. "Let's make sure I have all the details, then let's get you on a bus. Your parents are waiting for you. It's time to get you home."

CHAPTER 10

One. Two. Three. Four. Five. Six. Seven.

Logan counted off the shotgun blasts, only looking up once there was a pause in the shooting. Over their heads, the wall now held a line of jagged, gaping holes. He judged the hole furthest to the right as where the classroom ended about four feet to the right of the door and ordered the team to scuttle back beyond that marker. They jumped to their feet once they had cleared the shooter's sight line.

That was it; they were given no choice. The shooter had tried to kill the whole team, assuming they were on their feet and aiming to take them out midbody, only missing because they had the presence of mind to hit the dirt. Logan had hoped for a brief second that they'd be able to talk the kid down—the last thing he wanted to do was kill a child, though he wouldn't hesitate to do so for the protection of others, if given no other option—but that hope had been blown away with the corridor wall. The best he could do was take the shooter down and not out, but the shooter's own actions would prescribe how the next few minutes played out.

He gave the hand signal to Lewis to toss a flash bang. Lewis pulled a short black cylinder out of a front pocket of his vest, pulled the pin, and brought it up in his clenched fist beside Redding's head so he could see it. As the man in front, Redding often missed Logan's hand signals and had to be looped into each stage of the operation.

Lewis threw the stun grenade through the doorway, his aim true even at this distance, and they all turned their faces away from the blinding burst of light that was accompanied by a blast louder than the roar of a jet engine. Their headsets protected them from the deafening noise as the light flashed through their clenched eyelids, even with their faces turned away.

The moment the light faded, they were on the move, six officers moving as a single coordinated body. They only had about five seconds of flash blindness and sensory overload disorientation to work with, and every fraction of a second counted. Redding went through the door first, shielding the team in case of a blindly fired shot, Logan went next, and the rest of the team followed behind. "NYPD, get on the ground!" Bellows from the team members added to the disorientation, making them seem like a larger team than they were in reality.

But Logan was barely three steps inside the door when the percussion of a gunshot sliced through the classroom still echoing with the flash bang. Logan swung toward the far side of the teacher's desk, leading with his rifle. He quickly circled the desk on the blackboard side as Turner came around the far side.

"Shit." Turner froze, her eyes locked in horror on the ground around the side of the desk.

Two more steps and Logan jerked to a halt.

He could identify the shooter from Nilsson's description of his clothing—black jeans, black hoodie, and wearing a waist pouch at his hip—but there was no identifying him by his light hair, as most of the top of his head was missing where he sprawled in a pool of his own blood. The shotgun, a shorter home-security style with a tube magazine to hold extra cartridges, lay on the floor a few feet away. A matte black handgun lay beside the body within reach of the lax hand. Logan recognized it as a Glock 19, one of the three standard handguns NYPD officers carried.

The dead resource officer's missing handgun?

His gaze traveled up the boy's front, where a compact silver and black camera pressed against the center of his chest, held in place by an elastic harness, with a black wire winding into a pocket in the hoodie that held the boxy bulk of what had to be a power brick. The small screen beside the camera lens and above a bright red recording light slowly ticked the increasing recording time: 17:22, 17:23, 17:24...

Logan bent down and tapped the power button on the top of the camera. The screen and the red light went dark.

One live feed down, one to go.

Perez stepped up beside Logan and let out a low whistle. "You think this was the blaze of glory he planned?"

Logan shot him a sidelong glance. "He could have gone for suicide by cop. The fact that he didn't says he considered it a win to take his own life rather than let us do it. Surrender was never an option in his mind." He keyed his mic. "Unit 1 to Nilsson. Fourth floor east shooter is dead by suicide and his live feed is terminated. No other indications of any additional suspects. We need multiple teams of EMTs for casualties in multiple classrooms. It's clear to send them. Do you have teams to assist?"

"Affirmative. Unit 4 has just arrived and will accompany the EMTs."

"We need to begin the sweep of this wing to ensure no other hot spots. Is Unit 2 supported?"

"Unit 6 has been sent to assist Unit 2 with their active shooter. You are a go to conduct the sweep of the fourth floor. Unit 4 will assist. The east wing stairwell is clear for when you have students ready for evacuation. I'll send more officers in to assist evacuees into and down the stairwell."

"Ten-four. We'll bring students out that way." Logan ended the transmission, cast one last look at the waste of life—of what was once someone's baby boy, a new life full of possibilities—and turned his back on it. That was now a job for the crime scene techs.

He turned for the first time to study the room, already mentally bracing for the same carnage he'd seen in the art room. Instead, the room appeared empty in the thinning smoke from the flash bang.

It was a music room. A conductor's stand, with sheet music and a baton, stood at the front of three semicircular rows of chairs, the last row on wooden risers, each with its own music stand. Or what would normally have been rows—now the chairs and stands were haphazardly pushed out of position, some tipped over, with sheet music scattered across seats and over the floor and instruments scattered everywhere. But not a single student, dead or alive, in sight.

Logan's gaze tracked to where double doors marked *Instrument Storage* were set into the rear wall. Large holes pierced the door and wall, clearly from the shotgun. But unlike the hallway attack against him and his team, where the shooter had been making a concerted effort at targeted harm, the blast pattern was random, not a planned bombardment to facilitate entry.

The class had tried to hide away from him. The destruction to the hallway wall showed the shooter could have gotten through to them, but he was either too jacked to consider the officers who were coming after him, or he was having too much fun terrorizing the kids inside.

Logan was sure it was the latter—the massacre in the adjacent classroom might have temporarily blunted his need for blood, and had increased the chances of survival of anyone behind that wall.

Logan pushed through the chairs, clearing a path to the back of the room, his eyes on the largest of the holes, at about chest level—*Aiming for midbody to do the most damage*—five or six feet away from the doors. It was dark inside the room, with the lights out and no external windows. "NYPD, is anyone in there?"

"Here." The voice was that of an adult, shaky, but clear.

"We're coming in." Behind him, he could hear his team clearing a wider path through the classroom, making room for medical teams to come in, if needed. He reached the door and tried the knob—locked as expected. "Can you unlock the doors?"

"Can't get to it… they're blocked."

There was a thread of pain behind the words. *Shot?* "Perez! The Halligan."

He stepped out of the way as Perez pushed forward. Perez turned away from Logan, who unbuckled the heavy steel breaching tool strapped to the back of his vest—a large, slightly curved, two-tined fork at one end with an adz and a pick at ninety degrees at the other. Perez took the tool and wedged the double fork in between the door and the wooden frame, shoving it home with considerable force, about three inches above the deadbolt with the concave side facing the door. Then he braced himself and pulled. The bar inched slowly toward him, the teeth of the fork sliding in farther, forcing a space between the door and the frame. With a ragged tearing sound, the lock ripped from the wooden panel and the door popped open, only to hit something directly behind it. Perez set down the Halligan bar and braced both hands on the door.

Logan joined him. "Move away from the door." As he and Perez pushed, the objects blocking the door slid back with a screech of wood on tile until the gap was big enough for a team member and all their gear to slide through. "That's good." Logan slipped his rifle on its sling off over his head and handed it to Perez, leaving himself armed with only his sidearm. He pulled the compact flashlight off his utility belt, turned it on, and slipped sideways through the door, the spare rifle magazines in the front pockets of his Kevlar vest digging into his chest as he squeezed through the gap. Then he was on the other side and could draw breath again. He raised the flashlight, aided by fluorescent light filtering through the holes left by the shotgun as he took in the room in a single fast scan.

The room was lined with wooden shelves with different sized cubbies labeled with instrument numbers, some containing black instrument cases, some empty. In front of the door was a haphazard stack of larger wooden cases labeled *Drum Kit 3* and *Tuba 1*, among others. It was smart thinking—from the weight they'd just shifted, they were full, and blocked the shooter.

The indirect light from the classroom showed him no one standing, so he focused his light toward the floor. He found the missing class.

About two dozen students were huddled on the floor, lying flat or crouched down in a ball, trying to stay below the level of the gunshots. The only adult in the room, a middle-aged brunette, sat slumped against the shelves. Blood was a dark bloom across the right shoulder of her blouse and down her arm. "We need EMTs in here," Logan called. "And I need more hands."

"Right here." Lin squeezed through the gap to join Logan and found the lights by the door, brilliantly flooding the narrow space. "Redding's behind me."

Turning off his flashlight and snapping it into place on his utility belt, Logan picked his way carefully through the students. "It's clear out in the classroom." He had a flash of the ruins of the shooter beside the desk, but pushed past it. That couldn't be helped. The body would be there for hours as the crime scene techs came in, and they couldn't wait that long to evacuate the rest of the school. "Who's uninjured?"

Several voices identified themselves.

"I need you to exit this space. That will allow us to get to those who need assistance. More officers are outside to help you evacuate the building." He held out his hand toward the boy in front of him, who reached up to grasp his hand and be pulled to his feet.

"Thanks."

Logan waited until the boy had his balance in the cramped space and then released him.

The boy's gaze shot toward his teacher, and he winced at the sight of so much blood. "Can you help Ms. Beattie? She's trying to make it sound like she's fine." His gaze darted to Logan's. "She's not. She needs to be okay. She did everything to keep us safe."

"We'll take care of her. You can assist us by helping out any students who don't need medical attention."

The boy brightened at the thought of a mission, of something proactive, and of no longer being a victim. "I can do that." He bent over a student curled on the floor. "Brent, man, can you get up?"

As kids rose and made their way out to the classroom, Logan pushed through to the teacher on the far side. Reaching her, he squatted down to meet green eyes in a pale face framed by a short, dark bob. "Ms. Beattie. How badly are you hurt?"

"I'm okay. See to the students first."

Logan glanced over his shoulder to find his teammates helping the few injured students still in the room. "You're the most severely injured. Which makes you my priority."

She gave him a weak smile. "Thanks. We weren't as ready as we should have been. We didn't hear him coming." She winced as if in response to a stab of pain. "We were running 'Semper Fidelis' by John Philip Sousa. Lots of brass and cymbals and tympani. By the time we heard him he was practically on top of us." She stopped, almost panting. "We scrambled, but I took too long getting the students in, down on the floor, and the door locked and barricaded. I was still on my feet when the first blast came through and I got hit. Didn't need to tell the kids to stay down after that."

"Can I take a look so I know what we're dealing with?"

She nodded, her lips folded bloodlessly together.

Logan gently pulled the shoulder of her V-neck wrap blouse down to reveal a scatter of buckshot entry wounds. Each wound was bleeding sluggishly, but he knew from his first aid courses that there were major blood vessels in the area; he didn't want to shift her in case anything vital had been nicked and movement increased her bleeding. He carefully resettled the fabric. "I don't want to take any chances, so I'm going to get the EMTs in here to move you. We're going to clear a path for you."

He pushed to his feet. Only three kids were still in the room. One girl had a head wound and Turner was on her knees beside her helping her uncurl from the floor so she could be helped out. Two other boys had been shot and were being attended by Lin and Redding. One of them was bleeding steadily from his leg and Redding was using a folded rag, probably used for cleaning instruments, to apply pressure as he waited for EMTs. "Let me check on the EMTs' ETA."

Logan squeezed past them to step out into the classroom. The first thing he noticed was the riser, tipped upright to block the body from the students being led from the classroom. His team was always thinking on their feet and knew these kids had experienced enough today without witnessing what was left of the shooter.

They moved the kids out in a long line, through the classroom and past the crime scene, out the door, and down the hallway toward the stairwell. As he moved to stand in the hallway door, several pairs of paramedics jogged down the hall toward him, loaded with medical gear and backboards.

He wondered if the shooter on three had been neutralized yet.

CHAPTER 11

After Gemma completed her interviews with the girls, Morin sent her over to the school to assist in student evacuation, where they needed more hands getting kids out of the building and onto buses. She now stood on the sidewalk at the east end of the school, where the wing had been cleared. An A-Team officer she didn't recognize stood at the bottom of the stairwell as students came through, each with their hands on top of their head. He stopped each one with a hand to their shoulder, waited for a count of two, and sent them on their way before stopping the next student.

They considered it safe enough for a guarded evacuation, but were still not taking any chances, spacing out the students so if someone above opened fire, they minimized any potential loss of life. But no shots came from above and the students continued running from the school. An additional stream came from the rear of the school where another team was evacuating first-floor students through the gymnasium. Gemma and other officers kept the kids moving down the street to the rows of school buses awaiting them.

A flash of movement, of color where there should be none, attracted Gemma's gaze where she stood on the street. Turning, she studied the front of the school, for a moment not seeing anything. Then she zeroed in, and her heart stuttered.

Students had forced open a window on the third floor of the west wing and a teenage boy in a bright, kelly-green sweatshirt leaned out. Then he threw one leg over the window sill. Beside him, the second window slid up and another student appeared.

They're going to jump.

Caught between a shooter with a deadly weapon—and no respect for life—and what could be a deadly drop, Gemma couldn't blame the kids for taking their chances on the drop. Broken bones trumped death any day.

They might not consider that the drop might kill them, but she certainly did. Thirty feet was a long way to fall, even if you were landing on grass.

"We have jumpers!" She ordered a nearby patrol officer to take her place, then ran toward the command center. She scanned the vehicles lining both sides of the road and jamming the side streets—A-Team armored vehicles, patrol cruisers, SUVs. Then her gaze fell on the Emergency Services Squad truck, ESS 6. Smaller than some of the other rescue trucks, it had paired ladders that ran up its back to the roof on opposite sides.

That would work perfectly to get officers up and students down.

She sprinted toward the command center where Morin had heard her shout and was already turning away from the officer reporting to him. "Sir! Students are climbing out the windows on the third floor. Recommend taking the ESS 6 truck to get underneath them. We can get them onto the roof and then down the ladders."

Morin's gaze was fixed over her shoulder to the front of the school. "Agreed." He scanned the personnel around him. So many officers were already inside the school sweeping for additional shooters and clearing the school of students trapped in lockdown. His gaze finally landed on an ESU officer in full body armor and a helmet. "Kaplan, I need you to drive ESS 6!"

"Yes, sir."

"Capello, you'll assist. You." He drilled an index finger at a young officer in a navy patrol uniform walking toward the staging area. "You are?"

"Officer Henry Gregson, sir."

"Gregson, you'll assist Kaplan and Capello." He swung back to Gemma. "That's all I can give you."

"It's enough. Let's go!" Without looking to see if the two men were behind her, Gemma sprinted toward ESS 6. Instead of the blocky, fire truck format of some of the larger squad vehicles, ESS 6 had an extended cab in front of a large compartment with multiple storage areas behind latched doors, and the two ladders so well suited to the task at hand.

Dropping out of her run at the rear of the truck, she spun to point at the school. There was a kid at each window now with both legs dangling free. At one window, another kid had his head sticking out past the shoulders of the first. "Can you get us under those kids?"

Kaplan took in the scene in a single glance. "Yes. Get on those ladders and hang on tight. I'll get you there."

He jogged for the cab as Gemma and Gregson climbed on the back platform. Gemma slipped one arm through the left ladder between the third and fourth rung and locked her hands together, securing herself in place. A quick glance at Gregson found him facing the side rail of the ladder, holding on to the opposite side with both hands. The engine of the truck roared to life and Kaplan pulled out onto Bay Parkway, cutting through the narrow path left by the packed emergency vehicles as quickly as possible.

At the far end of the building, Kaplan slowed down. "Hang on!" His yell floated to them from the cab through the open window.

Gemma's body swayed as the front wheels lurched over the curb, followed by the rear. Then they were bumping over grass, heading for the school, arcing past the north edge of the west wing and then in toward the main body of the building.

Gemma looked up and quickly found the students. More heads were at the window, and she could see the student on the right was struggling to stay framed in the window as more students crowded him from behind, jostling him.

If we don't get there fast enough, he could not only fall and break his neck, he could end up under the wheels.

The rapid staccato of rifle fire sounded through the open windows.

Was the shooter trying to force his way in? Was he defending himself against the A-Team? Either way, all these kids would know was the battle was just outside their door and could be coming through to them, bringing death with it.

Even though they were still moving, Gemma clamped both hands to the ladder rungs and stepped up. One rung. Two. The truck hit a dip in the grass, heaving left and causing her to hang on for dear life. She looked up to find all eyes at the window locked on the truck's approach. "Don't jump!" she yelled, betting the shooter wouldn't be able to hear her and the class's imminent rescue over the sound of gunfire. "We'll come up under you so you don't have so far to go!"

She wasn't certain her words could be heard, but was assured when most movement at the window stopped. There was some scuffling inside the room, and even that halted as word filtered through.

Kaplan brought them along the wall of the school, the metal mesh–covered windows of the first and second floor whirring by and then slowly coming into focus as the truck slowed to a crawl. "How's that?" he called.

"Forward about another two feet to center the rear of the truck under the windows!" Gemma called. "And… perfect!"

Kaplan tapped the brakes, pushing Gemma into the ladder, and then she was moving, Gregson climbing in parallel. Reaching the top, Gemma grabbed the double metal loops installed in the roof and pulled herself up. The top of the truck had an additional long silver compartment that ran the length of the vehicle's body, stopping just short of the cab. Slightly narrower than the width of the truck, it allowed for two, narrow, full-length walkways on either side. Those walkways shortened the flat roof of the truck, but that still left them a roughly five-foot-by-twelve-foot open landing platform. Looking up, Gemma quickly gauged the distance. The truck had taken a full story off the jump, but they still had a long way to go. The drop would be easier on the kids if they could dangle from the window, dropping them another five or so feet, but the position of the truck wouldn't allow for that. They'd have to jump.

"Jump down one at a time!" Gemma called. "Keep your feet and knees together; that will make it easier to land on your feet. Concentrate on bending your knees to take the force of the fall. Don't worry about falling off because we'll move in to catch you. Once you're steady, get down the ladder, run along the front wall of the school, and then head for Bay Parkway by the end wall where there are no windows. Head for the command center, the big white trailer at the corner of Bay Parkway and East Third. Additional officers will help you there. If there are injuries, we'll deal with them as we go." She raised both hands, waving her fingers in a *come on* gesture. "Let's go! Aim for the middle of the platform." She met the eyes of the first boy to think of jumping, the first to have the nerve to throw a leg out into thin air. "You first. You can do it! We'll catch you." She moved toward the front of the truck as Gregson followed her lead and moved to the back, leaving a large landing pad. "Ready!"

Indecision shone for a moment in the boy's eyes, and then another double gunshot sounded behind him and he focused his gaze on the truck, braced his hands, slipped his feet onto the narrow window ledge, and pushed off. He was in the air for only a second, but he successfully kept his body in line. He landed on both feet with a metallic thud that shook the truck, but Gemma and Gregson immediately moved in, each catching an arm and steadying him when he pitched forward, limiting him to a single step.

The boy turned his wide eyes to Gemma. He was breathing hard, nearly panting and gripped her forearm with a stranglehold she suspected would leave bruises. But he was down.

"Steady?" At his nod, Gemma let him go and pointed toward where Kaplan stood at the bottom of the stairs. "Go. You understood my directions? Everyone else is going to follow you."

"I got it." He flashed her a smile that conveyed his relief and gratitude better than words ever could, and let go. He half-staggered to the ladder, climbed down, and then lit out at a run.

Gemma turned her face up to the window to find a girl had slipped into the open spot and the boy at the second window was ready to jump. She waved at him. "We're ready for you."

They got into a rhythm. In about twenty to thirty second intervals, they could get a kid down, steadied, and on their way down the ladder before getting ready for the next kid. Inside the classroom, Gemma got an occasional glimpse of an older man organizing the kids into two lines, occasionally stepping closer to give an encouraging word.

They made good time and had most of the students cleared out in short order, even as the sound of gunfire faded from the background. But with no guarantee of the shooter being apprehended—Morin could get word through to them via the truck radio, but hadn't—they kept going. The evacuation slowed down as one girl was reluctantly coaxed into the window, but then wouldn't budge, allowing only one window for egress. Finally, only this one terrified student remained with the teacher, who now leaned out the open window to talk to her.

"Come on down!" Gemma called. "We'll catch you!"

The girl shook her head frantically.

In the background, the sound of male voices rose. Commanding voices. Had to be the A-Team. She needed to get that girl out of the window before the shooter or tactical came through the door and scared her into a fall. The kind of fall that ended with a broken neck.

"You need to move now. Don't be scared."

Gemma couldn't hear what the teacher said, but she saw his lips moving. She nodded reluctantly once, then two more times.

"She's coming down," the teacher called.

"That's great! What's your name?"

"Melissa."

"Melissa, I want you to keep your eyes on me." Without looking, Gemma pointed down at the metal surface stretching between herself and Gregson. "You're going to push off and land right here beside me. On the count of three. One... two... *three!*"

With a muffled shriek, the girl pushed off. But as soon as she was in midair, Gemma could see the trajectory was wrong and she was going to only make the top platform if they were lucky. Gemma sprang forward just as the girl hit the top of the truck, only barely catching the edge of the roof and starting to fall backward, the solid brick wall of the school waiting to crack her head open only a foot away. Gemma and Gregson both dove for her, Gregson catching her flailing arm and Gemma her waistband. Gemma yanked as hard as she could, fighting to keep a hold of the denim as it slipped in her fingers, and threw herself backward as counterbalance. Melissa's feet slipped off the top platform as she crashed down a foot to the lower-level catwalk, but then she sprawled forward, dragged by Gemma as she went down herself on the top of the truck, taking Melissa's full weight and cushioning her fall.

The girl lay gasping, her head resting on Gemma's stomach, but her skull was intact and she was breathing.

Gemma raised herself up on her elbows as Gregson knelt down beside them. "Melissa! Are you okay?"

The girl scrunched her eyes shut and nodded her head.

"Come on, then, up you go," said Gregson, grasping her hand and pulling her vertical.

Melissa's weight lifted from Gemma, who then scrambled to her feet, looking up as Gregson passed Melissa off to Kaplan, who was halfway up one of the ladders.

Above her, the teacher was in the window and ready to jump. "That's everyone but me," he called.

Gemma checked to make sure Gregson was in position. "We're ready for you."

The man drew in a deep breath. "Here I come." He jumped.

They caught him as he landed, but he lurched sideways, rolling one ankle and falling toward Gregson, who neatly caught him and boosted him upright. "Are you okay, sir?"

The older man put a little weight on his left foot, but gave a yelp of pain and transferred it all to his right. "I may have sprained my ankle."

"We can get that looked at," Gemma said. "We'll get you down and then get you into the cab of the truck. We have EMTs on-site. They'll be able to fix you up."

Gemma waited as Gregson and Kaplan got the man down to the ground. Standing on the top of the truck, Gemma followed the path of the students. The first student—the boy in the green sweatshirt—stood at the edge of Bay Parkway, sending students toward the command center. As the last girl crossed to him, he turned with her and they jogged down the road, crossing the intersection at East 2nd Street.

Right past a gathering crowd.

Gemma could hear the shouts from where she stood, not the individual words, but the tone. And then she caught a flash of electric blue and had to hold back the growl building in her throat.

She took a protective step forward, but the two teenagers only slowed for a moment and then continued jogging past the group and farther down the sidewalk.

Her gaze jerked back to the crowd. That wasn't a harmless bunch of rubbernecking onlookers.

That was the media.

As Gemma stood there, hands on hips, she knew it was likely she was in the camera's eye. And that flash of blue told her that ABC7 was on scene, dressed in their station color.

And ABC7 meant Greg Coulter.

Gemma didn't like to think she had a nemesis, but if she did, it would be that perfectly coiffed, dressed-to-the-nines Rottweiler. Okay, not a Rottweiler, an investigative reporter. But he sure acted like a Rottweiler when he was going after a story. Greg Coulter, whom she didn't seem to be able to shake lately. The reporter who'd dogged her steps last August when she'd traded herself for a group of hostages and then the hostage taker had tried to escape using Gemma as a shield. It had nearly worked, until Coulter and his cameraman had spotted them and pursued. Coulter had ended up taking a bullet for his trouble that day. And then just last month, at the prison riot at Rikers Island, the inmates had asked for him specifically as the media contact to present their demands to. She'd had to play nice with Coulter, who hadn't wanted to play nice in return, and then had to practically blackmail him into not broadcasting his interview with the inmates to the world.

Coulter wouldn't be looking to do her any favors anytime soon. And this was currently the hottest story in town, so he was guaranteed to be on his way, if he hadn't already arrived. And while the majority of the action was inside the school, Gregson, Kaplan, and she had just staged a life-and-death rescue in full view of the cameras.

She hoped her father had the TV off. If not, he'd probably watched her save a class and then get flattened by one of the students. And if he'd seen it, it was only a matter of minutes until he showed up on-site.

Goddamn Coulter. He would never make her life easier. But he sure as hell could make it harder as this incident went on.

The NYPD just had to make sure he had absolutely no access to what was going on inside the school.

And that was easier said than done when it came to a junkyard dog like Coulter.

CHAPTER 12

Logan and his team quickly cleared the fourth-floor east wing. Each unoccupied room was searched, including every cupboard and closet and nook big enough to hold even a small child. Each area considered a hot zone, team members breached every space leading with their rifles, calling out their designation. Each occupied room was confirmed to have an adult present, each who confirmed a student head count, reported no injuries, and was then instructed to shelter in place until officers came to escort them to safety as they sequentially evacuated the school of more than four thousand students. Every team member was laser focused, each with a belly that burned with fury for those taken.

The east side of the floor cleared, it was now time to see if they were needed for the existing threat, or if that was under control. And if so, was it under control for the same reason as the fourth-floor shooter?

Logan wanted it over, preferably without additional loss of life, but if the death of the second gunman was what it took to save innocent children, then so be it.

He understood the cost of killing and personally bore the scars, smudges on his soul that would never wash away. But this would be one scar that would never form if it came down to him needing to take the shot. In his opinion, sometimes swift, sure justice in a concrete case like this was best for everyone involved.

Logan keyed his mic. "Unit 1 to Nilsson. We've completed the sweep of the east section of the fourth floor. Do you need us to relocate to the third-floor west wing?"

"Negative, Unit 1. Units 2 and 6 are in place and the shooter has gone quiet inside one of the classrooms."

Logan exchanged glances with Redding, who followed along through his own headset, recognizing the same caution in his eyes. "Quiet because he's gone passive or because he's down?"

"Passive, so we've moved to passive shooter protocols. Sims and Sanders are there and are trying to open up lines of communication."

"Is the classroom occupied? Has he taken hostages?"

"Unknown at this point."

"You know you have HNT right outside. Why aren't you bringing in Capello?"

"Sanders doesn't want to cross that line yet. He knows she's on-site, but he's trying to determine if the shooter is giving up or holing up. He doesn't want to force the guy's hand into holing up by bringing in a negotiator, which might signal a longer-term situation. Right now, the shooter only knows tactical is on the other side of the door, which may force his hand to surrender sooner. Sanders also wants to determine if he can get eyes in there to assist with negotiations if needed."

"We'll complete doing classroom checks for students and teachers to be evacuated after the wounded are moved while the hallways are clear. We'll also assist EMTs in bringing out the wounded from room 436. There are several critical who will need to be moved quickly."

"Ten-four Unit 1. Unit 4 is bringing up another pair of EMTs and a number of patrol officers to assist with the victims, and then Unit 4 can assist Unit 1 with clearing the floor."

"Ten-four." Logan turned to his team. "Redding, Turner, Lin, and Perez, clear every classroom from the center block down through the west wing on this floor. Check for any shooter who's holed up hiding, which could lead to a potential hostage situation. Prepare the classrooms for evacuation once we have the green light on this floor that the EMTs are finished. Unit 4 will assist. Lewis, with me. We're going back to the art room. The EMTs will need escorts out of the building and I want to know what happened in there."

They strode down the hall, Logan and Lewis leading the way. But as they turned the corner from the east wing to the main corridor, the sound of retching carried to them. Halfway down the hallway, a uniformed patrol officer in a Kevlar vest was losing his breakfast into a garbage can. He straightened to press one hand against the wall, his head sagging and his shoulders rising and falling as he fought to get himself under control.

Logan glanced sideways at Lewis, but there was no amusement at what could be considered the weak stomach of a junior officer. The grim set of Lewis's jaw echoed Logan's own determination. Logan had seen what this officer had seen, had mirrored his reaction, but years of seasoning had helped keep him steady. For a new officer in blue, this kind of horror could overwhelm and scar.

It could also scar the experienced; they'd simply already developed skills to keep their walls intact so those scars didn't show to the greater outside world. It was why he'd picked Lewis to step into the art room versus one of the newer team members. Because Lewis would hold.

You dealt with the massacre of children however you could. It was the stuff of nightmares, of PTSD, and Logan knew that previous brief glimpse was nothing compared to what they were about to see. He might be lucky to keep his own breakfast down.

Unit 1 split up at the door of the art room.

"NYPD, coming in," Logan called out just before he and Lewis stepped through the door. Still, the four EMTs in the room jerked and looked up when they entered. Jumpy, with good reason.

It was the smell that hit him first. Blood, urine, and feces. The smell of death.

He forced himself to step forward.

The scene wasn't so different than the one he'd seen the first time he'd entered the room. Blood still sprayed across counters, cupboards, and tables in the far corner from the door, and bodies still sprawled on the floor. But they were no longer in the same pile. Now a few still forms lay in straight lines on the floor, separated from the rest as the patrol officers sorted through the dead and the living as EMTs frantically helped those who still hung on. A pair of girls sat on stools pulled up to the tables, sobbing. They were blood-splattered and emotionally shattered, though otherwise looked physically whole.

Considering the slaughter that took place here, they may be the only ones.

"Over here." A patrol sergeant and several officers were scattered through the injured, helping the EMTs sort out who needed help first. And who was beyond help.

Tactical might be doing the majority of the heavy lifting today, but it was the core of the NYPD who filled in every gap, the men and women in blue who had turned out en masse, many off duty, to assist where they could. He was thankful for every one of them.

Logan circled the area, trying to stay clear of a crime scene where attention to the living trumped maintaining the integrity of the scene. "Sergeant, I'm Detective Logan. This is Detective Lewis. Where do you need us?"

A stocky man with a salt-and-pepper buzz cut jerked his head once in an acknowledging nod. "Sergeant Franco. We're trying to sort the victims as quickly as possible." Franco glanced over Logan's shoulder to give Lewis a nod. "Pretty much anyone in front was hit. Including the teacher, who it looks like was attempting to keep the class behind her. She died first, with the most catastrophic injuries." He kept his voice low, conscious of the ears around him. "Five gone so far, EMTs are working on three criticals. Two got up and walked away. We're sorting through the rest." He held up gloved hands, smeared with blood and head cocked toward the mass of students, some moving, some moaning, too many much too still. "We're working with EMT Pace"—he glanced in the direction of a young man with dark skin under a neat beard, his kinky hair in a trimmed flattop—"to determine who we can move and who needs to stay in place. If they're gone and are blocking other kids, we're shifting them. If they're mobile, we'll move them out on foot when we get a few more officers in here. If not mobile, the EMTs brought backboards to carry them down the stairs since there are no elevators."

"We'll give you a hand." Logan made sure the safety of his rifle was fully engaged, and pulled the sling around so the rifle lay flat against his back and stayed out of his way. Then he extracted a pair of black nitrile gloves from a pocket of his tactical pants and pulled them on over his tactical gloves. Taking a deep breath, he stepped into a small patch of open flooring, careful as he planted his boot not to slip on the blood-slicked surface. The boy he bent over was breathing hard through clenched teeth; the right side of his torso from hip to knee as well as his right arm were dotted with buckshot, the clothing around it saturated with blood. But not so much blood that Logan felt it was a risk to move him, not when the girl trapped under both him and a motionless boy was quietly moving and he couldn't determine her injuries. He met the boy's eyes, huge and dark in his pale, blood-specked face, and gave him a reassuring nod. "Hang on, buddy, we have you. Pace? This one was shot four times, twice in the leg, once in the hip, and once in the forearm."

Pace squatted down beside the boy and did a quick examination, asking the boy questions to assess the extent of his injuries. Logan could see he was checking to make sure there were no spinal injuries and that the bleeding could be controlled. It was a balancing act between each child's injuries, time ticking away, and the victims they were blocking who also needed assistance, potentially more critically. "He's clear to move, but he can't manage it himself. I need you to pick him up for transport. *Carefully.* I'd backboard him, but his spine is intact and there's simply nowhere to logroll him onto a board in this area. Carry him over to the area we've set up for triage." He pointed to the far side of the room where tables had been pushed together to give students a place to sit or lie down until they could be removed from the room. Standing, Pace picked his way over to Lewis, who was waving for his attention.

Logan looked down at the boy. "I'm Sean. What's your name?"

"Rob."

"Okay, Rob, I'm going to move you to a clear area where you can be examined more thoroughly. Can you help me? It's going to hurt, probably a lot, but we need to move you out of this area."

The boy nodded. "I can do it. I… I don't want to be here."

"I get that. Grab onto my shoulders. I'm going to lift you. I'll do all the work; you just hold on."

He moved the boy with relative ease—and he hoped relatively little pain to Rob—and then returned to the same place and the motionless boy. It was clear the boy had passed from his injuries, but Logan still took ten seconds to search for a pulse in his throat, just in case. Fury built as he gently closed the staring eyes and then he and Lewis shifted the body to lie with the other dead children.

His heart sank as he returned to the girl who had been trapped beneath. She no longer moved, but lay lax, rolled onto her side, her eyes open and fixed on nothing, her long red hair matted with clotted blood. *Is she gone? She was here only moments ago.* But moments were all it took for life to slip away. A curse rose in his throat, but he battled it back as he bent and pressed two fingers to her throat in search of the heartbeat he knew in his gut he wouldn't find.

But did.

His gaze snapped from his fingers to her face, but utter blankness remained. He scanned her form—she was blood-splattered, but her clothing was undisturbed and she didn't appear to have any injuries. He gently tapped her cheek. "Miss? I'm Detective Logan from the NYPD and I'm here to help you." There was no response. He gently tipped her face toward him, until her eyes should have seen him, but he instinctively knew she saw nothing.

She was alive but trapped inside the nightmare of her own mind. And as long as she was here in this room, she'd likely stay away as a form of self-protection.

Logan looked up to find Pace only about six feet away. "Pace? Could use you here."

The EMT sidled his way back. "Is she gone?"

"She's alive, but unresponsive."

Pace crouched down beside her, examined her quickly. "Respiration is shallow and pulse is thready. She's in severe shock. We need to get her out of here before it becomes life threatening. Can you carry her out? We can't spare a backboard for her to get her down the stairs. Too many others need it and there's only so many to go around."

"I can take her. She's fine to move?"

"Better than leaving her in here. If she's registering her surroundings, it may be contributing to the shock."

After stripping off his bloody nitrile gloves, Logan bent, slipped his arms under the girl, and lifted her. Her limp body sagged, her head lolling drunkenly until Logan stood and shifted her, cradling her closer to his chest, her head resting against his shoulder, her staring eyes fixed sightlessly somewhere over her knees. If she recognized what was happening, she gave no indication. If Logan didn't know better, he would have thought he bore the dead.

"Take her to any ambulance outside," Pace instructed. "They'll help her."

Logan carefully skirted the legs and feet of the bodies laid out on the floor, sidling sideways, his rifle scraping against the counter. Getting clear of the worst of the scene, he carried her into the hallway and past officers standing guard. He carried the girl carefully down two flights of steps in the stairwell, maneuvering through the few doors and then out onto the second floor and toward the main staircase. The whole time, the girl never moved.

Down the main staircase, past the body of Officer Kail still sprawled on the floor, awaiting the arrival of the crime techs to document his death, out through the main doors, and into the cool sunny autumn afternoon. But the brightness had no effect on the darkening pall shrouding Logan's emotions as the scope of the tragedy and his helplessness to stop it seemed to rest in the redemption of this one slight girl.

He strode down the front walk, past the blue tarp that draped the body of the boy in the band T-shirt, shielding it from public view, and toward Bay Parkway. Emergency vehicles jammed the street, lights flashing, and Logan scanned them, searching for ambulances. He found a cluster of them at the east end of the school. He speed-walked toward them, careful not to jostle his precious cargo, ignoring the lenses of the camera crews across the street.

A pair of EMTs waiting with a gurney spotted him and waved him closer. Logan gently laid the girl out on the gurney and then stepped away as both EMTs closed in around her, checking vitals, calling them out to each other.

He needed to return, needed to move, but he couldn't tear his gaze from the girl's face. All those students dead and bleeding in that art room and here he was, rooted in place, motionless with horror, transfixed, staring at this girl, splattered with so much blood that wasn't hers.

Those who were lost were beyond his help and were no longer in pain, though they left behind those whose agony was only just beginning. Those who were less seriously wounded could recover from their physical injuries. But the psychological impact of the attack would haunt these kids for the rest of their lives.

He was witnessing that impact in living color before his eyes. A girl with her whole life ahead of her, likely with a bright future, who was now trapped inside the hellscape of her own mind. Physically intact, but psychologically broken. He suspected this would be the hardest injury to come back from.

"We have her."

Logan pulled his gaze from the girl's inanimate face to stare at the EMT working on his side of the gurney.

She laid a gloved hand on his arm, just above the cuff of his tactical glove. "We have her," she repeated. "We'll take care of her. She's safe. Go help the rest." Her smile was gentle as she gave his arm a squeeze before letting go. Before returning to her own job of saving these kids.

Logan nodded, looked at the girl for another second, and then turned away to jog into the school.

He didn't look back.

CHAPTER 13

Raised voices attracted Gemma's attention, drawing her gaze toward the rear of an A-Team vehicle where Logan stood toe-to-toe with Nilsson. She couldn't hear their words distinctly, but Logan's tone carried frustration and anger. Which was surprising, because Logan's ability to stay cool under pressure was one of the main reasons he was so well suited to the A-Team.

He's rattled. And no wonder, considering what he's seen.

Gemma's eyebrows rose in surprise when Logan dropped his safety glasses into his upside-down helmet and slammed it on the floor of the truck just inside the open doors before striding away from Nilsson without a backward glance.

"I don't want to see you here in under ten!" Nilsson yelled after him. "Not until you've walked it off!"

Gemma exchanged a look with a nearby patrol officer. "Do you mind keeping the kids moving from here? I think I need to check on someone."

"I got it. Do what you need to do."

"Thanks. I won't go far in case something shifts with the second shooter. If anyone's looking for me, I'm with Detective Logan." Gemma rose and turned to track Logan as he stalked away from the command center down Bay Parkway. She hurried after him through the leaves that littered the sidewalk.

Five inches taller than Gemma and carrying a head of steam, Logan strode away from her in ground-eating strides she'd never keep up with at a walk. Breaking into a light jog, she took in his head-down posture, one gloved hand balled into a fist, and his shoulders set into a stiff line that rode close to his ears.

No wonder Nilsson wanted him to take ten. He's wound tight enough to pop. And anyone with that emotional level can't set foot inside the school.

"Sean!"

If he heard her, he didn't acknowledge it in any way. He just kept walking fast enough that she was barely gaining on him.

She picked up the pace as he turned the corner onto East 4th Street, striding down the sidewalk past a row of narrow two-story homes. It was a quiet, dead-end street, flanked on both sides by trees so old they towered overhead, their branches intertwining above the roadway in the last vibrant tones of autumn.

"Sean!" She finally caught up with him under the heavy bough of an oak tree and grabbed the crook of his left arm, yanking it to spin him to face her.

He came around, one fist white-knuckled around the stock of his rifle, the other raised to strike until he realized who stood before him. His hand dropped, fingers splaying wide as if throwing away his rage. "Damn it, I could have hit you."

"Not on purpose. Didn't you hear me calling your name?"

His blank expression answered her question.

"You're really wrapped up in your own head. When you didn't answer me, I had to run to catch you."

"When I didn't answer, you should have gotten the hint."

"I got the hint. I just didn't take it. What's up with Nilsson?"

"Saw that, did you?"

"Hard to miss."

"He wants a few of us to take a break. I want to go back in. The clock is ticking."

"Other teams are in there now. You can afford ten after what you had to deal with this morning."

"We need *everyone* in there now!" Rage overflowed in his tone and in the vicious clench of his fist as he spun away from her.

Gemma could see his intended target and reached for him before he could throw a punch at the wide trunk of the decades-old hardwood. She grabbed his wrist with both hands, letting him jerk her forward a step, but it kept him from following through. "Stop. You slug a tree and you won't be helping anyone because you'll be off the team while your broken hand heals. Take a breath. This is why you need to walk it off."

"Nilsson knows I'm pissed. Anyone would be."

"Of course they would. Even you, who has one of the coolest heads I know. Talk to me about what happened in there."

He gave a vicious head shake, flicked off her hold, and strode away, yanking off his tactical gloves and stuffing them in a thigh pocket of his pants. "Leave it alone, Gemma."

"Sean, stop." She took three steps to follow him and then, realizing the futility of chasing him, halted. She needed to appeal to him emotionally, because unless she tackled him to the sidewalk—something she'd done in hand-to-hand practice on mats at the academy, but she gave him the upper edge of rage this time—she wasn't going to physically stop him. "Talk to me. It's Gem."

Her use of his name for her finally stopped his driving pace. *Gem.* The name he called her in their most intimate moments. The name he used when he was bonded to her—or needed to be, like that moment at Rikers when a man's life was on the line and only their connection and shared past could save him.

He turned to find her about five feet away down the sidewalk. "You going to use your HNT psychoanalysis techniques on me?"

She took a step forward to meet him halfway. "No. I'm a friend asking you to lighten some of your load by telling me what you saw in there instead of holding it in so tight you're about to blow. You want to get back in there to help those kids, this is how you do it."

"You don't want to know what I saw in there."

"I can imagine some of what you must have seen, but that doesn't cut it. I want to know what's really going on in there." As disbelief streaked over his face, she amended, "Okay, I need to know. I need to know what Sam's going through in there."

"He's still in there?"

"No one knows anything for sure. We've heard nothing from him or from anyone who knows him. If he was out, surely he would have found a way to get through to one of us. Or NYPD command. The Capello name would move the message along quickly. Yet... nothing." She took a breath, battling back the terror that rose if she let herself consider what he might be going through. Or worse, what might already be past for him. The thought of Sam dying, today of all days, made her stomach threaten to lurch into her throat. She half-turned away from Logan. "God almighty… it's the wrong day for this."

Logan considered her quizzically, his head slightly tilted, his eyes narrowing as if trying to deduce her meaning. "It's never the right day for something like this."

"No, it's not. But… but…" She stuttered to a halt, unable to force the words out. She was struggling to compartmentalize and the dividing walls in her head were beginning to crack.

"But what?"

She closed her eyes and forced the words out, knowing that if she gave a little, he might as well. And she very much needed him to. "Because it's twenty-five years to the day since we lost my mother." She could hear the raw grief ripping through her words. "And here we are all over again."

"God, Gem." Logan closed the space between them. "I'm so sorry." He slipped his fingers between hers, gripping her hand palm to palm. She squeezed back with equal force. "Twenty-five years ago, you were almost as old as Sam, and you went through what he might be experiencing right now. You shouldn't be here for this."

Anger made her try to yank her hand free, but he doggedly held on and wouldn't let her break the connection. "Shouldn't be here? This is the only place I should be. Here's where I can help."

"Can you? With what must be going on in your head?" When she turned the full force of her fury on him, he held up a placating hand. "I'm not doubting your skills, but this has to be distracting you."

"You know what's distracting me? The thought of what my nephew might be going through in there."

"Is that why Chief Capello's not here?"

"Dad's not here because he took the day off and I'm hoping he's sitting reading a book or something and doesn't have the TV on or my ass is grass. I told Alex not to tell him. Worse, I'm on scene and *I'm* not telling him."

Logan winced. "He's going to be pissed when he finds out. And he will find out."

"Sure he will, but the original plan was that this would be wrapped in fifteen minutes, and I'd tell him once we already had Sam in hand." She tossed an acidic glare toward the end of the street. "But that's not how this has turned out." She moved to face him fully. "Tell me what you saw. I *need* to know. And you need to let some of it go before you'll be steady enough to go back in. We can help each other."

He deflated slightly, as if her pain and fury somehow let the pent-up air out of his sails. "I'll tell you what I saw if you answer me this first. Does Morin know? Or Garcia?"

"What today is? No. But they know Sam might be in there and don't have a problem with me assisting outside the school. Now tell me. I need to be prepared." The rest of the sentence—*for the worst*—hung silently between them.

"It's as bad as you think it is. Started off bad with a dead student on the front walk. Young guy, hard to tell how old because it was a headshot and the top of his head and a lot of his face was gone. But from what I could see..." Logan trailed off, his jaw clenching and his lips compressing chalk-white.

She stayed silent, giving him a moment to gather the emotion spinning in his head and to put it into actual words. She could feel his struggle from the ripple that passed from his fingers to hers.

"He could have been me at that age. Acne, a band T-shirt, ragged jeans, but brand-new expensive sneakers. Just some poor kid who got up and dragged his ass to school thinking it was a typical school day. Who then tried to escape someone nothing short of evil, and died in a pool of his own blood and brain matter on the school walkway. And we had to just run by him. Leaving him there, all alone. *Jesus Christ.*"

Gemma honestly couldn't tell if he was swearing or sending up a plea for help. What she did know was that Logan was describing the scene in a way he never would with his fellow A-Team officers. *Wouldn't want to look weak.*

"When we went in," he continued, "the SRO was dead in the foyer, but we had to run by him, too. I could hear the shotgun firing as we were going up the stairwell to the fourth floor. I knew it was going to be bad. You know, you work this job for years, you think you've seen it all. You think you're prepared."

"There's no way to prepare for this. They're kids."

"They wouldn't want to be called that, but yeah, they're kids. And they were slaughtered." He had to stop, take a breath, settle himself. "We ended up in the east wing on the fourth floor. The art wing. A lot of the doors were closed, the rooms dark. There were classes in there, but they were following procedure. You could see he'd fired into the ceiling every couple of doorways down the hall. He was trying to scare the living daylights out of those kids and teachers."

"Successfully, I'd bet."

"Yeah. It all went to hell when we came to a room where the door was ajar, the window blown out. At first I thought he'd gone into an empty room by mistake. From the doorway you could see backpacks and artwork out on the tables, but it looked like they'd evacuated. Until I took a few steps into the room. Then..." He swallowed hard, his Adam's apple sliding under the skin of his throat. "Holy shit, Gem. It was a massacre."

Gemma didn't say anything, just gripped his hand tighter.

"They'd done everything right, and were clustered together at the end of the classroom against the hallway wall so there was no way to see them, no way to aim at them unless you were in the room with them. And he took care of that pretty handily by simply shooting out the window in the door, slipping his hand through, and turning the knob. My guess is he never went in more than a few steps. He didn't need to. In fact, that produced the more effective shot pattern."

Logan would never use ten words when five would do, but now the story was pouring out of him, revealing only to someone who knew how he ticked how rattled he was. "He was the one with the shotgun?"

"Yeah, loaded with buckshot. My guess is triple aught. He was probably thirty-five feet away from the group when he shot into them multiple times."

Gemma winced. She could imagine the results in her mind, but that would have been nothing compared to what Logan must have experienced, seeing it with his own eyes.

"The death toll in that room alone is eight kids and the teacher so far, but when I left, they were still working on them. Some of the kids were critical and might not survive to the doors of the ER. You know what buckshot is like. The initial blast would have hit whoever was in front, and the pieces of buckshot would go through them, deflected out in a wider pattern to hit whoever was behind them. Catastrophic damage. Blood everywhere. Sprayed and splattered and running—" He had to stop, his head bowed, breathing hard as he collected himself before he could continue. "It's almost a miracle any of them survived, but they did."

"These kids aren't dumb. They would have been terrified, but some of them would still be thinking. They'd hit the ground and pretend to be dead, so the shooter would move on."

"God, I hope so. And he moved on all right. To the next classroom. The music room. And we had to leave those kids there in the art room, the living tangled with the dead and dying, to go after the shooter before he added to his kill count."

"You didn't have any choice."

"I know that! I was there!" The words exploded from Logan, hard and harsh. He sucked in a breath through clenched teeth and ran his free hand over his short blond hair, making the helmet-flattened strands stick up in every direction. For a moment, his hand fisted in his hair, then he let go. "Sorry. I'm not yelling at you."

"I know. Just tell me, however it needs to come out. What happened in the music room?" She knew the ending, but needed him to walk her through it. He needed it, too, because the injustice of the perpetrator getting away without what Logan would view as punishment had to be eating at him.

"As we got closer, we could hear him screaming."

"What did he say?"

"I didn't catch all of it. After a while all that mattered was the tone—there was so much rage—but the take-home message was that he wanted everyone to die. He wanted the world to burn, and was happy to set the match. Then we came face-to-face with all that rage when he tried to kill us through the classroom wall. Once we got in, we found the shotgun. A Mossberg pump-action."

"Reliable. That's not a weapon that's likely to malfunction on you."

"And the tube magazine that comes standard on that model holds six plus one in the chamber. He unloaded the entire magazine at us through the concrete block wall. Luckily, we were all down on the ground or we'd have had multiple casualties—or even fatalities."

"He used that weapon to commit suicide?"

"No. He'd taken the resource officer's handgun and that did the job neatly for him. Headshot."

She met his gaze. "I know you were prepared to do what needed to be done, but I'm glad you didn't have to. This day is already hard enough."

"Yeah. But, really, how do we compare what we're experiencing to the parents who've lost kids, or, more, the kids who survived, but will never be the same again? And not necessarily because of physical injury." His expression closed in, his eyes shuttered behind his narrowed lids.

Gemma waited for a few seconds, but he didn't continue. "What do you mean?"

"I helped carry out some of the critical victims. We split up Unit 1 with everyone but Lewis and I working with Unit 4 to clear the rest of the fourth floor. We circled back to check on the EMTs. They needed help getting the criticals taken out to the ambulances while they kept doing assessments, so until more hands arrived, we carried them out. The EMTs got them stabilized and strapped down to backboards. A school this old means there isn't true accessibility. Kids who are physically disabled are assigned to different schools instead. No elevator meant carrying them down the stairs, thus the backboards. One of the kids we took was bad. Hit in the leg, nicked the femur, he was bleeding out. They got the leg tourniquetted off and started him on fluids and then packed him. Lewis and I carried him down to the first floor and delivered him to an ambulance, which then took off at top speed."

"Likely had to, if they have any chance of saving him. Sounds like what he needs is a surgeon."

"And several units of blood. But that wasn't the one who bothered me most. That was a girl I took out to the ambulance. They couldn't spare a backboard for a kid who had no physical injuries, so I picked her up and carried her out."

"She was deemed more important than one of the shooting victims?"

"Because of mental distress. She was alive, but she... wasn't there. We found her underneath a couple of kids, one shot multiple times, one dead. And she'd been lying there until we dug her out. It wasn't just that she was in shock. I've seen lots of kids in shock today. You, too, I'm sure."

"Yes."

"But this girl. It was like what she witnessed closed her off. She just went away. Catatonic." Fury was building in his voice again.

Gemma understood that fury, and if they had more time, she'd have suggested something physical to dispel it. But that was a luxury they didn't have. "It may have been the safest thing for her to do. After what she'd seen—it's the stuff of nightmares."

"I think she's still stuck in that nightmare in her head."

"Or maybe she's finally found peace away from it."

"Either way, that's not how you live a life. And it wasn't the life she was leading two hours ago. How do you come back from that?"

Gemma pushed away the images that slid past her defenses—the wide eyes of terrified, huddled, adults; a cold marble floor splattered with blood; her mother's cooling hand locked in hers—in an attempt to stay focused on the present. "The strong can, but they need help. And she'll have support to help bring her back. Family, friends, counselors. You know what the response to an incident like this is like. The Department of Education will pull out all the stops, as they should. You did your bit to bring her out. Now let the medical and mental health experts bring her home."

"Yeah, I guess. If nothing else, I need to concentrate on that." Logan checked his watch. "I need to get back."

"Are you steady now? Or steady enough? Ready to take on round two?"

"Yeah, steady enough." He squeezed her hand. "Thanks."

"Sometimes you can't talk to your own guys this way, especially when you're in the command chain. But that doesn't mean you don't need to talk it out. I'm lucky, I have my family I can use as my sounding board."

"Thanks for being mine."

A burst of static came from the press-to-talk mic/speaker clipped to Logan's vest. "Sanders to Logan."

He dropped her hand to activate his mic, tipping his head toward it. "Logan here."

"Is Capello with you?"

"Affirmative."

"We need her back now. The second shooter has barricaded himself with hostages and gone quiet. Neither Sims or I can get him to talk to us, so we need to put together a negotiation team and Capello's the only one from HNT on-site. Ten-two." *Ten-two. Return to command.*

"Ten-four. On our way." Logan locked gazes with Gemma as he deactivated his mic. "You up for this?"

"Have to be. Garcia is sending at least one more team member and is incoming himself. But if the shooter is willing to talk, then we're starting immediately. Anyone else can catch up on the fly."

What Logan had told her now carried an entirely different weight. She now needed to use that knowledge to save the lives of every student in that classroom.

They sprinted back to incident command.

CHAPTER 14

Gemma and Logan were nearly at the command center when her phone rang. She slipped it out of her pocket to scan the screen and then looked up to meet Logan's eyes. "It's Joe. I'll make it fast, but I need to take this." She dropped to a power walk, Logan falling into step with her, and answered the call. "I've only got a minute. Have you heard from Sam?"

"Not me, and not directly, but Alyssa has been texting other mothers while she Ubered to Barclays. She said she was too nervous to drive."

Gemma immediately heard the lack of the steel edge of stress that had been in his voice every time she'd talked to him in the last half hour. "And that way she could multitask while in motion. Your wife is one smart cookie."

"Don't I know it. The Mom Network has been working overtime. Everyone has been tracking their own kids and all the kids they know. Some kids have their cell phones, some don't, but some of those kids are with others with a line of communication, so locations and names are being compiled."

"That's fantastic. Joe, that's the kind of list we need down here."

"I know. I asked Alyssa to put what she has into an email and shoot it to me so I can pass it on. Who's running the incident?"

"Lieutenant Noah Morin."

"Good choice."

"Lucky choice he was on today as the closest citywide patrol supervisor. Whatever you have, pass it to him. But where's Sam?"

"One of the kids spotted him evacuating from the school. For whatever reason, he doesn't have his cell on him or he'd have already made contact. But they've likely herded him onto a bus to head for Barclays. Alyssa will meet him there. But in case he's still on the grounds, I came here." There was a brief pause. "I'm just parking actually."

"How close are you?"

"I'm north on East 5th Street. Give me six or seven minutes to jog in. I'm sure I'll get stopped a few times, but I'll badge my way through. I'll head to the buses first since that's likely where he is. If so, I'll pull him off."

"I've been looking for him in the face of every kid since I got here. I can't wait to see his big goofy grin."

"Ditto. Okay, I'm coming in."

"I may not be here. The second shooter just took hostages."

"*Mio Dio.* How lucky are they you're right there? Of course, you'll be busy."

"You better text me the minute you have him."

"Which will hopefully be soon. Good luck."

"Thanks. Same to you." Gemma hung up and slid her phone into her back pocket, taking what felt like the first comfortable breath in over a half hour.

"Sam's out?"

"Sounds like it. No one's heard from him yet, but chances of him being separated from his cell phone are high."

"And most kids depend on their contacts list for phone numbers, though you might think a cop would have his kid memorize his parents' numbers. Though he probably never calls them from memory and today might be enough to rattle details like that right out of his head."

Gemma knew Logan was trying to keep a positive spin on things for her sake, so even though she didn't buy Sam's faulty memory, she gave the concept some leeway. "Possibly. Joe's here now; if Sam's out, Joe will find him." She studied the crowd milling around the command center. "Our task is to get through that."

"Don't worry about that. Just stay behind me."

True to his word, Logan cleared a path for them with relative ease. Even without the helmet, the sight of a tactical officer that tall and imposing with his equipment and weapons, and clearly on a mission, had people stepping back. One quick scan showed them Morin was nowhere in sight, so Logan took the short, narrow flight of stairs into the command center two at a time, Gemma running behind him. Logan opened the door and led her inside.

Gemma had been in different mobile command centers before and found this one to be similarly arranged. There was a large screen on the front wall and another on the side wall opposite the door showing different views of the outside of the school. A long desk with three computer terminals was tucked into the tip-out extension. Uniformed operators with headsets sat at their keyboards doing a variety of tasks from monitoring A-Team body cams, to coordinating and tracking incoming officers, to liaising with the different groups within the department as well as FDNY EMS. They also had control over the various cameras on the vehicle, including two mobile, wireless cameras, and the aerial camera overhead on the extendable mast that rose forty feet into the air. Each station was outfitted with police, Marine, and CB radios for full communication. Beside them, a full tech rack held all the hard drives they'd need for recording video, satellite connections, and the download components for the wireless cameras. At the rear of the space, a door led to a separate room for interviews or to be used for hostage negotiation.

Under normal circumstances, there would be four negotiators on the negotiation team—the primary negotiator; the coach who sat with the primary and counseled via written notes when calls were ongoing; the scribe, who, even though each call was recorded, transcribed each conversation for instant reference and acted as the team's situational historian; and the coordinator, the team member who stood in between the negotiator and everyone involved who wanted a piece of them, from the NYPD brass, to the media, to anyone else applying pressure because they had a vested interest in either the people or the location involved.

For now, there was only Gemma.

Come on, Garcia, I could use anyone you can send. Or I could use you *if you're closest. Just one more teammate would do.*

As they came through the door, Morin turned around from where he had been bent over the workstation desk, braced on one arm, studying the screen. He was surrounded by officers and support staff running the technical aspects of the center. With the exception of Logan, there were no A-Team members.

"Good, you're here," said Morin. "Have you been updated on the hostage situation in room 317?"

"Yes. Do we have lines of communication into the classroom? Do we know how many students are in there with him? Do we know what class was scheduled to be in that room at that time and who should have been in there?"

"No, and no definitive numbers or class information yet. Principal Baker got into the school system remotely from his phone and reported that it's a freshman math class, but he can't say if everyone came to class or stayed in class once the lockdown was called. And there's no way to know if any students caught in the hallway are sheltering in place with that class because it was closest."

A freshman math class. What if it's Sam's math class?

Stop it. He's out. Joe said he's out.

But what if he's not? Someone saw him, but Joe hasn't confirmed yet. What if that wasn't Sam?

Gemma pushed down the fear and concentrated on Morin as he continued to speak.

"Some kids might have panicked and run before the door was closed, or might have been in the bathroom. I'm going to need you to go in there and make contact with the shooter. Help him set up lines of communication. Sanders and Sims yelling at him through a closed door isn't getting us anywhere. Hopefully you'll be able to get some of that information for us."

Go in there and make contact with him. If there was a rule every negotiator tried not to break, it was no face-to-face negotiating with the hostage taker. Separated negotiations provided safety and allowed the negotiator a calmer emotional state because they weren't personally at risk and could concentrate solely on making a connection with the hostage taker. Garcia wouldn't be happy at an order from the incident commander to send one of his people in.

"We definitely need better communications than yelling through a door," Gemma agreed. "Every school has a public address system; why not use that? Lieutenant Garcia wouldn't want face-to-face interactions if we had any other options, especially considering what this shooter has already done today in that building."

"That makes sense. And Principal Baker is outside still. He packed the kids onto the buses but refused to leave himself and has instead been trying to be useful in any way possible. We could fast-track this by having Baker take Capello inside to show her how to use the system to only get 317, and to not broadcast to the whole school. We don't need every terrified kid still in the building listening in when we have no idea what the shooter might say."

"Sir." Logan waited until Morin's gaze settled on him. "Me and a few of my team can take in both Principal Baker and Detective Capello. And can remain with them assuring their protection until the school is cleared, as long as there are sufficient units on-site. The rest of Unit 1 can assist with clearing the school as long as the situation remains passive and contained at two shooters."

"Agreed. But even with your protection, I want them both in body armor. Until we clear the entire school, we have to still consider the entire building a hot zone."

"Agreed. We've already provided Detective Capello with a sidearm and vest, and will provide a vest for Principal Baker."

"Good." Morin turned back to Gemma. "Anything else you need?"

"A PA system is great for initial contact, but it doesn't provide privacy for negotiations. I need this boy to surrender with his head held high and every hostage unharmed. And that means not humiliating him in front of that class, or what he might feel is humiliation if surrender makes him look weak. Once I make contact, assuming he doesn't have a phone of his own, and won't use any of the phones already in the room, I'd like to arrange for a throw phone for him." A throw phone was literally that, a phone tossed to a suspect who had no form of his own technology for communication, just to start the conversation. "We'll want to record every interaction, and I can do that through the voice recorder app on my cell for conversations via the PA system, but if we can get him to agree to a throw phone, I could put a call recording app on my cell to record every call. Or if he'd use a student or teacher phone, that would work, too. But we need to be prepared for all options."

"I can get you the tech. You just need to convince him to use it."

"Absolutely. He may be digging in because of what he sees as a heavy-handed A-Team presence outside his door, so a gentler and less aggressive voice—especially a female voice that he may view as less threatening—might draw him out and leverage cooperation. We can begin with me, but Lieutenant Garcia will want to establish a larger team. One of the most important places to start is with identification of the hostage taker. I gave you two names. Did you get confirmation on either of them?"

"The fourth-floor shooter was Hank Richter." Morin's tone was definitive.

"Based on...?" Logan asked. "I saw him. He wasn't ID'd from his face."

"He was carrying his wallet. Driver's license gave us his name."

"Hank was the dominant presence in the dyad," Gemma said. "He didn't feel the need to be anonymous because he never planned to leave the school alive. He may have even wanted to leave a trail for officers to follow." A thought occurred to Gemma, sharpening her tone. "You must have already deployed detectives to investigate his home. Is there any chance it's booby trapped? You're not sending officers there who might be in jeopardy?"

"Good thought, Capello, but we're already on-site. We're about to send in explosives dogs first with the bomb squad. Once we know it's safe, then the investigators will move in."

"Good. Please ensure they pass along anything important in real time. I don't know how long this negotiation will take and any clues as to motive and means will be invaluable. So that leaves our shooter. Is it the other boy? Russ Shea?"

"We don't know. But I think there's a good chance. Your girl wasn't the only one to suggest that name. Richter and Shea were ID'd by several different students."

"No teachers though."

"No."

"That may have been a deliberate choice. Any teachers who knew them might have been targets. Harder to do with all the kids who may have known you over four years. Sims and Sanders don't know the shooter's identity yet, so they haven't called him by name?"

"No."

"Good. I can make that reveal have a greater impact. Teams have been deployed to the Shea house as well?"

"Yes. We'll pass along anything useful."

"I may not always be available on comms if I'm actively negotiating. Please keep Detective Logan informed of any updates and he'll pass them along when I'm available. There's been no other indications of additional shooters?"

"Correct. The school is now quiet. More than that, students are telling us they're not hearing anything."

"Telling you? How?"

"Social media. We've been monitoring and communicating with students directly."

Morin looked toward the three officers bent over their keyboards, and Gemma realized in glimpses of the monitors that she was looking at TikTok and Facebook.

"These kids live on the internet," Morin continued. "They're using the hashtag #SGShooter, and figured out fast that if they bombarded the 66th Precinct's Facebook page, they'd get our attention pretty quick. And it's how they got word to each other. A lot of kids thought the lockdown was a drill, but these messages straightened them out fast. At this point in the incident, what we're hearing is that no one is picking up any more shooting. Hopefully we have this nailed down, but no one moves until we've cleared the building and are sure it's safe."

"What about the live stream?" Logan asked. "I terminated the stream on the fourth-floor shooter. Is the third-floor shooter still streaming?"

"No. He cut the stream as he was entering 317. At that point, it was only a detriment to him. He couldn't take the chance we were watching—and we were—and could have used those visuals against him."

"That's too bad. That would have given us an advantage." Gemma looked up at Logan. "We need to get going."

"We need to find Baker. You may have to talk him into going back in."

Gemma shook her head. "I don't think so. I had a hard time getting him to leave the school when we were evacuating the front foyer. He just wants to do whatever is needed to keep his kids safe."

"That would help." Logan turned to Morin. "Did you get Sanders's request for building schematics? Specifically the schematics for 317 and the surrounding areas?"

"Baker is working on that for us."

"It's an older building—is it going to be a problem?"

"The building is from 1914, but Baker knows schematics exist because they had to update the building for newer HVAC systems, and electrical and data wiring. I'll let tactical know as soon as I have it."

"Sir." One of the computer operators turned around. "Chief Phillips is on line one."

"Be right there." Morin met Logan's gaze. "Pick the officers you want and take Capello and Baker in now. If additional negotiators arrive, we'll bring them in separately."

"Yes, sir."

But Morin already had his back to them and was reaching for the handset to talk to his chief.

Gemma wound her way through the packed command center, out the door, and down the steps, Logan immediately behind her. "Where are your guys?"

Logan scanned the crowd over Gemma's head. "Nilsson will know. I don't want too many for this. Actually, one other should do it. We need officers out in the rest of the school, and two of us could hold the office in a worst-case scenario. Not to mention, you're armed and armored, and anyone else who shows up will also be, or we'll make sure they are. Now let's find Baker."

A few minutes later, they congregated behind the armored A-Team vehicle as Nilsson helped Baker strap into a bulletproof vest. Baker stood unnaturally still, his gaze shooting from Nilsson to the school and back again.

"You're sure you're willing to do this?" Gemma asked. "You could talk us through this on the phone."

"No, no, I'm fine. I want to help." His voice was tight and pitched a little higher than previously. Before, in the foyer with his students, adrenaline and his natural protective instinct would have carried him through. Now the trauma of the day was wearing on him. It would be much safer in the school now with body armor, an A-Team escort, and all the other officers present for the incident. Yet he was still walking into a building in lockdown, where he'd seen the death of his SRO and a number of his own students.

"We'll only keep you with us for as long as we need to figure out the system. Logan, Perez, are you ready?"

"Affirmative."

"Great, let's—" Gemma cut off as her cell phone sounded. She pulled it out to find Garcia's name splashed on the screen. "It's Garcia. I need to take this." She answered the call. "Lieutenant."

"Morin filled me in. Are you going in now?"

"Yes, sir."

"With tactical support?"

"Detectives Logan and Perez. Lieutenant Sanders and Detective Sims and their teams are outside the classroom and will remain there while we go to the school office to contact the classroom via the PA system."

"Good scenario for both separation and communication. Capello, you know we have only two options here."

"Yes, sir. Surrender with all the hostages intact, or a tactical breach."

"Yes. Are Logan and Perez with you now?"

"Yes, sir."

"Then I'll assume you can't say everything you'd like to say without ruffling a few feathers and you don't want anything getting back to Sanders, so I'll say it for you. A tactical breach is most likely going to cost lives. The shooter for sure. But possibly some or all of the hostages, depending on how many there are."

"My thoughts exactly, sir."

"I thought they might be. Which puts you in a tough situation."

"I admit I have concerns. This isn't a planned situation. The dominant partner took himself out. That was probably the plan for the submissive as well, but then he couldn't or didn't do it. He seems to have turned away from suicide. Not at his own hand, not by tactical."

"Or it would already be over."

"Exactly. It's doubtful he'll have demands. He's not making a point. He's already killed, so he knows the best he can expect is a long jail sentence. He's cornered, and, I suspect, lost. Russ Shea wasn't the planner—Hank Richter was. And now he doesn't know what to do next."

"Which makes him unpredictable. The real question is how long will he feel cornered and lost before he tries to leverage the hostages? But one thing is for sure—the moment gunfire is heard inside the room, tactical will go through the door."

"Agreed."

"Get in there and get started. Your biggest challenge may just be getting the kid to talk to you. I'm incoming and am arranging for a larger team. I'll be in contact as soon as I get to the command center. *I* know we're in good hands. Now show everyone else." Garcia ended the call.

Gemma switched her phone to vibrate and slid it into her back pocket. "Ready."

They jogged away from the vehicle, Logan leading, followed by Gemma, Baker, and Perez. There were enough officers in the school and enough of it had been cleared at this point that they no longer had to use the ballistic shield, and, as a result, could move much faster. Down the street, up the front walk, past two tactical officers stationed at the main doors, and in.

Minus the lack of students, the scene in the foyer hadn't changed to Gemma's eye—the resource officer still lay staring sightlessly at the ceiling, and the two trench coats were still piled at the bottom of the stairs. However, a few steps inside showed officers stationed in each of the first-floor hallways and open doors as far as the eye could see. An additional officer stood at the bottom of the main staircase running up to the second floor. It looked like they'd managed to clear the entire first floor, which was now held by the NYPD.

"The office is there." Baker pointed past the slain SRO's body to the frosted glass door beyond. "I'm not sure if anyone is in there still. My vice principal is off campus today at his brother's funeral in Jersey, but my admin staff was with me when the shooting started."

"They're out," Logan said. "Officers cleared the entire first floor of staff and students."

"Good." Relief relaxed some of the tension from Baker's face, until his gaze tracked up the open staircase where muffled shouts of "NYPD!" filtered down to them as officers continued to clear classrooms, cupboards, and supply closets.

Logan led the way to the office, giving the fallen officer a wide berth.

"Why is he still here?" Grief thickened Baker's words. "It doesn't seem right to leave him here, just lying there like that. Out in the open, for anyone to see."

Gemma caught at Baker's arm when he slowed. "I'm sorry, Principal Baker. This is a crime scene and it needs to be fully documented, but that can't happen until the school is cleared. It seems disrespectful to leave him like this, but it's actually what needs to happen to give him justice. Normally only law enforcement would see him like this, but you've offered your assistance. I'm sorry it comes with this extra burden. We only cover the deceased when they're in full public view because you can inadvertently add trace evidence by draping the body."

Baker let himself be led past Kail, but his eyes stayed locked on the body for long seconds before he turned away. "I understand. Still feels wrong though."

"I know."

"And, please, call me Adam. After everything you've done for my students and my school, we hardly need any kind of formality."

"Then I'd like you to return the favor. I'm Gemma." She followed Logan through the office door. Unlike so much of the rest of the school, which showed its age, the office had been recently renovated. The walls were a clean white, contrasting the windows along the rear wall outlined in deep burgundy. A long, semicircular wood desk sat opposite the front door, and behind it in silver on burgundy was *South Greenfield High School* in a flowing script, over the stylized, sleek head of a dog and *HOME OF THE HUSKIES*. On the opposite wall, four padded burgundy chairs sat in a neat line, no doubt for any student who had to wait for an administrator. Behind the desk, a series of doors ran farther into the office. "Where's the PA system?"

"There, behind the top of Rose's desk. Go around that way." He indicated a path to the right.

Gemma circled the desk to find the PA system—a Dukane Compact 3200—behind the tall, raised edge of the desk. Unlike the newly renovated office, this technology looked straight out of the year 2000. The L-shaped unit had three long rows of toggle switches on the flat, lower section, and the upright section held a speaker and various buttons and dials: Intercom, Emergency, Program, Listen Level, Program Level, Output Level. An upright microphone on a stand sat on the desk beside the intercom unit.

She remembered a similar system when she went to school, and she'd thought it was old then. This plan had to be foolproof. If the PA system didn't work, or if it malfunctioned and cut out during sensitive negotiations, then the only way to make contact was the A-Team's method of yelling at a closed door. That was *not* optimal.

"I know, it looks ancient." Baker must have been able to correctly read the expression on her face. "It *is* ancient. But when we upgraded the office a few years ago, we couldn't update this system without having to deal with every classroom connection as well. And that wasn't in the budget. But don't worry, it's a workhorse and it functions, which is the important thing."

"They don't make 'em like they used to," Logan muttered.

But not quietly enough for Baker to miss his comment. "They sure don't, which is why it's still here. Take a seat." He waited while Gemma pulled out the rolling office chair and sat. "Let me do this." Reaching over her shoulder, he pushed the button to select a program, then found the toggle switch for room 317 and flipped it to intercom. The red light below the switch softly glowed. He touched the tip of an index finger to the Listen Level dial. "Turn this up and down as you need. This button here"—he indicated a square green button under the word *Intercom*—"is how you'll talk to the room. Pressing the button opens the microphone here, no need to do anything else. It also opens the microphone on his end. He doesn't need to touch anything else, and can simply talk to the speaker from wherever he is in the room. When you're done talking, or need to say something you don't want him to hear, push the green button again to turn off the mic at both ends."

"Can I cut my mic here but leave his end open so I can hear what's going on?"

"No, it's not that sophisticated. It's two-way communication or nothing. Also, so you know, on his end, there's a light on the speaker. It'll light up red when the intercom is open, so you won't be able to fool him. He'll know when the channel is open if he's a student at this school."

"And we think he is. What if he wants to talk to me through this system? He can do that, right?"

"Yes, he has one button that calls here directly. From here, if he needed another classroom, we could patch him through. But, in this case, you want him to have the option to reach out to you if he needs to talk."

"That's right. His biggest issue with reaching out to us, depending on how the hostages are arranged, is needing to physically get up and move to that button. Where is it in the classroom?"

"Near the front blackboard, in the corner by the door."

"He may not feel comfortable getting that close to the officers on the other side of the door, but at least it's an option." She looked up to where Logan had taken up position slightly behind and to the right of her chair, directly opposite the entry, and to where Perez stopped in the gap between the desk and the office wall. Both men held their rifles at the ready, and both had their gazes fixed on the office door. They were there to make sure no one walked into the room with the intent to harm her or to stop the negotiations. "Is everyone ready?"

"Affirmative," said Logan.

"Affirmative," Perez echoed.

Taking a deep breath, Gemma pulled the microphone closer and pushed the intercom button.

CHAPTER 15

The button flashed bright green and they were live.

"Hello, room 317." Gemma kept her tone calm and light, the voice of reason, one that didn't carry any of the aggression the A-Team conveyed simply by size, force, and the bulk of their equipment even before Sanders opened his mouth. Thus far, all communications with the NYPD had been at the level of a shout; she needed to distance herself from that. "My name is Gemma Capello. I'm not part of the tactical team. I just want to talk to you."

Gemma closed her eyes, concentrating hard, listening for any response, or even any hint of the hostages. What might have been a female whisper sounded for a fraction of a second before it was cut off. Then silence.

Walking the tightrope between invitation and oppression, she gave it another few seconds before continuing. "It's important you talk to me. The tactical team is still outside, but while there's a chance we'll have a conversation, I can keep them out. If you want to keep them out as well, please talk to me." More silence, but Gemma let it breathe, giving the armed boy inside the classroom time to consider her words and what her presence might mean. "Please let me know you can hear me. You can speak from wherever you are in the room and the PA system will pick up your voice. Do you see that red light on the PA speaker?" Gemma knew it was information the shooter should know, so she used it to make her look open and transparent. "When that light is on, you and I are connected and you can say anything you like to me. And if you need to talk to me, you can use the intercom button to contact me directly."

She glanced sideways at Baker, who sat with one hip on the desk beside her. His eyes were fixed on the PA unit as if he could see through the toggles and lights to the classroom at the other end. His jaw locked tight, he was shaking his head back and forth in a minute motion she doubted he was aware of, yet fully expressed how he felt the situation was stacking up.

We've barely started. Don't doubt the process. Give it time.

"Let me tell you a bit about myself and then maybe you can tell me about you," Gemma continued. "As I said, my name is Gemma. I work with the NYPD as a negotiator and I've spent the last few years talking to people in crisis situations. Finding a way to meet people in the middle, finding a way to end a standoff like this with no bloodshed. That's what I want. I want you to be able to walk out of here safely. But to do that, I need you to meet me halfway. And that starts by you talking to me. You can safely talk to me. I'm not tactical; I'm just here for you. I promise I won't lie to you. I won't tell you stories to convince you it's safe, and then put you in danger the minute you walk out the door. You and I, we need to be able to trust each other. Together, we can finish this."

The silence continued, but Gemma didn't let it drag on too long.

"I understand you need some time to think about how to handle this. That's okay. I'm going to give you some breathing space for a few minutes, then I'll call again. And I hope you'll talk to me then." She pushed the intercom button and the light went dark.

Gemma sat back in the chair, marking the time on the large wall clock. *Five minutes, starting now.* Enough time for him to think, and possibly to worry that the nice lady wasn't going to call again and he'd be stuck with a strictly tactical response.

"That didn't seem to get anywhere," Baker said. "What if he won't talk to you?"

Both Logan and Perez had worked with the HNT before and knew the baby steps involved in making first contact—hell, sometimes with the entire negotiation—and understood the pace. Instantaneous compliance from the hostage taker *never* happened. But this was a new process for Baker. "The boy killed a number of students and possibly a police officer. I wouldn't expect someone in that position to open up as soon as I initiated the conversation. Keep in mind, the last interaction he had with the NYPD was Detective Sims and Lieutenant Sanders, so my tone will sound radically different and he may be suffering a bit of whiplash. This first part could easily take fifteen or thirty minutes, if we're lucky—it could take longer. But as long as there's no violence inside that classroom, we can wait him out. In hostage negotiations, time is always on our side. The longer the negotiation takes, the better our chances. Every minute that goes by is a minute in our favor."

"Because he has time to think about everything that's happened?"

"And that he now has a chance to pull this out of the fire. While we're waiting, and now we're back in the school, is there any way for you to give me more information on that class? Morin said it's a freshman math class, but how many kids are in there? Which teacher is in there with them? That kind of thing. Can you give me that?"

Baker brightened at the thought of proactive work. "I can. All attendance is electronic, done through a tablet in the class. They're supposed to have the attendance submitted within the first ten minutes of class, so that should have been in place before lockdown. Now I'm in the office, I can get you that data. Give me a minute." He crossed to the far side of the curved desk where a computer sat, its screen dark, the chair pushed back haphazardly as if its occupant had abruptly pushed away from her station and evacuated the space.

Because she had.

Baker pulled the chair into place and sat down. A shake of the mouse and the screen lit up, and he leaned in and got to work.

Gemma swiveled in her chair to face Logan, who was still focused unblinkingly on the closed office door. "Can we get Sims down here for a few minutes? I'd like to talk to him about how our shooter got closed up in there, and I don't want to do it over the radio where his half of the conversation could be heard inside the classroom. If he's going to have to move away to talk to me, he might as well come down here, which will make the conversation faster. Can Sanders hold the corridor on his own, especially if I'm distracting the hostage taker, trying to get him to talk to me?"

"Yes." Logan tapped his mic. "Logan to Sims. Detective Capello wants to talk to you. Can you come down to the office at the bottom of the main staircase? Yes, ten-four." He tapped off. "He's on his way."

"I have your information," Baker said, his eyes still fixed on the monitor. "We have twenty-three students in that class, which is led by Mrs. Martha Fowler."

"Good info, thanks. Can you print out a class list for me? Just in case while talking to him, there's a connection to someone in that class?"

"Sure, hang on." A few clicks and the printer under the desk between them whirred to life. Baker pulled off the single sheet and handed it to Gemma.

Gemma scanned the list—in alphabetical order—her eyes snapping to the Cs. No Sam Capello. Some of the tightness in her chest eased, but she knew until she could wrap her arms around her nephew, it wouldn't go away; it would steadily squeeze her heart until she had proof he was safe and well. It also justified her position in that chair, in front of the microphone. If there had been any other negotiator on hand, Gemma was sure Morin would have held her back and sent in another officer, simply because of what some might see as a conflict of interest with her nephew a part of the larger incident. Had Sam been inside that classroom, Morin would have pulled her no matter what, and would have been entirely right to do so, even though delaying the negotiation carried its own risks. Not having her nephew inside the classroom gave Gemma the calm to settle in for the long haul.

"That list okay?"

Gemma looked up at Logan's voice, reading the real question behind his vague wording. She knew her smile likely telegraphed her relief. "It's good."

"Glad to hear that." His gaze returned to the office door.

She started at the top of the list again, reviewing each name, starting with the teacher, Mrs. Fowler, then moving through the students. Roughly half boys and half girls, no names jumped out at her, not that she truly expected any would at this stage.

If the reason he was in that particular room was because of one of the students in the class, hopefully investigators would find evidence at one of the boys' houses.

A dark shape appeared on the other side of the frosted glass, followed by Sims's voice, calling out in the familiar language of the A-Team entering a protected space to avoid being seen as an intruder. "Sims, coming in." Sims stepped in and closed the door behind him.

Gemma checked her watch. Fifteen seconds to go. "Give me a couple of minutes. It's time to call in again, but I suspect he won't be ready to actually start talking yet." She pulled the microphone closer and hit the intercom button. "Hello, room 317. It's Gemma Capello again. I'm here, and I'm not going away. I still want to talk to you. Am I getting through?" She waited to a slow count of five before continuing. "Are you injured? Do you need medical care? Are any students or the teacher with you injured? We can care for all of you. You just need to give us the chance. We can call in EMTs to treat anyone who needs it." As the silence continued, Gemma decided on a different angle. "I'd really like to talk to you. For you, talking to me is the only way to keep yourself safe. I'm keeping the tactical officers in check. If you do anything inside the classroom to make those officers think you're harming hostages, they're going in. There'll be nothing I can do to stop them. And they'll only wait so long. But if you're talking to me, then the tactical option is off the table. Think about it. I'll give you a few more minutes."

She turned off the mic, marked the time, and spun around to face Sims, who stood with Perez. "Catch me up. What happened to get the shooter into this room? I know the layout. It's not a room at the end of the wing, so it's not like he got trapped by you and Unit 2."

"Not exactly. When we got onto three, we could hear banging from around the corner into the west wing."

"Like someone was forcing their way in?"

"That's how I took it. Then we heard gunfire and breaking glass and screaming. We came around the corner just in time to see the door close. When we got closer, you could see he'd shot out the bottom part of the window, shredding part of the poster covering it. By the time we got there, he'd moved another poster over the window, covering the broken section so we couldn't see in."

"Breaking the window allowed the shooter to reach a hand in and open the handle from the inside."

"If he covered the window that fast, whatever he used was likely already on the door," Perez suggested. "Fire exit routes, that kind of thing."

"That would make sense. What about since then? Any noise from anyone? Seeing as the window is broken, you'll be able to hear better."

"There was some initial rustling and low voices," Sims said. "But since then, nothing. No voices, no gunfire. That's when we held position."

"It may be having officers that close made him realize he was finished," said Gemma. "And maybe, unlike Richter, he didn't have the guts to pull the trigger. Or possibly, he just doesn't have the same level of conviction because this was never what he wanted in the first place."

"For someone who didn't want to do this, he participated fully," Sims bit out. "He contributed to the trail of dead kids in the second-floor hallway and shot into two classes on his way down the hallway on the third floor. One was already empty." His eyes went to flint. "The other was not."

"How bad was it?" Logan's tone reminded Gemma of all he'd seen and how much he hadn't been able to fully verbalize for her.

"Bad enough. It actually kind of looked halfhearted. Like he stepped into the room, let fly with the rifle and backed out again without much thought, and moved on. It could have been worse, but..." His words trailed off, but the bleakness in his eyes implied the rest.

"Any kid dying is one kid too many." Logan released his white-knuckled grip on his rifle, flexed his fingers several times, and then let them fall back into position with a lighter touch.

"To be clear, I'm not justifying his actions," Gemma said. "I'm trying to get into his head. I need to do that to make the connection. He stopped for a reason. I need him to tell me why, but in the meantime, I need to form a theory." She checked the time. *Two minutes.* "Any chance we can get eyes into that classroom? Not talking to him is one thing, but I'd feel better if we could at least see, and now that he's not live streaming, we can't see inside that way. Do we have options? We can't go through the broken window, but could you put a fiberoptic camera under the door?"

Sims shook his head. "Too high a risk it would be seen. That happens and we risk the guy taking out his rage on the hostages." He turned to Logan. "We have the building schematics. We might be able to figure out something related to the air vents, but we need to know the setup."

"Are you thinking of the mini-CALIBER?" Perez asked.

"It came to mind."

"What's a mini-CALIBER?" Gemma asked.

"It's a small tactical robot, basically a mini version of the NYPD bomb robots," Logan explained. "About two feet long, and sixteen inches wide and high. It has an extendable, jointed arm with a number of different attachments, including a three-hundred-sixty-degree rotating claw with a zoom camera. It would fit in the vents, but it'll be too loud. It runs on rubber caterpillar tracks, similar to a tank. It's smooth, but it won't be nearly quiet enough in a duct system. We'd be putting those students in more danger by giving the shooter the heads-up." He paused, his gaze fixed on nothing. "Let us work on it. I'll let Sanders and Morin know we need to take a closer look at the schematics with that in mind."

"Thanks. Time to make contact again."

The next forty-five minutes went exactly the way Gemma thought it would. In rounds, she opened the intercom to room 317 and talked for several minutes, repeating over and over why she was there and how she could help him if he would only talk to her. Gemma could tell Baker was worried she was getting nowhere, and had to explain to him that with an unresponsive hostage taker, it could take an hour or more to make contact, and silence from inside the room from the hostage taker and the hostages was actually a good thing. Yes, it was hard on the hostages to be kept in there under that level of stress, but the main goal was extracting everyone safely. If that meant it took longer, so be it.

She was relieved to take a break from talking to hear Detective Pattison call out his designation from the foyer, and then the door opened to reveal fellow HNT officer Detective Gina Shelby. Wearing a bulletproof vest, she had a notebook in hand and was clearly ready to jump in. In a navy pantsuit with her long blond hair contained in a low knot at the back of her head and her Glock in a holster at her waist under a short blazer, Shelby at least appeared to have been on duty.

Gemma grasped her arm in greeting. "Am I glad to see you."

"I bet. I got here as fast as I could. I didn't want to come in until you took a break, but all I could hear was you. No response from the hostage taker. Has it all been like that?"

"Yes. It kind of feels like I'm shouting into the void, but you know what these first contacts can be like." Gemma sent a sideways glance at Baker, who'd moved aside to make room for Shelby next to Gemma, and dropped her voice even further. "I thought we'd make progress faster than this just because of the change of tone. I thought the shooter would find some safety in dealing with me versus Sanders and Sims. But it looks like I'm wrong. Logan is keeping the teams upstairs in the loop, but I'm sure Sanders and Sims are getting restless."

"It doesn't take much with them. You're doing fine. Consider who's inside that room, and I don't mean the hostages. It's a kid."

"It's a kid with a high-capacity rifle."

"You have me there, but the brain we're dealing with is that of a teenager, one who's high on hormones. A teenager who tried to act like a man, but then at the end didn't carry through the way his friend did."

"Yeah."

"He's digging in and trying to figure a way out of a closed box. Just keep doing what you're doing."

"Familiarity breeds comfort."

Shelby gave Gemma a half grin at her twist on the familiar catchphrase. "Yeah, I think that's how that goes. But in this case, that's exactly what it is. The more you talk, the more familiar you get, the greater the bond you're forging, even if it doesn't feel like it." She waved her notepad. "And I'm right here with you. Double duty for me as coach and scribe."

"Are we expecting anyone else?"

"No. Because we're inside an active situation, Garcia wanted to keep the team smaller than usual, thus the double duty."

"Bet he'd never try that with two guys," Gemma said dryly.

"No kidding. They just can't multitask the way we can. So it's going to be a three-man team with Garcia as coordinator staying at the command center, because that's the best place to liaise. Everything for this incident passes through there. We can do this."

"You got it, girlfriend." Gemma was simply grateful it was Shelby. They'd worked together on multiple HNT incidents and she always appreciated Shelby's steadiness, logic, and sarcastic sense of humor when her spirits were sagging.

It was as she was approaching the one-hour mark that things finally shifted.

"Hello, 317," she called, careful to keep her voice easy and light, letting none of her own building frustration show. There was only so many times you could say the same thing before you began to sound bored and frustrated yourself. "It's me again, Gemma Capello. I wanted to see if you were willing to talk to me now." A pause. Silence. *Come on, work with me here. I can do literally nothing for you unless we can have a conversation. Otherwise, I might as well just get out of Sanders's way.* "It will go easier for you if you talk to me. The A-Team is getting impatient, but they won't go in as long as I can tell them there's a chance we can talk and—"

"Stop."

The single word coming from the speaker had Gemma clamping down on the rest of her sentence. She froze, waiting for more.

More took about fifteen long seconds to arrive. "He wants you to stop talking."

The voice belonged to an adult—the teacher, being forced to speak for the hostage taker. Gemma reminded herself that though she was speaking to an older woman, she was really speaking to a teenager, maybe only seventeen or eighteen, who was possibly panicking and not thinking things through. "I can stop talking, but the tactical teams outside your door won't go away. If I sign off, they're in charge. If I stay on with you, I can help you all."

Another long pause. Closing her eyes, Gemma concentrated hard on the sound drifting through the speaker and caught just the barest murmur of a male voice. The voice was deep, that of a mature man, but the request revealed the cognition that had yet to mature to match the physical.

"He says he needs a break. Your constant talking doesn't let him think."

"I can do that. But he needs to understand we're in a holding pattern until he talks to me. No progress gets made. How about I give him thirty minutes? I'll take a break, but he needs to understand that the A-Team officers will remain outside the door of the classroom. No one will bother him as long as nothing happens. The first sign of violence, the first scream or cry, and tactical will charge in and it likely won't end well for him. I'm his best chance. To help him, I need to talk to him. Not you. Him." Gemma paused as the same voice, now at an even lower level, murmured in the background. She waited until there was silence inside the classroom. "Does he understand?"

"Yes."

"I'll give him his break." She glanced at her watch. "Tell him he needs to deal with me then or I may not be able to hold tactical back. Thirty minutes, starting now."

Gemma turned off the intercom. Without meaning to, Russ Shea had given them a mental break and possibly enough time to get a camera into place. Eyes and ears suddenly became a possibility.

It would make all the difference in the world.

CHAPTER 16

Gemma and Shelby stepped out of the east wing stairwell and into the bright sunlight that chased away the scudding cloud cover. Standing on the concrete walkway, the brisk November breeze was gloriously cool against Gemma's damp, overheated skin as it blew her hair into a cloud of curls. She caught at it with both hands and pushed it away from her face.

It was a break everyone needed.

Beside her, Shelby tipped her face up to the sun. "That feels good."

"Sure does. Come on. Everyone needs to take a breath and calm down, but we have to check in at the command center. We only have a few minutes to take a break and then we need to get organized. If anything happens while we're out of the building, Sims will let us know, and we can be back inside at a sprint in under two minutes. They're right outside the door. If anything goes south, Sims, Sanders, and their teams will go through it."

Gemma pulled out her cell phone. She hadn't felt it vibrate, but was still waiting for word from Joe that he'd found Sam. Maybe she'd missed his text. She woke the screen to find no word from Joe. Surely he'd have found Sam by now or her nephew would have joined his mother at Barclays.

The lack of an update made her gut clench.

However, there was a text from Garcia, saying he'd arrived and was working with Morin. "Garcia's arrived. He's at the command center. We can talk to him and Morin together." She tucked her phone into her pocket and started down the sidewalk.

They'd selected that exit as it would put them far away from the ever-growing media crowd—the last thing Gemma needed at that moment was Greg Coulter thrusting a microphone into her face. Safe within the secured zone, they speed-walked toward the command center, awash with blue and red lights. They had just reached the cross street separating the school from incident command when an older man stepped out of the command center. Of medium height, he had gray hair, and, as an exception to nearly everyone else on-site except herself, was dressed down in a navy NYPD hoodie and blue jeans.

Gemma would have known him at five times the distance.

Busted.

She'd known this moment was coming but had desperately wished the situation had been resolved long before now.

Chief Tony Capello was on-site.

"Shelby, I'm going to need a few minutes."

Shelby stepped off the curb, turned, and looked up at Gemma, then followed her locked gaze to the man who stood frozen, staring directly at them. "Is that Chief Capello?"

"Yes."

"Do you want to update him on…" Shelby trailed off as she turned back to Gemma and registered the look on her face. "Oh. Maybe not." She glanced toward the command center to see Tony Capello striding toward them with an intensity that bellowed *GET OUT OF MY WAY.* Shelby took a step farther into the intersection. "What say I nip into the command center and update them for us, then?"

"That would be perfect." Gemma took her eyes from her father's granite expression to give Shelby a wan smile. "It's okay. I'll be there shortly."

"I'm not so sure…" Shelby muttered and headed across the street, meeting Chief Capello halfway across. "Chief."

Tony gave her a sharp nod and continued without so much as a hitch in his stride.

Gemma waited to speak until Shelby was nearly at the far side and her father was about to step up onto the curb. "Hi, Dad."

"With me, Detective." Ignoring her familiar salutation and without waiting for her to reply, he turned north and crossed Bay Parkway to stride up East 3rd Street.

Nearly the same height as her father, Gemma fell into step with him.

When she left the apartment that morning, rage wasn't the emotion she expected to face from him, but here they were. And she was the first to say she deserved it.

Tony waited until they were a good half-dozen driveways down the street before rounding on his only daughter. *"Per tutto ciò che è santo,* Gemma. What were you thinking? I wouldn't expect Joe to concentrate on anything but Sam right now, but why did *you* leave me in the dark? I turned on the TV about a half hour ago for a little company only to find out that my grandson's school was under attack. Worse than that, I was watching a replay of my *daughter* rescuing kids jumping out of windows. My daughter, who said nothing to me even though I was only twenty minutes away and am her chief!" His voice was rising nearly to a shout. "And then when I get here, I find out you've been on-site practically since the beginning. And said nothing to me, the man who would normally be running this op."

Fury was pumping off her father with such strength, Gemma could practically see it as an undulating red aura. Tony didn't lose his temper often with his children, or with his officers, preferring a cold head and a serious tongue lashing, but she'd evidently shoved him one step too far.

Leave it to family to hammer the most painful emotional buttons.

She'd known if he found out before the situation was quickly resolved—which it clearly wasn't going to be, in this case—he'd rightfully expect an explanation as to why she'd left him out of an operation that affected his family, his very heart and soul.

That was precisely why she'd tried to leave him in the dark. To spare him that agony. The chance for life they'd won with the hostage crisis had lost her the chance for a fast resolution. Considering the lives on the line, she'd gladly take her father's wrath in exchange for the time required to save those children.

She didn't have time to prevaricate. She needed to take the cut down and get back to work.

"I was thinking of saving you the agony of worrying about Sam. When Alex called me to tell me—"

"Alex!"

"Yes, Alex. And don't get mad at him. I told him not to tell you."

"And he listened to you?"

"Amazingly, he actually does sometimes." At her father's narrowed eyes and clamped jaw, she pushed on. "I was only minutes away when he called to tell me, so I changed plans and came right here. I was going to let you know, but things have moved quickly since then and I've had my hands full with evacuating or interviewing kids, or I've been trying to communicate with the hostage taker, and haven't been in a position to call."

"Sei pazza. That's BS and you know it."

Gemma turned her head toward the school. Fear scratched at her as the silence of the dead air coming from Joe started to scream. For the first time, she had an inkling of the hell Tony had gone through twenty-five years ago as he stood outside the bank where his wife and daughter were being held hostage.

Time to show him the respect he deserved and speak the truth.

"Yes, it is." She met his gaze to find simmering anger backed by hurt that she would have cut him out of something so important. She reached for his hand, only to find it clenched into a rock-hard fist, so she simply wrapped hers around it, holding tight. "I told Alex not to tell you because I was banking on you being at home with the TV off and was hoping that by the time you found out about it, I'd be standing on your doorstep with Sam." She forced herself to hold his gaze. "I know what day it is as well as you do. We lost Mom twenty-five years ago today, and now we're at risk of losing Sam." She pulled in a deep breath, feeling it catch slightly on the inhale. *You've been holding it together up to now. You can't let it slip or you'll never find your balance again today. You have to hold steady; lives are depending on it.*

"You and I both know how fast these active shooter situations can go down. Fifteen minutes is usually the maximum time before the shooter either surrenders or is eliminated. I was banking on it being finished ten minutes after I arrived. But then it turned out to be two shooters, and while the first shooter was down inside of the usual time, the second took hostages." She stopped, closed her eyes. "And then I was even more terrified to tell you. To drag you into that kind of hell all over again, especially today of all days." She sucked in another breath and forced herself to open her eyes, to meet her father's gaze and take the well-deserved wrath. Instead, the anger seemed to have drained away, leaving devastation in its place, which, if anything, wounded her more. She let go of his hand to throw her arms around him, his body stiff in her arms. "I'm sorry, but I just couldn't do it to you. Even if that meant you'd hate me."

His arms came around her, hard. "*Mia passerotta,* I could never hate you." He pressed a kiss to her hair. "But I was angry at you."

The use of his nickname for her from when she was young—*my little sparrow*—was another kick to her composure, but she bore down, forced herself to stay steady. "Was?"

"Was." He pulled away from her, catching her hands as they dropped to hold them in both of his. "I'm sorry, too, for jumping into the deep end. Normally I wouldn't. But today…"

"Yeah. Today."

"I think you and I are both walking a knife's edge." He waited while she nodded. "An already sad day, terrorized by"—he looked over her shoulder, toward the school—"this. Garcia says you're negotiating. Does he know?"

"He knows Sam is in there; so does Morin. He was shorthanded because things went sideways so quickly, but I was here and we knew Sam wasn't in the class, so Morin wanted me to go in." She paused, frowning. "He doesn't know about Mom."

"Do I need to tell him?"

"Are you asking if I can do my job? Yes, I can. He doesn't need to know any more than that. I'm not in your command position. I'm the one talking to the second shooter with Gina Shelby beside me and Garcia ready to assist. I'm not alone. I can do this. I'll end this, and we'll bring Sam home. And if I feel I can't, it would be a risk to change negotiators after that first conversation, but I'll be the first to step back and have Shelby take over. Have you seen Joe?"

"No, but I haven't been here long. He's coming here?"

"He's here already. Somewhere. They're sending the kids to the Barclays Center and that's where the parents are supposed to go. Alyssa's probably there already, but Joe can badge his way through the police lines. Someone reported that they'd seen Sam outside the school, but…"

"But what?"

"That was an hour ago. And I haven't heard from Joe in all that time."

Tony's face pulled in, tightened, worry deepening the lines around his eyes. "He should have him by now."

"Or Alyssa should." She pulled out her phone and shot off a quick text to Joe—**Dad is on-site now, too. Any word about Sam?**—before pocketing it again. "I'll text you if I hear anything from Joe, but now he knows you're here, he'll know you'll be around the command center and may come looking for you. I wouldn't be surprised to see Alex here, too, at some point. He didn't say he was coming, but I can't imagine anything holding him back. Or Mark, or Teo, really. If they're on shift, they'll find a way to get off. Either way, I bet everyone is incoming." She gave his hands a squeeze and let them drop. "I have to go. We're only giving the hostage taker a half hour break. Shelby will have checked in with Morin and Garcia at this point, but I need to do the same. They won't let you take command with your grandson involved, but are they letting you observe?"

"Yes, but Morin's in charge. He knows I'll advise, but it's his call."

"He's good, but I'm sure he'll appreciate your experience." She headed down the sidewalk. "Logan and Perez are working on a way to get eyes into the room."

"They'll have to do it carefully so they aren't seen, or things could get rocky, but it's definitely a good idea. If you can get visuals, you'll have a much better idea of what's really going on inside."

"It will make a huge difference into how I'll handle the situation. I'll have visual cues to direct the conversation."

"I wonder if the visuals will help in another way?"

"What do you mean?"

"What's special about that room? From what I've heard, he could have ducked into any classroom if he was sheltering from the A-Team. And some of the classrooms would have been unoccupied and unlocked. Why did he pick a room that was not only occupied but locked? Was it closest? Did he get trapped? Did he already have a hostage taking planned? Or is there something special about that room, or the occupants in it, that directed his action? If so, that may be a key to getting him to surrender."

"Sims says they heard him shooting out the glass from around the corner, and by the time they ran to where they could see that part of the wing, the door was closing. Sims also doesn't know why he picked that room, and whether it was by chance or by design, even if on the fly. You raise excellent questions." Gemma grinned at her father and slipped her hand through his arm as he walked, his left hand in his pocket. "When did you get to be so smart? It's almost like you run this unit."

"Almost like."

As he smiled at her, Gemma realized a large part of the stress she'd been carrying had been worry about her father, and that weight was now gone, leaving her clear-eyed and regenerated. This incident happening on the anniversary of his wife's death was terrible, but Tony Capello knew how to handle it. "I'm sorry."

The look he threw her was questioning. "You've already apologized, there's no need to do so again."

"For underestimating you. Yes, it's an extra stressor, but I didn't give you credit for managing it. And I should have."

He rubbed her fingers where they rested on his forearm with his free hand. "Next time you won't." He picked up the pace. "Now, let's go see how the A-Team is planning to get you the visuals you need to get the upper hand and bring those kids home."

CHAPTER 17

"This'll do nicely." Logan studied the coiled black cord tipped with a metal cap, and the handheld console, complete with joystick, nestled in foam in a heavy black metal case. He glanced up at Sanders. "Who'll be best at navigation?"

"Boone, from Unit 5. He's a whiz with electronics, from robots to listening devices to cameras. He'll be able to get this into place without being detected, no problem. And then get us the best view of the room." He tapped his mic on. "Sanders to Boone." A pause. "Ten-two. We need you for the snake cam." Another pause. "Ten-four." He clicked his mic off. "He's nearby, so he'll be here soon." His gaze flicked toward the large red clock numbers on the wall. "Seventeen minutes to go. We'll start the briefing as soon as he gets here."

The door to the command center opened, flooding the cold blue light of the well-lit space with the warm glow of natural daylight.

"Excuse me, officers."

Logan would have known that voice anywhere—Gemma's chicken had come home to roost.

Chief Capello stepped into the narrow space, and officers jostled to make room for him. To Logan's surprise, Gemma stepped in behind him. She scanned the room, past him, and then snapped back to answer his unspoken question with a chagrined smile. Then her gaze moved on until she found the negotiators standing near the large smart board at the front of the space. She broke off from her father and headed for Shelby and Garcia.

Guess they sorted it out.

Garcia, Gemma, and Shelby went into a huddle, then Garcia handed Gemma a cell phone. She immediately flipped through the phone's settings.

"Good. There's Boone."

Sanders's words pulled Logan's attention to where stocky, solid Detective Orren Boone came through the door. He made a beeline toward Sanders and Logan, his gaze dropping to the open case on the desk. A smile curved his lips at the sight of the borescope.

Tech geeks.

Granted, tech geeks had their place, and Boone would have his today.

Boone laid his hand down on the edge of the case. "Where are we taking her?"

"We're just about to run the plan with Morin." Sanders nodded in Morin's direction. "Looks like he's ready to start."

Morin squeezed through the officers packed in the command center to get to the smart board. "Attention, everyone!" The buzz of conversation in the command center died down. "Sorry to squeeze everyone in here. I'd prefer to do this on the board outside, but the media are too damned close and every one of them has zoom lenses. We can't afford to let any of this get out onto the general airwaves where the shooter could possibly hear about it. Now, we have fifteen minutes to get this into place before the HNT is expected to make contact again. And expected to make progress."

Three sets of eyes narrowed on Morin. No one said anything, but Logan knew Gemma well enough to hear the curses streaming through her head. They all knew what pressures they were up against. Morin didn't need to add to it.

"Principal Baker was instrumental in helping us get the schematics for the school," Morin continued. "Can I get those schematics on the board, please?" There was a brief lag, and then the screen flashed on with the school's blueprints. "Lieutenant Sanders, can you walk us through your plan?"

Sanders sidestepped a few people to get close to the board. "Principal Baker walked us through some of the design aspects of the school with the help of one of the custodians, who was evacuated from the first floor. Together, we've devised a plan of attack to get visuals of 317. Like so many schools from this era, the school is heated by electric baseboard heaters. They're the old style a lot of us saw as kids—running along the outside wall under the windows to counteract any cold air leaking in. They're about two and a half feet tall, flattopped, with vented slats along the upper surface. But most importantly, they sit about three inches off the floor, and all the electrical wiring goes through the concrete floor to the dropped, T-bar ceiling on the floor below. That means if we go through the ceiling tiles on the second-floor classroom directly below 317, we can make use of those electrical access points."

Sanders glanced in the direction of the computer operators, but no doubt couldn't see them due to the standing room only crowd. "Can I get this enlarged to the schematic for 217 and 317?" he called. The screen behind him enlarged and then shifted to those two rooms, stacked one on top of the other. "A little larger, centered on the floor between them... stop." With an index finger, Sanders circled an area of the floor where lines indicating electrical wiring dropped through the floor to run along the top of the ceiling in the classroom below. "We can take advantage of this design. The heaters are powered by electrical lines running through pipes embedded in the concrete floor. However, when they originally bored holes for the pipes, they left a narrow space to allow for natural expansion and contraction of materials. We're going to use that space for the borescope. All we need is a quarter inch to pass the probe through."

He sketched a path from the ceiling of 217 to the floor of 317. "We'll run the cable up through this gap. The top is covered with fire caulk, but the custodian has assured us it's so old, it can literally be pushed out of the way. The caulk is essentially useless now, and a lot of it has crumbled away, but it's never been repaired. We'll run the probe into 317 and then Detective Boone will manually control it, because it's fully articulated. That means we'll be able to precisely control the view. If for some reason that location is blocked, there's a second location to try between 217 and 317."

"Any chance that you're going to make enough noise that you'll attract the shooter's attention?" Garcia asked.

"That's where the HNT comes in. We shouldn't make much noise, but there's the chance the probe moving between the pipe and concrete wall might produce some limited sound. So we're going to need to coordinate with you to make sure that the PA system is being used at the time. That should give us enough noise to cover."

"How long will you need?"

"No more than forty-five seconds. Once the probe is through to the other side, movement is silent, so we'll be able to adjust without giving away our position. But if you could go sixty seconds, just in case, that would probably be best."

"I'm going to need access to what that camera sees," Gemma said. "Then I'll know when you're through. But, more importantly, we need to confirm suspect ID, and I need to be able to track his movements and any physical manifestation of anxiety or rage. That will give me a considerable advantage."

"The control device itself has a tiny LCD screen, but it also has capabilities to broadcast a signal up to three hundred feet. Schematics say from room 217 to the office is just over one hundred fifty feet. Boone, can we set Detective Capello up with a monitor?"

"Yes, sir, we can."

"That's what we'll do then. Go in and set up in 217. Remove ceiling tiles, get the tech set up, test the broadcast. Then when Capello begins to talk in"—Sanders's gaze flicked in the direction of the clock—"thirteen minutes, we'll start the operation. Logan and Perez will stay with Capello in the office in case of any additional risk factors as well as to be the go-between for the A-Team and HNT." He met Logan's eyes. "Logan, stay with Capello on the monitor and report any problems or changes you need made. Boone, you'll have Leishman with you for support. Garcia, are we a go with the throw phone?"

"Yes. Capello is going to tell him over the PA that we're going to move to the throw phone to save him from yelling at the PA speaker. The phone is ready, so if you can take that to the third floor, we'll let you know when you can push it under the door. But we can't do that until he's prepared for it."

"I'm with Capello already," Logan interjected. "I'll radio when he's ready to receive."

"That works. Clock is ticking. We're clear to enter via the east wing to avoid the media gaggle. Get into position."

Logan met Gemma's eyes across the command center and gave her a nod.

Let's move.

CHAPTER 18

Eight minutes later, Gemma was settled once again in the administrative assistant's chair in the office, Shelby pulled up next to her, a pen in hand and paper at the ready. Gemma swiveled in her chair to study the eleven-inch monitor Logan was angling toward her on the desk. "That's perfect. Are they ready to go?"

"They'd better be; we're running out of time." Logan activated his mic. "Logan to Boone, we're ready to test the broadcast feed." He stood silent for a moment, staring at the screen. "No, nothing yet. Why don't you—" The screen flashed on, an image of window panes and the edge of a sky-blue wall filling the screen. "Wait. We have your signal now. Coming in crystal clear." He smiled at what was coming down the line. "Maybe ask her out to dinner after this if you love her that much." He chuckled, then went serious. "Ten-four. Good luck. Capello will start in four minutes." He tapped off his mic and watched the screen for a few seconds as the picture held momentarily fixed on the floor and then turned upside down and began to rise. Pause. Rise again. "Leishman is going up the ladder. He'll feed the line through on my mark of a double mic click once you're talking to 317. Boone has the control unit and will monitor from the ground." He tapped the edge of the screen. "And we'll watch from here."

The image now showed a hand holding a short-bladed knife reaching for a spot in the ceiling where a steel pipe penetrated from the floor above, before taking a sharp turn to run along the ceiling to join with several other pipes that then disappeared through the wall into an adjoining classroom. A ring of red caulk circled the pipe, plugging any gaps between it and the ceiling, blocking flame or smoke from moving from one class to the other in the event of a fire. The tip of the knife slipped under the caulk and a large chunk easily dislodged and dropped out of view.

"The fire caulk looks intact from the outside, but wouldn't stop anything," said Logan.

"It's totally lost its integrity. If the other side is like that, it will be easy to push against it and pop it off." Gemma checked the time. "One minute to go. They need to get into position."

"They got this." Logan's voice carried the calm of hundreds of successful missions, many of which were just-in-time productions. "There they go."

On the monitor, a bright LED light came on, illuminating the ceiling, and then dimmed under Boone's control. The camera rose, pushing into the narrow gap between the edge of the drilled concrete hole and the pipe. The light revealed inches of pipe and concrete rising above.

"How far does he have to go?" Shelby asked.

"About six inches from the schematics. You both ready?"

"We are." Gemma answered for herself and Shelby. "Sanders is in place?"

"Affirmative. He'll go on your command."

"That'll be nice for a change," Shelby muttered.

Gemma's lips twitched, always appreciative of Shelby's sass. "Ready to record the conversation?"

"And transcribe it. My recording app will mark the time. You need to talk for at least forty-five seconds straight."

"Aiming for the sixty they suggested." Gemma's attention was attracted when Shelby's cell phone lit up where it sat, face up, next to Gemma's and the NYPD phone, off to one side of the desk. Both personal phones were silenced, but were on to receive messages if needed from the teams.

Shelby pulled her phone closer and flipped to the incoming message. "Ah, well done, Garcia."

Gemma leaned in. "What's he got?"

Shelby opened a photo and angled the phone toward Gemma. "Russ Shea's yearbook photo from this year."

"Excellent." Gemma took the phone, studying the face, trying to elicit as much information as possible before she actually spoke to him, assuming it was Russ Shea in room 317. Pale skin, widely spaced dark eyes, clean shaven, hair a little shaggy and decidedly overlong in front, as if it was a shield to hide behind. He was unsmiling, his face holding an expression close to blank. *Disconnected from everything around him?* He wore a blue plaid flannel shirt over a gray hoodie, both slightly worn in a way that said either he forgot when picture day was, or he was making a statement that both it and school were unimportant in his eyes.

"This is good. If we can get a view of the shooter, we'll know for sure if it's him." She turned the phone around and held it up first for Perez and then Logan. "This could be our guy." She handed the phone to Shelby and checked the clock one more time. "Let's get started." She flipped the toggle for room 317 and turned on the mic. "Hello, room 317." Behind and to her right, she heard the quiet double click of Logan keying his mic, putting the camera in motion. "It's Gemma Capello again." Her eyes tracked to the phone Shelby turned around so she could see the large glowing red record symbol, and, more importantly, the seconds ticking up. "I hope you've been able to use this time to think about how you'd like to handle this situation. If I may, I'd like to make a suggestion." A glance at the monitor showed the camera in motion, so she barreled on without actually waiting for acquiescence.

"Yelling at a PA speaker isn't the best way to have a conversation about what happened today and how we can bring everyone in 317 out safely, including you. You're going to get hoarse and frustrated and tired. I'd like to provide a phone to you with absolutely no contact. It's not meant to put you in a position where you're in jeopardy; it's meant to provide a means of communication in a safe manner so you and I can talk. Most importantly, it means you and I can talk privately." A quick flash from side to side: The recording time read 33.62 seconds; above the camera, cracks of light filtered through the caulk that blocked their way. "We can pass this phone to you under the door. There are no tricks here. It's a basic cell phone with nothing special on it. There are no trackers or recording devices. It's simply meant to be a phone so you and I can talk. Would you consider this?" The camera's guiding light went out before it pushed through the caulk. It crumbled, leaving the camera looking straight into the grimy pipes and metal fins of the electric baseboard heater. The camera moved a little higher, then the view pitched down. "Alternatively, if you don't like that idea, you likely have several phones in there with you, from the students or Mrs. Martha Fowler." Gemma purposely used the woman's full name—the more familiarity there was between the hostage taker and the hostages, the harder it would be to harm them. The camera's view dropped toward the floor—they were in place, which meant she could stop talking and allow the hostage taker to think and respond. "That would work as well. What do you think?"

Silence filled the space over the intercom. Gemma was willing to give him fifteen or twenty seconds to answer, but there wouldn't be breaks this time. She'd given him a half hour; it was time to fish or cut bait. He didn't have to walk out the door, but he had to be willing to work with her.

Gemma used the time given by her question to do a quick study of the room. Her view was partially blocked by a number of desks in straight rows from left to right in the foreground, those table-chair combinations with the rack underneath the seat for a student's belongings that never fit the backpack they actually carried. But her gaze was drawn through the desks to the far side of the classroom. A number of desks looked like they had been pushed together to make not only a barricade, but an open space in the far back corner of the classroom. And, in that space, she found both the hostages and the shooter.

Still mostly focused low on the floor and the bottom part of the classroom, the camera panned left through empty desks and the open aisles between them to the closed door, and then it panned back again, this time past a pair of black army boots and green fatigue pants, all the way to the right where it stopped on the hostages. Done with the floor sweep, the camera then tilted up and Gemma got her first look at the shooter.

Despite the fact that he was clutching a semiautomatic rifle on a two-point sling, he looked young. His finger lay along the trigger guard, but Gemma wasn't fooled into relaxation at that pose—she knew how fast a shooter could get into shooting position and open fire. He wore a black T-shirt and green fatigue pants, the pockets bulging, likely with additional ammunition. Held in place across his chest with an elastic harness was the compact camera he'd used for live streaming until he'd terminated the feed.

There was no doubt in Gemma's mind that she was looking at Russ Shea. His hair was longer, hiding even more of his eyes from the world, though currently, he'd pushed most of his bangs away from his forehead. It was the same flat mouth and the same dark eyes, though now instead of being blank, they held a combination of mania, caution, and uncertainty. *Still coming down from the high of all that power, and now realizing he's backed himself into a corner.*

She needed to tread carefully.

The hostages sat on the floor, in a space made clear by pushing desks out of the way, without a backpack or a phone in sight; likely the first thing the shooter had done was make sure they were separated from any and all forms of communication. Some students sat cross-legged with their backs to the camera, their heads bent. Some leaned against the far wall, many of them pressed together in twos and threes, some holding hands, some holding each other. One girl sat slightly separate from the group, her arms wrapped tightly around her knees, as if there were no one to hold on to except herself. There was one adult in the crowd, a middle-aged blonde in slacks and a blazer sitting with her students, but closest to the standing figure. Her head was tipped up toward him, watchful, calculating, but not defiant. She was flanked by two teenage boys and had reached out to hold a hand of each. To comfort? Or to restrain? The view was too far away and not sharp enough for her to judge the strength of her hold on the two boys.

Gemma remembered her own brothers when they were that age and considered how they'd have handled a situation just like this. Joe would've been the one they'd have to hold back, the eldest son looking out for his tribe, whose first reckless impulse would be to go toe-to-toe with the intruder. Mark would have been the peacekeeper, the one who would talk his way out of a situation using logic and heart. Teo would have concocted some cockamamie scheme to escape the threat. Alex would have been the last to go, determined to stay until everyone else was safe.

Teenagers could be unpredictable, a whirlwind of hormones and actively rewiring brain connections. And that unpredictability applied to both the hostages and the hostage taker. As the sole adult in the room, Mrs. Fowler must know she was in the middle of what could be a ticking time bomb.

On top of that, teenagers could be emotional and would try to hide that emotionality behind sometimes brutal words. Hostage negotiators were trained to listen to a suspect's words, but, just as importantly, to listen to the emotion behind them. That was even more crucial in this case.

Gemma did a quick head count of the kids she could see and reached nineteen, though she knew with the kids sitting in clumps, some kids were simply out of her sight line. She would have to assume all twenty-three kids were still in the room.

She'd given the boy long enough. Time to push. "I need an answer, 317." She decided to apply a little pressure, even if it wasn't absolutely true. She fixed her gaze on the shooter's profile where he stood apart from the rest of the occupants, stared as if she was making actual eye contact. "Tactical is going to need to know you'll meet me in the middle. If not, I can't hold them back if they decide to move." Gemma took care to keep herself out of the decision structure. She was here to help, but the final call wasn't hers. "What do you say?"

Gemma was concentrating so hard on the shooter that she jerked in surprise when Shelby's hand closed over her forearm in a quick squeeze to catch her attention. Shelby then pointed at a single student, a girl with dark hair, shaved short on the sides with the top drawn off her face, dressed in black and charcoal with heavy black eyeliner and dark lips. Gemma jolted when she realized the girl's gaze was laser focused on the camera. So much so, it was like they were making eye contact.

Someone had seen the camera moving into place.

But then the girl did something curious. Making a thumbs-up sign with her left hand, she seated that hand in the open palm of her right hand, paused for a moment and then moved her hands up a few inches before laying her hands loosely in her lap.

Beside Gemma, Shelby gave an almost imperceivable gasp and scrawled *ASL for help* on her pad of paper.

American Sign Language. They had someone who not only knew law enforcement had a presence inside the room and was trying to take control of the situation, but someone who could communicate.

Gemma reached for her own pen and paper, tapped Logan on the thigh to attract his attention, and wrote *Tell Boone to nod the camera up and down once.* Logan didn't question the request, but stepped several feet away, turned his back, and whispered into his mic. Almost immediately, the camera tipped up, then down, then back to level. Through the movement, Gemma kept her eyes fixed on the girl, reading the relief as her eyes fluttered closed and her jaw relaxed. Then she opened her eyes, raised the fingers of her right hand to her chin, and then dropped it in a forward motion.

Beside her, Shelby wrote *Thank you.*

Message received. Now they had to hope that student kept the presence of the camera to herself, because loose lips sank ships, or in this case, invited a slaughter at the hands of a killer with a high-capacity rifle.

"What's your answer, 317?" Gemma prodded.

"Fine." The single word was low, clipped, and angry, but it brought a smile of relief to Gemma's lips.

It was a step forward.

"Thank you. Please move to the door of the classroom. I'll have an officer push a phone under the door."

On the monitor, the shooter turned toward the door, took one step, and then stopped dead. "No."

"Pardon?"

"No. You want to get me to walk to a spot where the cops outside know where I am so they can open fire. Not happening."

"That's not how it will go. You can trust me."

"Are you standing outside the door?"

He had her there. "No. I'm in the office with the PA system."

"So you have no control over them. You just said you can't hold them back."

Cazzate. The boy was paying attention. There was no sign of him crumbling under pressure.

"I'm not doing it," the boy continued.

Movement to the right of the boy caught Gemma's attention as Mrs. Fowler scrambled to her knees. "I'll do it. I'll get the phone. They won't shoot me." Bracing her hands on the floor, she pushed off to stand, disappearing behind a desk to reappear as she straightened. "Let me by and I'll pick up the phone. Then I'll put it down wherever you want it in the room and they won't know where you are."

Gemma and Shelby exchanged a glance and then both turned back to the monitor where they and the rest of the NYPD tuned in to see exactly where he was.

Mrs. Fowler took a step forward, her hand extended. "Just let me—"

"*Stop.*" The boy barked the word and Mrs. Fowler froze.

Even from the distance of the camera, Gemma could see the teacher's chest rising and falling with her rapid breaths, and she leaned in, as if she could control the situation from afar.

Mrs. Fowler held up both hands, fingers splayed, to placate or to stave off. Or both. "I'm just trying to help. I don't want anyone to get hurt, including you."

"I can tell the officers in the hallway that it won't be you picking up the phone," Gemma said. "It's a good compromise. All she needs to do is walk to the door, grab the phone, and bring it back to you. It would be a sign of your good faith."

Indecision narrowed his eyes and flattened his lips. Then, "Do it." The rifle fixed on her torso as he backed away, winding between desks or kicking them out of his way until Gemma could no longer see him from his shoulders up. He stood with his back to the camera, his boots planted and only the end of the rifle barrel visible, locked on Mrs. Fowler.

"Can I tell the officers to push the phone under the door?" Gemma asked.

"Yes." He scowled at Mrs. Fowler. "But you stay there until it's on this side of the door. And if you attempt to open the door and let the cops in"—he swung the rifle toward the kids—"they'll pay the price."

"I swear I'll only do as you ask. Just don't hurt them."

Gemma didn't want that conversation to go on any longer. "I'm telling them to push the phone under now." She looked up at Logan and nodded.

Logan keyed his mic as he turned away. "Logan to Sanders, you're a go on the throw phone."

Gemma didn't need to ask Boone to follow the action. The camera view was already sliding sideways, past the shooter and to the door. A scraping sound came through the intercom, and then Mrs. Fowler looked at the shooter. He must have indicated his approval, because she ran to the door, picked up the phone, and ran back. She set the phone on a desk and then stepped away from it, her splayed hands in the air, returning to the students and sinking down again between the two boys. This time they reached for her, helping her down, holding on to her as she settled beside them.

Probably terrified to lose the only adult in the room.

But the shooter didn't move—he simply stayed locked in place, gun still pointed at the pack of students in the corner of the room.

"Do you have the phone?" Gemma asked, hoping to break his concentration on the hostages.

That seemed to bring him around, and he pushed his way to the far side of the room, snatched the phone, and pulled back a few feet again. "Yeah. I have it."

"Turn it on. You'll see it's a simple base model phone with no special apps or features. There's no data plan. It's only good for talk and text." She didn't tell him that the Wi-Fi had been physically disabled. The last thing the NYPD wanted to do was to give this kid any form of communication to the outside world. Gemma needed to be his world; she didn't want him to have outside distractions. They knew he could gain that by taking the phone of anyone else in the room, but they wouldn't make the task easy for him by putting a connection directly into his hands. "It's just for you and me."

Gemma picked up the NYPD phone and flipped to the phone app installed on it, double checking the settings to ensure it was set to record all incoming and outgoing calls automatically. Then she moved to her contacts and brought up the information for the throw phone.

"Phone's on," he called.

"Excellent. I'm turning off the intercom and then I'm going to call you." She slid the microphone away, pushed the intercom button on the PA system, and the green light extinguished. "Finally."

"I hear you," Shelby said. "Now we're in a position to make some progress."

"I need to call him right away, but quickly, you said that girl was signing. You know ASL?"

"My brother is deaf. The whole family is fluent in it."

"Good to know. That may come in handy. I know you're already doing double duty as coach and scribe, but I need you to keep an eye on that student as much as you can. I will, too. She may attempt more communication now that she knows we can understand her. We can't talk to her past a rudimentary yes or no, but at least we can listen. If she says something in ASL, write it down and underline it. That way I know it's communication from her." She craned her neck over her shoulder. "Logan, please tell Boone I need the goth student on the right there, the one beside the boy in the navy and white striped shirt, in view at all times."

Logan didn't respond; he simply contacted Boone directly. "Logan to Boone. No, it's all good. We need you to keep the goth female on the right side of the screen in view at all times, if possible. The one beside the male in the navy and white striped shirt. Affirmative. Because she's sitting on the floor, she noticed the camera installation and is communicating to us in American Sign Language, so we need to keep an eye on her. Ten-four." He looked down at Gemma. "He'll keep her in view unless he has to follow the hostage taker."

"Understood. Calling in now." Gemma slid her pad of paper closer, pulled up the number she'd stored in the phone's contacts, and placed the call, putting it on speaker and setting the phone between herself and Shelby so they could both hear. As the phone rang, she studied the boy who moved to sit on top of one of the desks so he could balance the rifle over his right knee, freeing up one hand for the phone.

He tapped it, and raised it to his ear. "'Lo."

"Thank you for taking my call." Gemma sat back in her chair, settling in for the long haul, and, with calculation, began with a jolt to the boy on the other end of the line. "Now, Russ, please, talk to me."

CHAPTER 19

There was several seconds of silence before the boy spoke. "You know who I am."

"We do. You were identified by several people. You didn't think your identity would remain a secret when you walked into the school that way, did you?"

Onscreen, the boy shrugged, but only silence carried down the line.

Russ's unawareness of the camera was a huge advantage for the negotiating team. They could see his body language and judge what he was hiding when he thought the only message he conveyed was verbal. He sat frozen, his body stiff, his shoulders riding high, exuding tension. Defiant attitude came through loud and clear in his few words, but it was clear to Gemma that a large portion of that was teenage bravado.

The most important aspect of a successful negotiation was the connection that needed to be forged between the negotiator and the person on the other end of the conversation, be it a hostage taker or a despondent individual seeking to end their own life on the edge of a bridge over the Hudson. For Gemma, that was job one.

"First of all, I'd like to know how you'd like me to address you. Can I call you Russ?" She wasn't naïve enough to think he'd consider her friendly, but she at least wanted to soften her position of authority.

"Sure."

"Thank you, Russ. Now, I want to stress a few things before we really get talking. The rules haven't changed. Tactical officers are still outside the door and aren't going anywhere, even while we talk. But, while we continue to talk, even if we take a few breaks to think things over, they'll continue to stay out and to give you space, as long as you don't hurt anyone inside the room. That starts now. Do you understand?"

"Yeah." More monosyllables, thick with that uniquely teenage derision.

That was fine. Gemma had lived with four teenage brothers; she had a bone-deep understanding of this temporary base attitude. "Excellent. Thank you, Russ. Understanding that starts now, I'd like to ask if anyone one in the room, including you, requires medical care. I can offer medical care freely with no pressure on you because everything that came before now doesn't affect our conversation." She was careful not to use the word "negotiation," because she didn't think he would like the context around it. "Does anyone require care?"

"No. No one's hurt."

Gemma scanned the students in view onscreen. No one appeared to be injured or in distress, so she felt a little safer taking his word for it. "Very good."

Shelby tapped Goth Girl onscreen, who sat with her shoulders angled to block her hands from Russ's view. The girl drew a semicircle from one collarbone to the other, then curved her fingers to meet her thumbs, then made a *V* of her first and second fingers, the tip of her thumb between then. Shelby jotted down *We're okay*. The girl was signing again, confirming his answers.

"Let's get down to it, then, Russ," Gemma continued. "You're holding a number of students and a teacher hostage. My goal is to end this peacefully and with no injury to anyone, including yourself. And I can only do that with your cooperation. You and I, we need to be a team."

The rough laugh that carried across the phone line told Gemma about the wall she was going to have to dismantle.

"I ain't going to team up with no cop." He practically spit the words. "Cops aren't my friends."

"I don't know you, Russ, so even I would think I was handing you a load of crap if I said I was your friend." Gemma let herself use more common language, purposely shifting her vocabulary to strengthen her connection to him in ways he wouldn't detect.

"Why wouldn't you hand me a load of crap?" He turned her own words back on her. Onscreen, his lip curled in disgust. "You'll say whatever you need to get what you want."

"That's not how this works. First thing I want you to know is whatever I say to you is the absolute truth. Sure, I could lie to you, but that could bite me in the ass later, and you have the power to make me pay for it with the hostages you're holding. That isn't a chance I'm willing to take. The truth only, Russ, I swear to God. When I say you and I need to be a team, I mean it." She took his continuing silence for acquiescence. "It's just you and me, talking. There's no time limit. No deadline. However long it takes for you and I to work through this, that's fine. And the officers outside your door know it, too."

Gemma glanced sideways to find Shelby tossing her a look from under her eyebrows that said *I hope Sanders is listening to you.* Sanders was known to lean on the side of wrapping up a situation sooner rather than later, even if it meant using force to do so. Sometimes, especially if it required force to do so. But even Sanders would view the twenty-three kids inside through a more patient lens.

"And you and me talking means you need to actually talk to me," Gemma continued. "If we're making no progress, the decisions are made by going around me. What happens now, how this ends, is entirely up to you. You're in charge. So let's start with the basics. With today." Gemma needed to get him talking. The active listening technique the negotiators used was paramount to building a bridge between hostage taker and negotiators, but it was just that—listening. Gemma needed to not be the person speaking, but sometimes it could be hard to get a suspect talking. "Tell me your story."

"No one wants to hear that."

"I do." Gemma made a snap judgment—time to let Russ know he was on his own and had only himself to depend on. "I have questions only you can answer now."

A few beats of silence passed. "Only me."

"Only you. Hank killed himself." She let that sink in for a several breaths. "You're the only one who can tell your story now." She kept her tone mild, with no hint of disrespect. She didn't have to befriend this boy, but she needed to be entirely nonjudgmental or he'd shut down. Her rage and sorrow and horror had no place here, not when twenty-four lives depended on what she did in the coming hours. "Why did you do it?"

"Because we could."

Gemma let silence ride for a moment, enough to make him want to fill it, then gave him a little push to remind him she was not only there, but listening. "I see."

"Because we have power."

"What gave you that power?"

"Our guns. They demand respect."

"It sounds like you felt you didn't have that before."

Silence. *Doesn't want to admit to any failures.*

"I remember high school," Gemma continued. "Friends were everything, but other kids could sometimes be brutal. Was Hank your best friend?"

"Hank was everything." There was a slight tremor in Russ's voice. Onscreen, while he still sat on the desk, his rifle across his knees, he curled into himself.

He's lost his touchstone, his reason for being here, in this place, with that weapon. He's shaken.

"Tell me about your friendship with him," Gemma prompted.

"Hank was smart. He knew what he wanted. He knew this world wasn't good enough for him."

"So he didn't want to live in it?"

"He didn't think anyone should live in it. *Burn it down.*"

Russ's last words were a whisper, so quiet that Gemma wasn't sure she'd heard it. "Burn it down? That's what he wanted to do?"

"Yeah."

"Hank wanted to burn it all down. What did you want?"

"To burn it down with him. To make everyone pay."

"For what?"

"For everything they've ever done to us."

"What was it anyone did that hurt you so badly?" Onscreen, Russ snapped upright, his hands restless on the rifle. Gemma knew she'd hit a pressure point too early. "Maybe that's too specific a question. Let's back up, Russ. Tell me about your family."

"Nothing to tell. I live with my parents."

"How would they feel about what's happened today?"

"They're not going to care."

Gemma let her surprise show on her face, two floors away, but didn't let it flow through her voice. "They won't care? What would make you say that?"

"If they don't care about me, they won't care about what I do."

Gemma and Shelby exchanged glances. This was the first hint of inward-peering self-esteem issues. "Why do you think they don't care about you?"

"Because they're just like everyone else."

"Everyone but Hank."

"Yeah."

"Hank was your friend."

"Hank was my brother."

"You considered Hank family."

"Yeah. Hank gave a damn."

"You sound like you didn't feel anyone else did."

"Does that matter?" For the first time, defensiveness crawled into Russ's tone.

"Of course it matters. Everyone wants to be loved."

"So you find your own tribe."

"And your tribe was Hank."

"Yeah."

"Anyone else?"

"Hank was enough."

Clearly, Hank was all. Having grown up in a loud, loving, Sicilian family, Gemma couldn't imagine the bleakness of feeling you were unloved, especially during the sensitive and formative teenage years. If Russ felt no one in his life loved, trusted, or valued him, he would seek it elsewhere, and would have been an easy target for Hank's overbearing personality.

"Do you have other friends?"

"Sure."

"But they weren't part of the tribe."

"No."

"What about girls?"

Russ had been shifting restlessly on the desk, perhaps made uncomfortable with talk about parents and friends who didn't value him enough, but now he went dead still. He stayed silent, his face blank.

Another sensitive issue.

"Russ? What about girls? Did you have a girlfriend?"

"No. Look, this is bullshit." His tone rose, the words sharp-bitten. "What more do you want from me?"

"Just to talk. How about the guns? Where did you get those?"

"Hank's dad. We don't have guns at home."

Tread carefully. Here lies a host of other charges. "He gave them to you, or they're his guns?"

Russ's left hand stroked up and down the barrel of his rifle. "His dad has a collection. And would let us target shoot with them."

"He took you target shooting?"

"Nah. He didn't have time for that. But he let us take them when we wanted them."

"Does he know you took them from his house this morning?"

"No. Hank did it after his dad went to work."

"And you were comfortable bringing them to school?"

Russ shrugged carelessly. "Sure. Why not? It's our right."

Her eyes fixed on the screen, Gemma studied Russ. He still sat on the desk, his feet on the seat, facing the kids and teacher at the rear of the room, who would have been able to hear every word he said. He may have still held the rifle in a position so as to pull the trigger at a moment's notice, but Gemma was picking up a disconnect between his words, his tone, and his physical stance.

He wanted the world to burn and was happy to set the match.

Logan's words came back to Gemma. Such rage was evident in the way Hank terrorized and killed. But that's not what she was getting from Russ. He was saying the right words, but without the rage that should have accompanied them.

"Whose idea was it to bring guns to school today? Was it Hank's?"

"He suggested it, but we planned it together. We…" Russ drew in a harsh breath. "We were a team."

You were an acolyte. "He didn't drag you along in his plan?"

"We were a team." Anger was rising in his voice.

Important for him to make sure he's seen as Hank's equal, even though Hank likely didn't think that. "Okay, you were a team. But now it's you calling the shots, Russ. When you come out, it needs to be on terms you can agree on." Gemma was careful to sow the seeds of when Russ surrendered—when, not if. If that became a question rather than a certainty, Gemma was going to lose her hold on Sanders and the tactical team. "Tell me this—what assurances do you need to leave room 317 with everyone inside uninjured?"

"You can't give me any. I walk out this door, those cops will kill me."

"Russ, do you remember at the beginning of this conversation I told you I wouldn't lie to you? I mean that. And that means when I say that those cops won't kill you, I mean it. They won't. If you leave the room unarmed with everyone inside untouched, you won't be harmed." Gemma purposely left unsaid that he'd be taken into custody, tried as an adult, and wouldn't see the outside world for decades, if ever again. If Russ thought too much about that, suicide might start looking like a favorable option.

"So you say."

"You can believe me."

"Uh-huh." Distrust lay heavy in his tone.

"The outcome is entirely up to you, Russ. If you and I can work through this, you'll remain unharmed. If we can't, or if you stop the conversation, the officers outside your door are in charge. You've come this far; meet me in the middle."

The guttural sound he made expressed his doubt more clearly than words ever could. "I'm done talking."

"For now," Gemma pressed. "That's fine. But remember our deal— everyone inside remains untouched and I'll keep the officers out in the hallway. Take a break. But that phone you're holding? It has one phone number in the contacts. This one. If you want to talk to me before I talk to you, just call me. If I'm not in the room, my friend Gina is here and she'd be happy to talk to you, too. I'll be back in thirty minutes. Do we have an agreement?"

"Yeah." With a click he was gone.

Onscreen, Russ held the phone in a clenched fist, and, for a moment, Gemma thought he was going to hurl it at the nearest wall, but he shook his head and slid the phone into his back pocket. Then he seemed to crumple into himself, as if reverting to a small, scared boy who was in over his head.

"He's not feeling it, is he?" Shelby asked.

"No, he's not," Gemma agreed. "And I'm picking up something… I'm not sure what yet, but something he's saying isn't sitting right with me."

"Surely you don't expect them to just open their hearts in a situation like this?" Perez said.

"Definitely not, at least not in the first moments. But for a lot of hostage takers, this is their moment to be heard. They've done what they've done because they feel powerless and they're trying to take that power back."

"That's certainly what the shooting looked like," Logan said. "An effort to exude power, to prove they had it. He said it himself. The guns demand respect. Those holding them demand it, too. Anyone who didn't respect them, died."

"That likely was part of their mindset," Gemma agreed, "though I suspect for Hank it was long past that. He wanted people to die. It gave him a high. According to reports, he was laughing as he gunned kids and teachers down."

"The power of life and death." Shelby frowned down at the monitor. "That's what they wanted." She paused, her head slightly tilted as she stared at Russ. "Or at least Hank did."

"That's the issue, right there. Hank did. I'm not sure what Russ wanted. He was a willing partner, but I don't have a handle on his motive yet." On the desk, her phone lit up with an incoming text. She scanned the message, then texted a reply. "That's Garcia. Morin has identified two kids who were friends of both boys and they've agreed to talk to Garcia and me. I'm going to run over there and will be back inside of thirty."

"If Russ calls in that time, I'll answer and pick up where you left off," Shelby said. "I'll text you and you can get back in a flash."

"Thanks. This could be enlightening. We need the straight goods on these boys, and I'm not getting the whole truth from Russ. These kids could change the conversation and give us exactly what we need to turn this around."

CHAPTER 20

Gemma stepped from the overwhelming quiet of the first floor into the cacophony of the ongoing evacuation and police action. Standing at the top of the steps at the main doors of the school, she saw how the efforts to evacuate the school from the wings, maintaining the crime scene in the front foyer, was evident. There were now closer bus locations so kids could exit from either wing, be quickly questioned by NYPD officers, and be loaded onto buses headed for the Barclays Center if they had no information related to the incident. Evacuation of the first two floors was complete, and A-Team officers were still clearing classrooms on the upper floors. The officer stationed inside the front doors had told her they were making good time, but with more than four thousand students to evacuate—minus those they'd lost and those in the west wing of the third floor they didn't dare move during an ongoing police action—it was going to take considerable time.

Gemma strode down the front walk, keeping an eye on the media throng on the far side. The crowd was thinner now, some of the groups spreading east and west, hoping for the winning shot of the evacuation, perhaps an injured student helped out by a classmate, or a still of a devastated student, her face frozen in a wail of anguish.

Vultures. Picking on the weak at a time of crisis.

Part of Gemma knew she was being unfair, lumping the entire category of media together in a single group, when she knew some reporters were respectful, thoughtful, and diligent about making sure their stories were factually accurate. But as she looked across the street at the bright blue of the ABC7 team, she wished all reporters embraced that same level of integrity.

Instead of aiming for the story that brought the reporter the greatest glory.

Across the street, Greg Coulter was looking straight at her. Not wanting to talk to him, not even wanting to be a part of his shot, she cut across the grass in front of the school, angling away from him and toward the command center.

"Capello!"

She glanced over her left shoulder to see Coulter had left his team and was jogging down the sidewalk parallel to her. The street was full of police cars and A-Team armored vehicles, all still with lights swirling, washing him in waves of blue and red. She looked away from him and walked faster. With this imminent student interview, she didn't have time to spare for him, and even if she did, she certainly wasn't about to give him the inside scoop about her negotiation. She suspected he'd already inferred there was a hostage negotiation going on—it was one thing that she was on-site, she'd been there since the beginning after all; it was another thing that she was spending large amounts of time inside the school unrelated to the evacuation.

As much as she disliked Coulter's attitude and dogged aggression, he was a smart guy and she bet he'd already put two and two together, even though the NYPD had released nothing to the media besides the obvious basics of the incident, and they'd successfully kept the students away from any media. The only tiny bits they'd gleaned had been through social media posts. And while Gemma hadn't seen those public accounts personally, she wouldn't be surprised if the fact there were multiple shooters was widely known. So how much did he really know?

"Capello! I know you can hear me."

She ignored him and kept walking, her mind already rolling ahead to the friends. They had to know something crucial that could assist in her negotiation, in her understanding of Shea, or Garcia wouldn't have pulled her away at this particular time. An experienced negotiator like Garcia would know what was important and would know that for it to really impact negotiations, Gemma needed to hear their stories with her own ears. To hear the emotion and to understand the personalities. Then she could turn that around on the hostage taker. And that, in turn, would—

"I have something you need. If you're smart, you'll stop and talk to me."

Her jaw clenched and her hands balled into fists, Gemma stopped and turned to face Coulter over the hood of the SUV they'd hidden behind only a few hours ago, its side riddled with bullet holes. "I don't have time for a media ask, Coulter. Talk to the Office of the Deputy Commissioner, Public Information."

"You don't have time for me to do that. Not with what I have. And unless you want me to let every other media organization on-site know what it is by yelling at you, you may want to get off your high horse and meet me over here."

Gemma counted to ten in her head but did it so quickly she doubted it cooled her temper at all. What was it about this man that got under her skin so quickly? Well… maybe that was obvious. How about that every time she had anything to do with him, he caused some sort of chaos? Actually trailing Garcia at a negotiation and trying to argue his way into an interview with him. Chasing her and a suspect, and catching a bullet in the shoulder for his trouble. Being requested by the inmates at Rikers during her sensitive negotiations following the riot, and letting his ego run the interview until Lieutenant Cartwright put him in his place.

But no matter how much she disliked him, she couldn't let this turn into a media circus—any more than it already was, at least.

Presuntuoso figlio di puttana…

Swearing under her breath, Gemma stalked across the road, slipping between vehicles and emerging to see a patrol officer pushing Coulter back onto the curb when he attempted to meet her halfway. "Thank you, officer." She met Coulter's angry gaze. "He's going to stay on this side of the road." She stepped up on the curb, forcing him to take a step backward. She gave the officer a nod and he turned away, returning to the line of cops watching the far side of the street, ensuring that no media or lookie-loo civilians vied for a better view of the incident.

She turned back to Coulter. "You're catching me at a bad time."

"You're in there negotiating? One or both of the shooters have hostages?"

"No comment. Now, if that's all you have…" She started to turn away.

"No. I have something you want. It'll be worth your while."

She stepped off the curb. "I don't have time to deal with vague inferences."

"Then how about video footage of Hank Richter and Russ Shea prepping for this event?"

That stopped her cold. He had their names and God knew what else. She turned around slowly to face Coulter. "You have what?"

"You heard me. Video footage of Hank Richter and Russ Shea prepping for this event. This was a planned attack."

Gemma stepped closer and lowered her voice. "I know this was a planned attack. I want to know how *you* know that."

"Social media is an investigative reporter's friend, especially during a time like this." His smile was full of self-confidence. "Especially when a student slides right into my DMs. You know, all those billboards I have up around town," he said, referring to his tipster line advertising, complete with his grinning, perfect face. "Everyone knows me."

That smile was the final feather drifting down to land on the detonator of Gemma's temper, tipping it into red. "You son-of-a-bitch, this isn't the time to boost your own career. Children are *dead*."

Coulter's arrogant smile melted away to be replaced with a snarl. "You think I don't know that?"

"I can't tell by listening to you. Now if you have something relevant to this ongoing incident, something that could save the lives of the kids in there—"

"There are hostages. I thought so."

It took all of Gemma's self-control not to slam her fist into his perfectly straight, bleached teeth, but she hung on, knowing her reaction was way over the top, pushed to extremes because of everything she'd seen today, the pressure of the lives resting in her hands combined with time ticking away, her missing nephew, and the anniversary of her mother's murder. "No. Comment." The words slithered through gritted teeth.

"Don't worry, I won't pin that tidbit on you. I'll put you down as an NYPD source."

"The video, Coulter. We need to see it. *Now*."

"I can arrange that. But I need something in return. Access to the school and the room where the hostages are stashed with a cameraman. That way I can catch the real NYPD response in action."

Gemma fought not to goggle at him stupidly, but his presumption and arrogance almost left her speechless. "You're out of your mind. Not a chance."

"That's not your call."

"No, but I can tell you that it'll be Lieutenant Morin's call."

"I heard he was in charge. He's a hard ass."

"He's a good officer and a better leader. We're in good hands. He won't allow media in the school."

"That doesn't help me."

The urge to hit him came roaring back from wherever it had crawled for the past few seconds. "This isn't about you. This is about so much more than you."

"I totally agree. It's an awful situation and I'm not responsible for it, but why not take advantage of it? And it just so happens, that helps you, too."

"And if we don't let you take advantage of it, you're going to keep your information to yourself?"

"I'm not sure yet. I need to think about that."

"The fact that's even something to consider says worlds about you, Coulter." She turned away from him and stepped into the street. "I have to go."

"Think about my offer. It's still open."

She strode away without looking back.

CHAPTER 21

Gemma stepped into the command center and let the door slam behind her. For a moment, all she could do was stand there, trying to let her anger dissipate. She couldn't meet those students like this. She had to calm down. She closed her eyes and ran through the ingredients and complicated steps required to create her *torta setteveli* cake.

"What's wrong?"

Garcia's voice jolted her out of the steps to create the hazelnut paste and her eyes flew open to find Garcia and Morin standing opposite. "Sir?"

"What happened? You look like you're going to explode."

Gemma met his gaze. "I ran into Coulter."

Understanding lit Garcia's eyes, and his lip curled. "Asshole."

Morin looked from one to the other. "Greg Coulter from ABC7? That asshole?"

"Yes, sir."

"But there's no way you 'ran' into him," Garcia stated. "He should be on the other side of the police line with the rest of the media."

"You're right, he is. I crossed the line and went to him when he yelled that he had something for us. I didn't know what he knew and I didn't want him to blurt out crucial information in front of anyone else out there." She looked from Garcia to Morin. "He says he has a recording of the shooters prepping for the attack. And he knew Richter and Shea's names."

"Shit." Morin dragged a hand through his hair. "The last thing we need now is that getting out, interfering with our investigation, and making those parents' lives any harder than they already are. How did he get it?"

"He said he was contacted directly in a private message."

"Those goddamn billboards," Garcia muttered. "His face is everywhere. Kids don't use their phones for actual telephone calls, but he's easy enough to track down through a bunch of social media accounts, I bet."

"It sounds like someone either sent him the recording or told him where to access it. And God only knows what else they might have sent with it."

"So he didn't tell you anything specific?" Morin asked.

"No, he wants to trade the information for access to the school and the third-floor operation with a camera crew so he can catch the NYPD in action."

"No. Fucking. Way." Morin's words were backed with steel.

"I told him that, sir. He told me to think about it."

"Not your call, Capello."

"I told him that, too. He knows it's yours. But he still seems to think he has a shot at it."

"Where is he?"

"I assume by now he's returned to his crew directly opposite the school."

"I think Mr. Coulter and I need to have a talk. I've never met him, but his face is plastered all over town, so I'm sure he'll stand out in the crowd. But if someone sent him a video, we need to see it, and anything else they might have included." He looked toward the closed door to the interview room. "The two students you need to interview are back there. Take a breath, then go deal with them. Head in the game, Capello."

"It's there, sir." She turned to Garcia. "Ready, Lieutenant?"

"After you, Detective. You take the lead when we get in there to make sure you get the information you need. I'm just there as a second set of ears and for support."

She opened the door to the interview room to find two teenagers sitting side by side at the computer stations on the right side of the room. The space was set up with two long desks on opposite walls, each with a computer terminal and chair. The room could be used for negotiations or as an interview location simply by turning the chairs in. The two boys had already turned their two chairs toward each other.

"Good afternoon, gentlemen." Gemma gave both a pleasant smile and then moved to take the rear chair on the left side.

Garcia slid the door closed behind him and nodded at each boy.

Gemma took a moment to size up each teenager. The boy opposite her was pale, thin, and gangly, all awkward arms and legs it appeared he still hadn't quite figured out how to handle. He wore a navy Henley draped loosely over his bony frame, dark wash jeans, scuffed sneakers, and a ball cap backward over dirty blond hair that needed a shampoo. He slumped in his chair, one knee bouncing, and had picked at the cuticle of one thumb until blood smeared the nail. The other boy sat motionless in his chair, his head slightly lowered, his eyes watchful and wary under his drawn brows. He had his dark hair cut short on the sides, with just enough on the top to fall across a forehead a few shades darker than his friend's. He wore a sweatshirt, once likely black, now an overwashed charcoal, with the image of a T-Rex chasing the figure of a sprinting man and the slogan *Running—sometimes all we need is a little motivation,* and faded jeans with tattered hems paired with scuffed Doc Martens.

They both looked young, shaken, and scared.

Some of that she couldn't help with, some she could. "My name is Detective Gemma Capello, and this is Lieutenant Tomás Garcia. We're part of the NYPD Hostage Negotiation Team. First of all, I'm sorry about what you've been through today. I'm sure it's been a terrifying experience."

"Yeah." The dark-haired boy now had his head up and was looking right at Gemma, while the blond kept his eyes averted.

She grabbed a clipboard and pen from the desk. "I understand you have some information to share about the shooters, so thank you for offering to speak to us today. Let's start with your names."

"I'm Lino Ruiz. He's"—he tossed a hand in the blond's direction—"Curt Kavanaugh."

"Thank you for offering to meet with us."

"When we heard it was Hank and Russ…" Curt finally spoke, but seemed to need to gather his thoughts. "Are they… are they…" He stopped, gathered himself, spit it out. "Did you kill them?"

"It's not our goal to kill anyone, though our officers will do what they have to do to keep the students inside safe." Gemma considered for a moment, and decided they needed to lay their cards out on the table. "Hank Richter killed himself about three hours ago." Lino swore viciously; Curt simply bent his head, hiding his eyes. "Russ Shea has taken a class hostage. I'm talking to him, trying to get him to release the hostages. Twenty-four lives are on the line between the students and the teacher. Twenty-five, if you count Russ."

"Who is it?"

"Who is who?"

"The teacher. Who's the teacher?"

"Mrs. Fowler."

Both boys' heads snapped up.

"You know her?" Gemma asked.

"Had her for sophomore math," said Curt.

"I had her for freshman. Mrs. F is really good. She actually gives a damn. And doesn't make you feel stupid when you don't get it. She just explains it again or another way, until you understand. Russ is in there with her?"

"Yes. That's why we need your help. I need to talk Russ into surrendering and letting everyone walk out of there, alive and uninjured. Anything you can tell us about the boys would be helpful."

The two boys exchanged looks, but both stayed silent.

"Were either of you aware of the attack?"

"You're not going to be in trouble," Garcia clarified when the teenagers still hesitated, "unless you directly contributed to the attack. If you did, we're going to find out. Helping us now could lessen any sentence that could come downstream. There's no negative here for you helping us."

Lino's eyes were wide with horror. "No, man, we didn't help."

"But…" Curt pressed his lips together, frowning at the floor. "I think Hank tried to get us to join them."

"How so?" Gemma asked.

"Hank and Russ both loved to shoot. And my uncle has a farm out in Jersey, about an hour and a half from here. Maybe once a month, once every two months, we'd drive out there. Could target shoot in the backcountry as much as we wanted."

"And it was on one of these trips that he talked about the attack?"

"He didn't really talk about it straight-out," Lino clarified. "He made it kind of a joke. Like, 'Wouldn't it be great if we went to school one day weaponed up like this and shot all the jocks?' That kind of thing."

"That's called 'leaking,'" Gemma explained. "It happens almost all the time before an incident like this. The perpetrator sounds out others to see if they'll join him. Or is so full of plans that he can't resist telling. And then if he's met with scorn or horror, he's all 'Hey, man, don't be so serious. I was only kidding.'"

Curt's eyes flared wide. "That's exactly what he did. We both didn't know what to say to that, and sort of fumbled around. He didn't even let us get out a real answer before laughing and telling us we couldn't take a joke."

"That's how it often goes. You didn't immediately sign on, so he made light of it. He couldn't afford for you to think he really had something in mind and be so alarmed you'd go tell someone. Chances are good he may have asked others a similar question. Or sometimes shooters leak in other, less obvious, ways. Did either boy seem obsessed with death or violence?"

"You mean like in video games? That kind of thing?"

"No. There's a belief that school shooters learn to kill using first-person shooter games, and that revs them up, but the data doesn't support it. No, what I mean is, did they talk about it a lot, or write stories about it, or draw about in in art class?"

Lino glanced sideways at Curt. "Hank told me once about a paper he wrote for English class that got him called into a meeting with the teacher. I don't know the details, but it had to do with death. A lot of death. But apparently he explained it away and she let it go."

"And remember when Russ showed us some of his manga storyline sketches? Some of those were heavy on death and violence."

"Lots of imaginative kids use the arts to express their thoughts, and lot of kids your age can be preoccupied with death and explore it through art. It's not a red flag on its own, but it can be indicative, looking back. It sounds like both boys may have laid this groundwork. And it sounds like both were comfortable around firearms?"

Curt ran his index finger down his thumb, smearing the half-dried blood. "Hank more than Russ."

"Hank could have been born with a shotgun in his hand," said Lino. "He was a natural. Russ... not so much. He wasn't bad, but..."

"Didn't have a good eye?" Gemma asked.

"Good eye, good hands, good stance. He tried hard to please Hank, but he never quite measured up in Hank's eyes."

"I don't think Hank minded that," Curt commented.

Now we're getting somewhere. "Hank liked to win?"

Lino let out a rough laugh. "Hank needed to be best at anything that mattered to him. At least in his own head. Nothing else was good enough for him."

"The world wasn't good enough for him," Curt sneered. "He would cut down anything and everything."

Gemma and Garcia exchanged glances, and she could tell he was thinking the same thing as her. *Narcissist?*

"If the world wasn't good enough for him, why did you hang out with him?"

"He never cut us down—"

"At least not while we were with him," Lino interrupted. "I bet he did behind our backs though."

"Probably. Considering how he always talked about everyone else to us. The only one he probably didn't talk about like that was Russ."

Gemma considered both boys. "They were best friends?"

"I guess. Though Russ kind of disappeared when Hank was around."

"Meaning?"

Curt shrugged. "He kind of *became* Hank. Whatever Hank said, Russ would be parroting it by the next day. It was like he was a giant sponge, but just for Hank. If Russ had an opinion, and Hank thought differently, Russ would suddenly flip-flop to Hank's opinion."

Puzzle pieces snapped into place for Gemma as the disconnect from her first discussion with Russ crystallized. *He could become Hank while Hank was there to emulate. Now Hank's gone, he's drifting somewhere between his own personality and what he's still clinging to of Hank's.* "That kind of adulation through emulation must have made Hank feel good. So they were friends with each other, and friends with you. Did they have friends besides that?"

"They weren't the popular kids at school, but they knew lots of kids. They were both involved in stuff at school."

"Like what?"

"Hank was in the drama club, was in some theater productions, and did some stuff with the school newspaper," said Lino. "Russ played the trumpet in band and was in the manga club."

"What about girlfriends?"

"Neither of them had one," Lino said. "That was a sore spot for both of them."

"In what way? Because of status? Look at me and who I have? That kind of thing?"

"I don't think so. Hank really wanted to get laid. It was all about sex for him. Russ wanted the relationship."

"One wanted sex, one wanted intimacy," Gemma clarified, and Lino nodded. "What about jobs?" Gemma asked.

"Russ works at CVS after school and on weekends."

"Hank used to work at the local sub place, but he quit a few weeks ago," Curt added.

That caught Gemma's attention. *Knew he wouldn't need the job long term.* "Did he say why?"

"He said they didn't treat him well enough. He had ideas about how to make the place run better and the manager didn't take him seriously." Lino shook his head. "Nothing pissed Hank off more than someone not listening to his opinion."

"Did he have a temper?" Both boys laughed, which Gemma took as assent. "I'll take that as a yes. Was it bad?"

"Fuck, yeah." Curt immediately flushed. "Sorry, ma'am. Yeah, it was bad. He'd lose it all the time with us."

"With you? But not with others."

"Not us specifically, just with other students and friends. People knew not to cross Hank. He was scary."

"Not as scary as Russ," Lino muttered.

Gemma sat forward. "Pardon?"

"Russ didn't seem to have a temper. People called him Eeyore behind his back because he was so gloomy. Always down, always negative."

"Unless he was with Hank," Curt cut in.

"Yeah," Lino agreed, "unless he was with Hank, because Hank didn't want a black cloud hanging with him, so to win Hank's approval, Russ had to buck up. Being with Hank always revved Russ up."

"Could that have been an act?" Gemma asked.

"Sure, but Hank didn't care. He got what he wanted and was satisfied."

"So how was Russ scarier than Hank?"

"I saw Russ lose it once. Just once. We were hanging out at a park, and some girl said she'd seen some of his alternate reality manga and he must be jacked in the head. He flipped out, screaming and throwing bottles, and pounding his fists on the picnic table. Just went nuts. The girls made a run for it, some of the guys, too."

"I wasn't there," Curt said, "but kids talked about it for days and didn't get near Russ in case he went off again."

"Everyone except Hank," Lino added.

"Right."

"You said the girl made a derogatory comment about Russ. Was he bullied generally? Was Hank?"

"Definitely not Hank. If anyone was going to be the bully, it would be him. People talked about Russ behind his back, thought he was weird, but mostly no one said anything to him. Besides, he had Hank's protection."

That made sense to Gemma—this was part of the payoff of merging Russ's personality into Hank's. "Was Hank a bully?"

"Not really…" Curt dragged his words out, looking unsure. "But no one could hold a grudge like Hank. If you wronged him—or what he thought of as that—he'd never forget. Once when we were walking home from class, he spotted some kid and told me about an incident in like first grade where the kid swiped something from him. He was still pissed about it." He met Gemma's eyes. "I thought it was weird then. I still do. Who thinks about stuff like that years later?"

Someone whose entire existence is grounded in their own superiority. "Some people have a hard time letting go. What do you both know about their family lives?"

"Russ has an older brother. Hank has… had… *Fuck.*" Curt stopped and dragged in a breath before completing the thought. "Hank had an older brother and sister."

That caught Gemma's attention—Russ had erased his brother from his family story, instead giving that role to Hank. "What were they like, the older siblings?"

"Russ seemed a little in awe of his brother David. He was really smart and popular with the teachers here and was one of the stars on the basketball team. They only overlapped when Russ was a freshman and his brother was a senior, then his brother went off to Cornell on a partial scholarship."

"Hard to be in the shadow of an older sibling." Gemma couldn't help but think of her own time in the academy, the third Capello in five years, each of whom had excelled in their own way, so it seemed like every instructor had a story. Added to that, being the daughter of a high-ranking officer layered on even more expectation. The kind of expectation that made you push harder, as Gemma did, or collapse under the weight, as Russ may have. "Especially if he's well rounded, so no matter what you do, someone has a story about said sibling. What about Hank's older brother and sister?"

"The oldest brother was a bit of a screw up, but the middle sister, Clara, she was a star. She was only a year ahead, and was in everything. Debate team, math club, physics club, anything the brainiacs joined. She was the valedictorian at graduation last year, and got a full ride to Columbia."

Gemma couldn't help but be impressed. "Must have been hard for Hank to live with that kind of competition."

"He didn't talk about her much directly, but he said his parents gave him a hard time about his grades. They weren't the best, but they weren't terrible, unless you compared his grades to his sister's. Then they sucked."

"It's all relative," Gemma said. "I have one more question for you. It's come to light that there's a video of Hank and Russ prepping for the attack. Do you know anything about it?"

Curt and Lino stared at each other, then started to talk at each other instead of Gemma.

"They shot some short video clips a few times at the farm, but that was just target practice. And we were there, so they didn't discuss anything like that in the open."

"But they had to have spent time planning the attack," said Curt. "Date, time, what weapons, who to target. They had to have scheduled a post about it ahead of time."

"Or just sent out a link to where it was already posted somewhere private?" Lino suggested.

Gemma jumped in while the seconds were ticking away. "So you don't know anything specific about it."

"No."

"I've never seen anything and they never said anything to me."

"Thanks." Gemma ripped the top sheets off the clipboard and folded the papers in half. "If you'll stay here for a few more minutes, an officer will take you over to the buses, so you can meet your family at the Barclays Center." Gemma stood and held out her hand and shook with both boys. "Thank you very much for your time. It's been extremely helpful."

They stepped into the communications center and Garcia closed the door behind them. "Have you got a good picture of them in your head now?"

"Yes. Killing dyads aren't that common, but at first glance this looks like a classic setup. The narcissist and the depressive. Hank was crafty, and played all the adults around him perfectly. To them, he was polite and respectful, playing the power hierarchy just right. Those were the people who had power over him, so he appeared in his best light to them. He let his real personality rip with the kids around him because they had no power over him, so he could be verbally and emotionally abusive. Russ was isolated even though he was surrounded by people. He, too, may have only shown his true self to his peers, rather than the adults around him. I wonder if his parents knew he was in such a bad place mentally. If his own sense of identity was so fragile, he may have simply gotten sucked into Hank's delusions of grandeur."

"He's still responsible for his actions."

"I agree, one hundred percent. Don't get me wrong, I'm not making excuses; I'm just trying to understand where things went off the rails."

"With an ego like they described, Hank's intention may have been a spectacle murder."

"To qualify for that, they'd need to get into the Top 10 with the number of dead victims." A chill ran through Gemma at the memory of Logan's description of the art room. "We don't know how many we've lost today. We may never know their intentions, but if they were going for straight-up performance violence, they hit the mark dead-on. Go out with power and glory, that was Hank's goal, I suspect. And one he tried to instill in Russ, but it didn't take in the end. Russ couldn't do it, couldn't pull the trigger on himself. I wonder if we'll find other failed suicide attempts in his history."

"Possibly, but his inability to do it opens the door for us."

"It does. And what Hank didn't take into account is the current media environment. There have simply been too many shootings, and media outlets now go out of their way to focus on the victims and not the shooters. Some won't even name the shooter. If fame and name recognition was what he wanted, he's not going to get it."

"What's your next angle?"

"Knowing what I do now, I'm going to push for the first hostage exchange. The world wasn't good enough for Hank; he wanted to end it all for everyone. I'm no mental health expert, and we'll need one later to help us break this down, but what I'm seeing from these stories about Russ and from talking to him myself is that he didn't feel he was good enough for the world, and he got pulled into Hank's grand plan. But that's the key—it wasn't Russ's plan. The girls I talked to told me Hank was egging Russ on, telling him who to shoot. Hank's mistake was letting them split up. If they'd stayed together, they'd both be dead right now, because Russ would have stayed with the plan under Hank's insistence. But he didn't and now he's in this situation. He doesn't want hostages, he just ended up with them and now he doesn't know what to do with them. Trading a few of them for something he wants may not be too difficult an argument to make. So that's where I'm going to start." Gemma heaved out a heavy sigh. The weight of the day and pressure of the ongoing negotiation were wearing on her. She straightened and squared her shoulders. "I need to get back now. Past this first exchange, now that I know all this, I'll be better able to talk to him and hopefully talk him down."

Time was usually on a negotiator's side, but Gemma had the feeling that for this situation, time was working against her. Russ's own lack of conviction in Hank's larger mission had kept him from pulling the trigger. But if this dragged on too much longer and he saw no way to extract himself with his head high, he might see that as a viable option again.

And if he was taking himself out, why not take the whole class with him?

CHAPTER 22

Logan's grip on his carbine tightened at the knock on the office door, but then relaxed when Gemma's voice came through the frosted glass. "Capello, coming in."

Gemma opened the door and stepped into the school office, closing it quietly behind her. For a moment, she stood, hand resting on the knob, scanning the room to see if anything had changed. To Logan's eye, she looked worn, her shoulders drooping and her dark eyes flat. Her eyes rose to his, and met his expectant gaze with a wan smile.

"How'd it go?" Shelby asked.

"Minus a confrontation with Greg Coulter that made me want to hit something—preferably him—not bad."

"Coulter?" A sneer streaked heavily through Shelby's single word. "What did *he* want?"

"Access to the third floor so he could film the NYPD in action."

Perez made a sound that was halfway between a snicker and derisive snort. "Like that's going to happen."

That brought a smile to Gemma's lips. "Exactly." The smile dissolved. "The problem is he actually may have some leverage. Someone contacted him through social media. He says he has a video of the two shooters prepping for the event. The kids I just talked to didn't think that was an impossibility."

Logan didn't let his jolt of surprise show. "You think he's putting one over on you? Or he actually has it?"

"I think he has it. He knows he doesn't have a chance of getting in without showing his cards first."

"You think it came from the shooters themselves?"

"Yes. Hank Richter hated the world and everyone in it, and wanted to go out in a blaze of glory. Thus, the song, which was entirely too on-the-nose. The glory part may have been key for him, and how better to ensure his story is told the way he wants than to send exactly what he wants revealed to the media just before he carries out the crime?"

"Some media types wouldn't take advantage of that kind of material because it elevates the killers," Shelby said. "But not Coulter. He'd get the bit in his teeth and run with it."

Gemma circled the desk. "Which would be exactly why they sent it to him. Anyone who's seen more than a couple of his reports understands the kind of reporter he is. They could be assured he'd want to break the story highlighting them. Not the victims—them. Anyway, when I left, Morin was going out to have a come-to-Jesus moment with Coulter, so I expect that will be the last I hear of it." She pulled out her chair, her eyes on the monitor. "No changes here? Or any communication from Goth Girl?"

Logan had been only periodically checking the monitor, knowing Shelby was staring at it for the whole twenty-five minutes Gemma had been gone, but he had seen zero movement from anyone onscreen minus some minor body rearrangements.

Shelby rolled her chair sideways to give Gemma more room. "No, it's been quiet. Russ pretty much hasn't moved except to pull off his camera and harness, which was buckled on so he could do it with one hand. And he seems to be relying on us calling him. He's not in any rush to resolve this."

"Because he doesn't have any motivation to. He knows what he's done. And even knowing more about him, I still don't have a handle on what the key is going to be to get him to let everyone go. I'm going to have to feel my way through this."

"What's your tactic for right now?" Logan asked.

Gemma swiveled her chair to look up at him. "I'm going to try for the first exchange. They've been in there for just about three hours at this point and no one has eaten since breakfast. The teens may start to get restless and whiny, and Russ could get short tempered. I need everyone's energy level up and their brains firing on all cylinders. But I'm going to couch it in terms so it looks like I'm doing him a favor. And in exchange, I want hostages out."

There was some ease for Logan in knowing they were in good hands. Gemma might be concerned about her nephew and terrified for the kids in that room, but she was 110% in the game. "I like it."

"Good, because you're going to be the one upstairs getting them out."

Another jolt of surprise. "Me, specifically? I have no problem with that, but there are already two extremely competent teams up there."

"I know that. But you're going to talk to him on the phone first. Let him hear your voice, learn it, know I sent you. He sees the officers outside his door as a threat. I need you to be marked as different. He has to open the door to let the hostages out. That would be an A1 moment for Sanders to be standing just outside the door to either take him out or simply stage an incursion. I need someone to be my representative. More than that, I need it to be someone whose actions I have a hope of foreseeing. Someone I can speak to in shorthand in case of crisis, and who can do the same to me."

"Gem, your hand! Thomson's live-fire training exercise."

An image of the scene at Rikers filled Logan's head. An inmate with a noose around his neck, slowly strangling to death. Gemma, himself, Lieutenant Cartwright, and five other officers sprinting into the high-security unit to prevent the murder happening before their eyes. Logan's unorthodox plan described in only seven words, and Gemma's instantaneous understanding. Their teamwork saving Alvaro Vega's life.

That was the kind of speed she knew she might need.

He gave her a single nod of agreement.

"I'm glad we're off the PA system, because I can mute the phone at this end to talk to you via radio without him knowing what's going on in the background." She turned to the monitor and pulled the NYPD cell phone in front of her. "It's time." She dialed the phone, switched it to speaker, and kept her eyes on the boy onscreen who sat alone and apart from his peers. He'd left his phone sitting beside him on the desk he perched on, and his hand automatically lifted as if to pick it up in response to the ringing, then hesitated, hanging several inches over the phone.

Gemma murmured something in Italian he didn't catch—and wouldn't have understood even if he had—and leaned into the monitor as if she could compel him with her mind. Her shoulders rose on an indrawn breath, held high until the boy's hand finally dropped and he picked up the phone to answer.

"Yeah."

"Hi, Russ. It's Gemma."

Logan had always admired the way that no matter how discouraged or stressed Gemma was—or any of the HNT negotiators, for that matter—she could make a conversation sound light and free from pressure so the hostage taker at the other end of the line didn't immediately shut down. He had lots of skills—from long range sniper tactics to explosives control and high-level rappelling—but managing that kind of delicate communication wasn't one of them.

"It's time you made a good-faith exchange with us to show the NYPD that you're open to continuing our conversation," Gemma continued. "Can we talk about that?"

"What do you mean 'good faith'?" Russ's voice was pure suspicion. Onscreen, his knee bounced.

"I'll promise you something, you'll promise me something, and we'll both carry through. This conversation we're having can take as long as it needs, but, occasionally, I need to show my commanders that we're moving forward. Does that make sense?"

"What you gonna give me?"

"I figure it's been a few hours that you've been in there, and it's a long time since anyone in the room ate or drank anything. Including you. I'd like to give that to you. Whatever you want, for everyone in the room. Your choice. We'll get it to you as fast as we can put it together."

"Like McDonald's?"

"If that's what you want. Big Macs, fries, and Cokes for everyone. And then I'll give you some space while you eat so you won't have to worry about my hounding you through lunch."

"And what do I have to do to get this food and space?"

"Release six hostages."

Logan stared at the back of Gemma's head as if he could see inside to the inner workings, wondering how fast food equated to human life on that scale. He expected her to start high, but that was *high.*

Russ seemed to be on the same wavelength as he simply laughed at her suggestion. "Six? Are you out of your mind?"

"It's a nice round number." If Gemma didn't like being laughed at, Logan couldn't hear it in her tone. "I'm sure you're hungry. And thirsty."

"Not that hungry and thirsty."

"Four, then."

"Two."

"Three." The lightness was gone, and there was steel behind Gemma's tone. "Good faith, Russ. Give me something to show the officers outside your door that we're making progress and they need to back off. You don't want them coming through that door."

Seconds ticked by, stretching further and further until Logan was sure Russ was going to flat-out refuse.

Then, "'Kay."

"You agree to three?"

"Yeah."

Beside Gemma, Shelby gave a silent fist pump.

"Big Macs, fries, and Cokes are okay?"

"Yeah."

"Then that's what I'll arrange. Same rules apply, Russ. The hostages stay safe and untouched and we can proceed."

"I got it."

"Let me get back to you in about ten about how fast we can set this up. Talk to you then." Gemma ended the call.

"Nice going!" Shelby looked exultant. "Worked that nicely."

"She wanted six hostages out and only got half that." Perez's tone didn't share Shelby's jubilation. "It's good, but she was aiming for better."

Logan winced. *Stop while you're ahead, man.* Perez was one of the newer members of the team. A solid guy, quick on his feet, calm, a great shot... but, apparently, he hadn't worked enough large-scale hostage negotiations this up close and personal to know how they really worked.

Shelby fixed Perez with a glare so glacial it gave Logan chills, and he wasn't even a direct target.

"Maybe you're new," she said, in that tone reserved for mothers explaining complex topics to a toddler, "so I'll give you the benefit of the doubt. Have you ever negotiated for anything? A car? A salary?" She didn't even give him time to answer. "You never start with what you think you're going to get. You have to look flexible and willing to give way to the other side." She turned her back on Perez and gave Gemma an eyeroll that clearly said, *Men!* "What were you hoping for?"

"Two at most. Three is fantastic." She grabbed her own phone, called up a number, and placed a call. "This is Capello with HNT. I need Lieutenant Morin." She waited for about fifteen seconds before he came on the line. "Sir, the hostage taker is willing to exchange food and drink for three hostages. Thank you, sir. McDonald's. Big Macs, fries, Cokes. For twenty-two. I also need Principal Baker in here again, if you could have someone bring him over. He can help me with hostage selection. We need to know if anyone is medically vulnerable in there. If so, we want them out first since there aren't any injuries to take into account. And I need a spare tactical radio set. Perfect. Yes, I told him I'd call back in ten minutes and we'll give him the names of the selected students then. Thank you, sir."

The next eight minutes were busy as arrangements were made. Officers were dispatched to get boxes of fast food. Logan made plans with Sanders around delivery to room 317. Principal Baker arrived carrying a spare A-Team throat mic and earpiece, and then he and Gemma huddled around the school computer reviewing the class list. At one point, Gemma called Baker over and showed him the student who had communicated to them via sign language, but with Baker's negative head shake, Gemma looked relieved.

Logan suspected she wanted that girl to remain to allow for emergency communication. Looked like she got her wish.

Just before the ten-minute mark, the printer whirred to life and Baker pulled a piece of paper off the tray and handed it to Gemma. She returned to her seat and laid the paper on the desk. On it was a list of three names.

"What's the status on the food?" Gemma asked.

"Two patrol officers are picking it up right now at a restaurant about four minutes away," said Shelby. "It's going to be packed into boxes that can be stacked and pushed into the room. You have the students you want released?"

"Yes. Two females with health issues—one is diabetic and the other has diagnosed anxiety issues—and one male Adam recommends removing from the situation because he may be unpredictable. Neither of the females is our ASL signer. We would have pulled her out if we had to, but since she's not at immediate risk, we'll use her to our advantage, if needed." She turned to Logan. "You're ready to go up?"

"Yes." Logan pointed at the mic and earpiece lying on the desk. "You're ready to give me instructions?"

"As needed." Gemma slipped on the throat mic and pushed the earpiece into place. "Keep in mind, I can't let him know I have visuals or this whole thing could implode. So I'm going to be making calls balancing what he's telling me and what I can see."

"If we have to go through the door, we don't have to give him an explanation."

He knew even before she spoke that his standard tac team response was pushing all the wrong buttons with her negotiator outlook. The tightly pinched corners of her mouth and the crook of her eyebrow spoke volumes.

"If you go through the door, he could take out every hostage before you take two steps."

Irritation prickled as his own buttons were pushed. "I realize that. I'm just saying that if we go in, it's going to be to end it. There won't be time to talk about you having a visual advantage."

"You guys don't talk, you bellow. And you're missing the—"

Shelby's hand slapped the desk with a sharp crack. "Enough. You're both traumatized and stressed, and this is a ridiculous conversation. Remember you're on the same side. Don't use each other as handy sniping targets to blow off steam."

Logan's cheeks warmed under Shelby's sharp stare. "Traumatized? That's overly dramatic."

"Think about what you've seen today, and ask that question again."

Images of broken bodies, smeared and splattered with blood, and the devastated, haunted eyes of the survivors rose like specters. Logan closed his eyes for a moment to clear his mind, but the images only followed him into the dark. His eyes snapped open again, and he silently raised a hand in capitulation. *You win.*

Gemma blew out a breath. The eyes that turned up to his were smudged with fatigue, relaying the exhausting effort to maintain the happy negotiator persona when she probably wanted to pound something. "Sorry. I know you know what you're doing, and won't push to end this earlier than needed."

"I'm sorry, too. Guess I'm spoiling for a fight."

"Tell me about it."

Logan gave her a half smile. "Want me to go find Coulter? I'll hold him and you can hit him. We'll both feel better."

Gemma chuckled. "You have no idea. Sadly, I don't think the brass would look kindly on that." She turned back to the phone. "Let's introduce you to Russ. Keep it brief." She met his eyes and he felt the intensity of her gaze as if it was a physical touch. "You've seen too much today. This is going to be hard, but you can't let that show in your voice. If he feels persecuted and shuts down, we lose it all, possibly including the hostages. This is part of the skill of negotiating—no matter what you feel about the hostage taker, or what he's done, you can't let it show. Connection is everything. Without it, it's game over. You need to tell me now if you don't think you can pull that off. It's no negative against you, but I need to know."

It was going to be hard, especially with the sights and sounds of the day and the emotions they drove entirely too close to the surface. However, he had the skills to control that emotional response, and fell back on the logic and steadiness he used as a sniper. Sometimes to take the shot ordered by the commander in your ear, you needed to disconnect. You had to trust that voice—trust it had a fuller picture of the incident than you did, trust it to guide you. Gemma would be that voice. "I can do it."

She didn't say anything, just gave him a single nod and placed the call.

Logan noted this time there was no delay by Russ in picking up the phone. *Anticipating his reward.*

"Hi, Russ, we're ready to do the exchange on our end," Gemma said. "Are you ready?"

"Yeah."

"Before we do this, I wanted to introduce you to the officer who will make the exchange." She waved Logan in.

Logan braced a hand on the back of Gemma's chair and leaned in over her shoulder toward the phone. "Russ, this is Sean Logan. I'll be delivering your food and meeting the three kids you're releasing."

"You'll be unarmed?"

He didn't want to be entirely unarmed, but he could compromise. There would be enough firepower behind him if it all went to hell, and he wouldn't actually be entering the classroom. "I'll leave my rifle here."

"And how will I know it's you?"

"By my voice. And we'll double up. Give me a word I can give back to you. Something... unusual. Something only I would know."

Four or five seconds of silence passed, and Logan was beginning to think he'd made an error.

"Isekai."

"Isekai?" Logan repeated the strange word, emulating Russ's pronunciation of *ee-sec-eye* with the emphasis on the initial vowel. "Am I saying it right?"

"Good enough."

Gemma gave him the hand signal for *enough*, and he straightened.

"Are you ready then, Russ?" she asked.

"Yeah."

"Sean will bring the food in ten minutes. He'll knock on the door and announce himself. You open the door and let the three students out. Then the food is passed in and the door closes again. Do you understand?"

"Yeah."

"These are the three students you will send out. Azumi Yamazaki. Lia Vilar. Jake Terret. All right?" Gemma looked at the phone expectantly, and then when no answer came, her gaze shot to the monitor where Russ sat motionless on the desk, his gaze fixed across the room. "Russ?"

"Got it. We'll do the exchange. Send it up." Onscreen, he lifted his phone and jabbed at the screen to disconnect the call.

"What happened there?" Shelby asked.

"I have no idea. But we have his agreement, so I'll take it. Logan, do you have that word?"

Logan had been repeating it in his head to cement it in his memory. *Isekai isekai isekai.* "I have it. I don't know what it means, but I have it."

"My nephew is nuts for manga and anime," said Perez. "Isekai is some kind of fantasy world. He goes on and on about it, and I don't really follow most of what he says, but I do know that much."

"He's in the manga club, so it makes sense, knowing that." Gemma stood. "Is the door going to be a problem?"

"He got in; I'll get in. There's always the broken window. But if that handle is like this one"—he pointed to the office door where a silver push button locked the door from the inside—"once Russ opened the door, it stayed unlocked."

"Good. Are you ready?"

Isekai. "Ready." Logan flipped the safety on his M4A1, slipped his rifle sling over his head, and laid the rifle on the desk beside Gemma. He lay his fingers on the receiver. "Keep an eye on this for me?"

"It'll be right here when you come back."

In a situation like this, Logan felt naked without his carbine. *If I make it back. If this goes pear-shaped, I've only got a vest and a pistol.* His hand fell to the grip of his Glock 19. *And the twelve guys behind me who would consider me in their way if I'm standing in the doorway.*

This had better not go pear-shaped.

A few minutes later, Logan found himself outside of room 317, staring at the broken window and shredded poster, covered with more paper. Three oblong boxes were stacked at his feet.

Gemma's voice sounded in his ear. "Detective Logan, are you ready?"

"Affirmative. Is he?"

"Yes. He has the three kids grouped between him and the door. His rifle is pointed at the floor. Calling now."

Through his earpiece, he heard her place the call, heard her tell Russ that he was standing outside the door. "Are Azumi, Lia, and Jake ready to go?"

A low murmur came from the other side of the door.

"I'm going to tell Sean to open the door," Gemma continued. "Sean? You can go ahead now."

Logan noted the positions of the officers in the hallway. Behind him, Sanders stood, rifle braced at his shoulder, already staring down the sight, getting ready to place the perfect shot if the hostage taker didn't follow the rules exactly. On the other side of the hallway, Sims was similarly braced, but didn't exude the same level of aggression.

At Logan's suggestion, Turner stood directly opposite the doorway. These kids were going to leave the classroom and walk into a hallway full of officers and guns; he wanted a woman to be there to soften the affect, especially for the girls. She, too, had handed off her rifle and had removed her safety glasses, slightly softening the overall look of weapons and body armor as much as safety allowed.

He knew without a doubt that every officer in the hallway was ready to react if needed.

"Russ, it's Sean. I'm opening the door." He started to turn the handle, but stopped when he heard the question from the other side of the door.

"What's the word?"

"Isekai." *Nailed it.*

"Okay."

Logan tested the handle and, as expected, found it unlocked. He opened the door one foot, then two. He instinctively swung his fist up on a bent elbow for the officers behind him—*Hold*—just as Gemma said, "He's now aiming at the kids."

Three kids stood in front of Shea, who held his rifle pointed at their backs. Behind him, on the floor, a huddle of wide-eyed teens was grouped behind the only adult in the room, who sat holding the hands of the kids on either side of her.

Logan loosened his fist and raised his other hand so they were both in clear view of the shooter. "Hi, Russ." He did his best to mimic the easy lilt he heard in Gemma's voice when she negotiated.

In his ear, Gemma was speaking. "Logan, he put down the phone, so you're our only voice now. Remind him it's a good-faith exchange. The three kids come out, the food goes in. Use his first name, it helps build the connection."

"Russ, I have your burgers and fries. But as part of our good-faith exchange, I need those kids first. Please send them out one at a time." A girl stood at the front of the group, slender and blond, in leggings and a long-sleeved T-shirt that came to midthigh. Logan motioned to her. "You first."

She looked over her shoulder, saw the rifle pointed at her, and froze.

Logan took a step into the doorway, his hand extended, but Russ only raised his rifle higher and hissed. Logan froze, his eyes locked on the finger threaded inside the trigger guard. *Too easy to twitch under pressure and fire inadvertently.* "Russ, you made an agreement and these three need to come out one at a time." He forced himself to look at the girl. "Are you Lia?"

"Yes."

"Give me your hand, Lia. It's time to go." More firmly. "Now."

Moving so slowly Logan had to check himself from directing her again because it would only slow her further, she placed her hand in his. He gripped it tight, drawing her forward, through the doorway, and toward Turner. Turner took the girl's hand and pulled her behind the line of officers as they waited for the second student.

Logan looked at the remaining girl. "You're next."

The girl practically flew past him and out the door, leaving only a tall, gangly boy standing in front of Russ's rifle.

"Come on out," Logan prompted.

Five steps and the boy was out as well, leaving no cover in front of Russ. But Logan kept himself between the boy and the officers behind him, even as he maneuvered around the boxes, and pushed them into the room with a booted foot on the bottom of the stack. Once they cleared the arc of the door, he stepped backward, closing the door as he went.

"Fall back." Sanders's voice sounded behind him.

Logan pulled back with Turner and the kids, coaxing the girls, who were holding on to each other, to move. "Logan to Capello, we have them. And the food is delivered."

"Good job, Detective. Please bring the kids here before they leave the building. I'd like to talk to them."

Down the stairs to the second floor, and then down to the first floor. There was no avoiding Officer Kail, but Logan and Turner kept the kids moving, through the foyer and into the office with a call of "Logan and Turner, coming in" before opening the door.

Baker, who had remained in the office for the exchange, rose from his chair behind the admin assistant's PC, a smile lighting his face. He scanned the kids, making sure they were okay, and the smile slowly slipped from his face.

Gemma couldn't see him, but Logan certainly could. "Principal Baker? What's wrong?"

Gemma jerked, her head swinging from Baker to Logan, Turner, and the kids, and back again, confusion in her eyes.

But Baker's eyes were fixed on the boy Logan had brought from 317. "Russ put one over on you."

"What do you mean?" Gemma asked.

"That's not Jake Terret."

CHAPTER 23

Gemma surged to her feet, her heart rate kicking high. "What do you mean that's not Jake Terret?"

Baker's face was cut deeply into grim lines. "I mean it's not Jake." His face softened as he stepped to the boy, standing frozen in front of Logan, his eyes wide and his pulse visibly beating under his jaw. "It's Clive, isn't it?"

The boy nodded.

Baker lay a gentle hand on the boy's shoulder. "It's okay, Clive. We're glad you're out, even though that's not the way it was supposed to go."

Gemma remembered Russ's reaction to being told the names of the hostages they expected in the trade. *A long silence, then agreement to the exchange.*

But not agreement to the hostages themselves.

Gemma glanced at the monitor, where Mrs. Fowler was passing out the food to students who remained in position on the ground. "Can you keep an eye on the monitor for a minute while we sort this out?" she asked Shelby.

"Of course." Shelby rolled her chair closer to the monitor.

Gemma circled the desk to approach the huddled teens. "Hi, guys, my name is Gemma."

"You're the one speaking through the PA," said the girl with a long, dark ponytail.

"Yes." Gemma had the advantage of having witnessed the exchange, knew which girl was which, or at least who exited under each name. "It's Azumi, right?"

"Yeah."

"We pulled you out because of your diabetes. Do you need medical care?"

"No. I haven't eaten, so I'm fine for now. To be safe, I should check my sugars, but my glucometer is in my backpack upstairs."

"We'll get you out to EMS in a few minutes and they can check your blood sugar. In the meantime, if you feel unwell, you let me know right away."

"Sure."

"Is your insulin in your backpack as well?"

Azumi lifted the edge of her sweatshirt to reveal a small black box with a screen and a row of buttons across the front clipped to her waistband. "I have a pump, so all the insulin I need is here."

"Excellent." Gemma turned a smile on the blond girl. "And you're Lia."

"Yes."

Taking care not to draw attention to her challenges around anxiety, Gemma gently asked, "Are you okay? It's been a pretty intense day."

Lia's eyes grew wet, and she blinked several times. "I want to go home. I want to see my parents."

"We're going to make that happen for you. Can you give me a few more minutes before I have officers escort you out?"

Lia's mouth wobbled as she fought back tears and nodded, making Gemma wonder if she didn't trust her voice.

Gemma gave her shoulder a quick squeeze. "Thank you. I know this is hard. Hang on just a bit longer." She had the flash of an idea. "You know your parents' phone numbers?"

Another nod.

"Do you all?"

Positive responses from all three.

That gave her a serious kick in the gut. She'd been trying to convince herself they weren't hearing from Sam because he couldn't recall his parents' phone numbers under stress. But these kids did, so he should be able to.

Why aren't we hearing from him?

She swallowed down the rising edge of panic. *Stay on task.*

"Pass me my phone?" Gemma crossed to the desk, taking her phone from Shelby. She unlocked it and opened a new, blank text message and extended the phone to Lia. "Send your mom or dad a text, telling them you had to borrow a phone so you can't talk, but you wanted to let them know you're okay, and you'll meet them at the Barclays Center." She looked at the other two students. "Then you guys do the same. That will take a load of stress off your parents. You may not see them for another hour or so, but they'll know you're coming, and they'll stop being frantic."

As Lia texted, Gemma looked at the boy. Tall and gangly, he had the same body shape as her brother Mark until he grew into his limbs. His shaggy hair fell into eyes clouded with guilt. "And you're Clive..."

"Birmingham." He hunched his shoulders and looked at the floor. "I'm obviously not the person you wanted out of there."

Gemma stepped forward so her smaller stature moved into his downcast field of vision. "Yes, we'd selected another boy to come out, not because you're not worthy, but because he was deemed a risk to the stability inside the classroom. Our primary aim is to peacefully resolve this incident. I'd have liked to have every one of you out of there an hour ago, but if all I can do is work to get you out three at a time, then that's what I'll do." The boy raised his gaze to meet hers. "I'm glad you're out, Clive, and I'm sure your parents will be as well. It's not your fault Russ didn't do as we asked. But now you've been in there, I'd like to ask you about what you saw." She glanced from face to face, read the exhaustion, and pointed at the row of chairs opposite the main desk. "Why don't you guys sit down? I know you've had a hard morning. Take a load off." Leading them over, she pulled the last chair around to sit opposite the students, waiting until they were settled and her phone had been passed to Azumi. "I don't want to keep you long, but if there's anything you can share with us about what's going on inside that room we're not hearing, it could go a long way to helping your classmates get released as well. Do you know Russ Shea, the boy holding the class in there?"

All three kids shook their heads in the negative.

"Was he targeting anyone specific in that classroom? Was he particularly threatening to anyone there?"

"Not anyone specific," said Clive. "He seemed more scared of us as a group."

"Even though he was the one with his finger on the trigger of a semiautomatic rifle. Because you could overpower him as a group?"

"Maybe. When he shot his way through the window and opened the door, we were all at the far end of the class. Not that he could see anything from the outside. Mrs. Fowler covered the window with a poster as we were locking down."

"He screamed at us not to move," Azumi added as she passed Gemma's phone to Clive. "And after all the shooting we could hear from a distance, we weren't going to."

The classrooms Sims reported on. The empty one and the halfhearted attempt. He didn't have Hank there to egg him on. He also didn't have Hank to perform for. Maybe he wasn't having the glorious time he thought he would?

"What did he do once he was in the room?"

"He made us stay in that corner. If there were backpacks in that area, he made us push them out of reach and then he kicked them the rest of the way. If anyone had their phones with them, he made us power them down and throw them across the room, onto the floor under the windows. But only a couple of us had them because they were supposed to be in our bags on silent."

"By that time the cops were outside the door and screaming at him," Clive said. "We thought they were going to break down the door and we were all going to die."

"Your safety is our top priority," Gemma said. "They're not going to enter as long as we have a dialog going, because they know to do so would likely sacrifice lives. What did Russ do when the officers in the hallway were yelling at him?"

Azumi shrugged. "Nothing much. He paced for a bit in front of the windows across from us. Mrs. F already had the blinds down, so that was safe for him, and he kind of avoided anything too close to the door. Except for the desk."

"What do you mean?"

"He was pacing back and forth, muttering to himself. He stayed to the rear of the classroom, and kept an eye on us the whole time. I assumed he was staying out of range of any rounds that could come through the window of the door, but then he sat down on a desk almost at the front of the class and only two rows over from the door."

Gemma thought about where she'd seen Russ sitting just before the exchange—she would have described it in roughly the same position. "And then he stayed sitting there?"

Clive let out a rough laugh. "God, no. He has energy to burn. He'd get up about every three or four minutes and pace and then go sit down again."

"He'd pick whichever desk was closest to him at the time? Or did he pick a desk closer to you so he could be more threatening?"

Gemma deduced from the puzzled look on Azumi's face that she was following her line of thought. "No," Azumi said. "He kept going back to the same desk."

"Like it had some kind of special significance to him?"

"I don't... know?" Her tone rose in question as she squinted down at the floor as if working it out in her head.

Clive passed Gemma her phone, which she slipped into her back pocket. "What about weapons? You said he carried a semiautomatic rifle." Her gaze shifted to Logan. "Did you get a look at it?"

"It's a Ruger Mini-14. That particular configuration gets around New York State's automatic rifle ban because it doesn't have a pistol grip, flash suppressor, or telescopic stock. Because of state laws, he can only legally use a seven-round magazine in it. He managed that by stuffing the cargo pockets of his fatigues with extra magazines for fast reloading."

"Any other weapons?" she asked the teens. "Another gun? A knife?"

"Not that I could see," Clive said, and the girls agreed.

"I don't want to delay you any longer, because your parents are waiting to see you, and, Azumi, I want EMTs to check you out before you head to the Barclays Center. Other officers will want to talk to you in more detail, but is there anything else you can add? Did he say anything or threaten anyone you haven't mentioned?"

"He seemed to be talking to himself more than anyone else," Clive said. "I mean... he knew we were there, but he didn't seem eager to kill us."

"What do you mean?"

Clive looked at the girls as if asking for help.

"He didn't seem to be looking for a reason to shoot anyone," Lia said. "He kind of seemed... lost? Sometimes. Not when he was talking to you."

The hairs on the back of Gemma's neck prickled. "He was focused when he was talking to me?"

Lia looked from Azumi to Clive, who nodded in encouragement. "More focused anyway. He would sit on that desk, talking to himself, but when you called, that stopped and he would pay attention to you."

"Did anyone hear what he was saying to himself?"

Negatives from all three teens.

Gemma stood. "Thank you for spending a few extra minutes here. There are officers in the foyer who will escort you and Principal Baker out of the school and to the EMTs so they can check you out. Then they'll get you to the buses and to the Barclays Center."

Baker was shaking his head, his expression set in stone. "I'm not leaving until every child is out. Wouldn't it be better if I stayed here with you? In case you need me again?"

"That's a generous offer, Adam, but the school isn't secured yet, so I'd prefer to keep civilians where they're safest." Baker gathered himself to argue, so Gemma jumped back in before he could speak. "But I appreciate the offer and you may be right. Would you stay at the command center so we can call you if needed? I'll make sure Lieutenant Morin knows. If we need you back, you can be here in two minutes. And that way you're still in the loop no matter what happens." When he still looked like he was going to dig in his heels, she hit him where she knew it would make the biggest impact. "The students are being escorted out to the EMTs, but I'd feel better if they had someone they trusted with them until we can get them on a bus. They've been through enough today."

Baker's gaze slid to the students and his face softened. "I'd be happy to stay with them. Let me leave you my cell number. I left it behind in the initial rush to get kids to safety, but I have it now, so you can contact me directly."

"That's perfect. Thank you."

Logan and Turner walked the kids and Baker out to the two officers waiting for them outside the office, and Gemma returned to her chair by the monitor. "Anything happening in 317?" she asked Shelby.

"Just eating and drinking. That was the right call. Faces that looked stressed are a little more relaxed now."

"Including Russ?"

"Hard to tell. He's mostly inscrutable. But since those kids mentioned the muttering, I've been watching for it. He is." Shelby pointed at the monitor. "Keep your eyes on his lips and you can see them moving as he's sitting on the desk without anyone within fifteen feet to talk to."

Gemma stared at the scene onscreen, focusing on Russ where he sat on the desk. He would take a bite of burger, chew, swallow, and then his lips moved as he spoke. *Who are you talking to?*

"What are you thinking?" Shelby said.

"I think I'm missing something. The kids mentioned that desk. I noticed where he was sitting, but not being in the room and seeing him from this odd angle, I don't have his exact 3D placement. But the kids are right. He's sitting somewhere where he could be more in jeopardy, so why there? It looks like it's a conscious choice, because he leaves and comes back to it. Why?"

"That might be a question for Baker?"

"Maybe, but it's likely too specific for his bird's-eye view of the school. He might be able to tell us if he ever had a class in that particular room, but he'd likely not be able to tell us if something happened there if it didn't require disciplinary action. What if he had a disastrous presentation and felt humiliated? Or had a teacher who also had his older brother and couldn't stop comparing them, making Russ feel small, stupid, and useless? We just don't have enough information yet."

"And likely won't on this kind of timetable. This incident isn't going to go on for days. Things will get tense in there just because kids will need to use a bathroom."

"And when things get tense, I may not be able to maintain control. I know. This isn't going to be a multiday incident like Rikers. This is going to be solved by dinnertime, my way or Sanders's way. The question right now is which way."

"We got this."

"Damn straight." Gemma looked up as Logan called out his designation and came through the door. "While you had a glimpse into the room, did you see anything there that set off warning bells?"

Logan stood at ease, feet planted, his hands clasped over the butt of his rifle. "No, but I didn't have a lot of time. I wanted to get those kids out, but Lia was terrified and I was focused on coaxing her out, then the other two. Then my focus switched to getting the food in and backing out without incident. He kept his rifle barrel on the kids' backs at all times and had his finger on the trigger. I was worried we were one careless twitch away from major trouble. There really wasn't time, plus my concentration was focused on the kids and that rifle."

"When even a hint of playing chicken with him would have been disastrous. Of course you didn't have time and couldn't chance breaking focus to scope out the room from another angle. I figured, but I needed to check, just in case."

On the desk, Gemma's phone lit up and she opened her messages. And froze.

"That's not a good look," Logan stepped to the other side of the desk, his hands automatically falling to the pistol grip and forestock of his carbine. "What happened?"

"He's... Morin arranged..." Gemma forced herself to stop and take a breath.

"What?"

"Morin had to make a deal with Coulter. Coulter wouldn't release the video to Morin—"

"Bastard..." Shelby muttered.

"—so Morin had to deal with Coulter for access."

Logan's eyes narrowed suspiciously. "What does that mean?"

"Morin wants me at the command center as soon as I can get free and Coulter will show us the video."

"There's no way he's doing that out of the goodness of his heart. But I can't believe Morin is giving him full access to the school in exchange."

Inside Gemma's head, a string of Italian invectives tumbled over each other, wanting to burst free. She swallowed them down. "No, just to *me*. Morin pressured him with the fact that he could get a warrant quickly under the circumstances, and there was no way in hell Coulter was getting any access to the school during the incident. But he offered him full access to me in an exclusive one-on-one interview about the incident sometime after the fact. Coulter took the deal."

"And you're basically being ordered to do it," Shelby stated.

"That's the basic gist, yes." She jammed her phone in her pocket. "I really hate Coulter. Morin knows that."

"He was doing what was best for the students inside. Who knows what might have happened if he had to take the time to get the warrant? Now you have instantaneous access to a video that could give you some significant insight."

"I know." Gemma glanced down at the monitor where most of the kids were done eating but a few still picked at their food. "Now is probably the best time to watch it. I told Russ I'd give him some space while they ate. I'll go to the command center now and be back as fast as possible."

"We'll hold down the fort here," Shelby said. "And if he calls and won't talk to me, I'll hold him until you return."

"Thanks." Gemma headed for the door.

It was time to see what Coulter had that he thought was so crucial, he could use it as a blackmail bargaining chip with the NYPD.

CHAPTER 24

Gemma stepped onto the front walk when her phone buzzed in her pocket. She pulled it out, and the text from Joe filled her with cautious hope. *Word, finally.*

She opened the message from him as she hurried down the front walk.

The kid wasn't Sam. No one's seen him. The class he was in has been evacuated. He's not with them. Must be inside still.

Gemma nearly stumbled and had to stop entirely as she read the text through a second time. The message was terse and bare-bones, a cop's communication of just the facts. This is what she'd been most afraid of. She'd been able to keep Sam compartmentalized in a corner of her brain while she worked because they thought he was out. And if that child wasn't Sam, there were thousands of kids who had already been evacuated.

And Sam wasn't one of them.

She slowly turned to stare at the school. The first and second floors were entirely evacuated at this point, as was the fourth floor once the injured had been removed, leaving only the dead behind. The east side of the third floor was in progress last she heard and was likely mostly clear.

That left the west side of the third floor, but his class was already out. *Where was he?*

Or was he among those who would never walk out?

For a second, Gemma could only stand frozen, her breath trapped in lungs that had forgotten how to work, her brain sluggishly sifting through scenarios. Caught in the hallway by one of the shooters and becoming a target. Or being out on a task and taking shelter with another class—a class that then came under fire. Or—

Stop it.

Your best way to help Sam is to end this situation. When the hostage taker is taken down or out, officers will find him.

Keep your head in the game. That's *how you help him.*

The breath she drew in was jerky, like teaching her diaphragm to expand as if it was her first breath out of the womb.

Move.

She put one foot in front of the other, moving faster with each step as they carried her to the command center.

Sam needs you to focus. You're doing it for him and for every other kid at risk in there. You can deal with Coulter for them.

Coulter. Her patience level with him was going to be below zero before they even started. And as much as she'd like to give him the cut direct, she needed him right now. More than that, she needed to work with him. Morin and Garcia both knew Sam was missing, even if he wasn't in that classroom. The moment they thought her head wasn't completely focused on the hostage taker, she'd be off the team and Shelby would be primary. She had to be at her most calm and most professional.

For Sam.

Striding down the sidewalk, her gaze fixed on the command center, she tucked Sam away into a corner of her mind and quietly pushed the door shut behind him, the click of the latch reverberating in her head like a gunshot.

She jogged up the steps of the command center, opened the door, and walked through. Inside, it was the same kind of intense action as before. Energetic, efficient, and, organized, if you knew what you were looking at. Otherwise, it might appear chaotic, but there was a rhythm to the chaos, and the pull of forward motion. Her eyes moved to where Morin stood with Garcia, her father, and two other officers.

Garcia, who stood with his back to her as he talked to Morin and Gemma's father, looked over his shoulder at the sound of the door and gave her a nod. "Good, you're here."

"I came as soon as I got the message. Is Coulter here?"

"In the interview room, but we need to update you first."

Gemma's gaze skipped from Garcia to her father to Morin. "On what?"

"We sent detectives to the Richter and Shea households."

The intensity behind his tone jangled down Gemma's already alert nerves. "What did they find?"

"Dead parents."

"*What? Where?*"

"At the Richter household. It looks like Hank warmed up by shooting both his parents last night."

"No one reported hearing shots fired?"

"Evidently no one heard it. Hank used a Walther P22 with a 22LR suppressor and subsonic ammunition. Headshots at close range for both of them."

"Brutal. Is there evidence he stayed in the house last night after the shooting?"

"There sure is. He ordered a pizza on Daddy's credit card and had it delivered to the house. Then ate it in front of the TV while his parents' bodies cooled on their bedroom floor."

"I suspected Hank was a stone-cold psychopath; this cements it. Interesting though that Russ told me they had to wait to get the guns to stage the attack until Hank's father went to work, because they were the father's guns. Hank didn't tell Russ he killed them; he just let him think everything was going according to plan."

"Looks like Richter didn't trust Shea all the way. Enough to plan the killing and carry it out, but not enough to show where Richter might be vulnerable."

"Russ definitely trusted Hank to a greater extent. Notice, too, that Hank's mother hasn't been mentioned at all. Not that he had to wait until both parents went to work, only the father. The mother wasn't considered any kind of threat."

"And that may be why his father had to die," Garcia said. "His mother may have simply been collateral damage. She had to die so she didn't blow the whole plan. It does make you wonder though if he planned parricide all along, if it was a spur-of-the-moment rage killing, or if the plan was threatened because Dad had figured out something was going down."

"That might be in their journals," Morin said.

Gemma's gaze flicked to Morin. "They kept journals?"

"Both of them. Maybe as a way to document this deed, but from what I hear, they both go further back than that. Maybe journaling was suggested to them by school counselors or something. Either way, they both have them."

"Clearly you've executed warrants already."

"That and we got cooperative parents at the Shea house. Christopher and Erica Shea were getting ready to leave for the Barclays Center when detectives arrived. They didn't believe their boy could possibly be involved and told them to go ahead and search." Morin met Gemma's gaze. "Russ Shea had no intention of going home. He left his journals on his desk, and the top one had a suicide note tucked into the front cover. He probably figured that way it wouldn't be prematurely spotted and they'd be stopped before they carried out the attack, but would be easy to find after he committed suicide."

Gemma had always suspected suicide was the final goal of the mission for both shooters, but an actual suicide note cemented her theory. However, without Hank's determination, Russ had floundered. "Was Russ's note in his own handwriting?"

"It was printed out from a computer document. But his mother said it was his signature."

"Did she read the whole note?"

Morin's eyes narrowed on her. "They didn't say. Why?"

"I want to know if the note sounded like it was written by him." She turned to Garcia, could see he was following her line of thought because he'd been following the negotiation as part of the team, versus Morin who was controlling the entire incident and was only getting updates. "I'd put money on the fact he didn't write it."

"I wouldn't take that bet. Chances are good I'd lose," Garcia said. "Everything we've heard and seen so far has him as the submissive partner."

"Meaning Richter was calling the shots, right down to writing Shea's suicide note," Tony stated.

"I'm leaning in that direction. I think Hank really had his claws into Russ. He encouraged him through the attack, and he was the one who was glorying in it, reportedly laughing as he gunned down other students and at least one teacher. But things got shaky for Russ when they split up."

"Hank probably thought they could cover more ground separately. Increase their kill count," Morin said.

"I agree, that was likely Hank's mindset, and it goes to show how wrapped up he was in his own narcissistic worldview. He gave orders he expected to be followed; what he didn't count on was Russ second guessing himself. He's not only still alive, so is the class he's locked in with, while Hank was gone hours ago." She caught her father's eye. "And there's something about that room…"

Tony nodded in acknowledgment. "Have you narrowed it down yet?"

"I think I'm getting there. I want to work with Baker on it, see if I can't get it completely figured out. Is he still here?"

"He's outside. You must have passed him on the way in," Morin said.

"My head was already on Coulter and I must have missed him. I'll catch him on my way out. Anything else the detective could tell us? Did they have a chance to look in the journals?"

"They're just starting to go through them at Shea's," said Morin. "I told them we needed even preliminary content ASAP. I'm hoping that comes by the time you're done with Coulter."

"What about at the Richter house? Did Hank leave a suicide note?"

"Yes. And this one wasn't tucked out of sight like Shea's. He left it on the kitchen table. His journals were in his bedroom, but weren't hard to find."

"He must have left them where they could be easily found, because it's doubtful that was his normal hiding spot or his parents might have stumbled across them and blown the whistle on him. It seems like he had them completely fooled." Gemma glanced at Garcia, got a nod of agreement. "The information we have so far on Hank Richter makes him sound like a narcissistic psychopath. And that type of personality often does an excellent job of hiding their true identity from authority figures. They may not have stopped him because they didn't realize how truly psychopathic he was."

"What is it with kids and handwritten journals?" Morin asked. "When they're otherwise never without a phone?"

"Handwritten journals are more personal, more raw, and the handwriting itself is a reflection of the mood. And they can illustrate if they want. Russ was into manga; I'll bet we'll find illustrations in his, likely in that style."

"Handwritten journals also aren't hackable, and can't be lost to a hard drive failure," Garcia interjected. "They'd want to review their feelings and relive them. It's part of how they hype themselves up for an event like this. Reliving past hurts and rages. It drives the emotion higher and cements their purpose. We definitely need a *Reader's Digest* version of those journals. It's going to take experts months to go through them all and diagnose what happened here today, but we need a snapshot of their own voices to get a handle on what we're dealing with if we're going to break through to Shea."

"The detectives on-scene figured you needed some idea about the shooters' mindsets, so they took a quick look at each kid's journals," Morin said. "Richter's is full of rage and homicidal thoughts for everyone, from his parents, to students, to teachers. He didn't feel he was liked enough, or respected enough when he was the best of them. He wasn't responsible for anything that went wrong; that was always someone else's fault. Shea's writings, on the other hand, were more mournful. He felt he was a failure and no one loved him. His parents, his friends, girls. Especially girls. He couldn't get any of them involved with him and he took that as a serious hurt. The investigator said he sounded extremely depressed but blamed himself for all his failures."

"Where Hank saw it entirely the other way," said Gemma. "That's helpful. The investigator said he sounded depressed—can we ask his parents if he's undergoing treatment for depression, either therapy or by prescription drugs? If he's medicated, they might not know if he's off his meds, but it might be something to consider."

"We can ask."

"Thanks. I may ask for more details later, but this is a useful start. What are the specifics of the agreement you made with Coulter?"

"He wanted access to the classroom with the hostages, which was immediately off the table." The disgust in Morin's eyes spoke to the fact the concept had never been on the table in his opinion. "But I think we need this video, and we need it now, not three hours from now. Or even one hour from now. Getting a warrant to search suspects' houses is one thing; getting a warrant for footage held by the media would take more time to argue. So I had to deal. Trust me, it was hard enough to get him to settle for this. I tried to get him to hand over the link, but he would take nothing less than showing it to you so he can get your reaction to it."

"Typical," Garcia muttered. "He wants to beef up his story."

Morin looked from Garcia to Gemma and back again. "I'm getting the feeling you guys aren't friendly."

"Not even remotely." Garcia's face was closed in, like he was holding himself back.

"Are you going to be able to work with him?" Tony asked.

"Of course," Gemma interjected. "We worked with him at Rikers."

"He mentioned Rikers," said Morin. "He's pissed about it and says we owe him for it. Says he got shafted. Blackmailed."

"Hardly."

"So why would he say that?"

"I may have commented that I was going to reach out to one of his competitors when he didn't like our terms. He got his story; he just didn't get his footage. I didn't have anything dirty on him to use as leverage. He just had to play by our rules if he wanted access, because if he got his way, he would have forever damaged hostage negotiations in every police force in the country. But he got a story afterward."

"In his opinion, his original story was so heavily redacted, it was hardly worth covering."

"Notice he did cover it, though."

"Of course he did. His kind of media type will do anything for glory."

"I see you have a clear picture of him," Garcia said dryly.

"In spades." Morin's tone was undergirded with disgust. "Rikers may have played into it, but he had no intention of making an easy deal. I had to threaten to make sure he couldn't come within a mile of any NYPD crime scene without being charged with trespassing for the rest of his working life if he didn't meet us halfway. It was only when I offered an exclusive with you that he started to bend."

"I bet." Gemma's tone was flat and utterly toneless.

"He's an asshole, I get it. But he has something we need, so I had to move on it."

"I get that. Doesn't mean I need to enjoy working with him."

"I'd think less of you if you did." Morin head-cocked toward the door. "Now get in there and make this bullshit arrangement worth our while." He turned away and wound his way toward the front of the command center.

Tony gave her a pointed look and a nod, then followed Morin.

"Let's do it," Garcia said. "And if I lose my temper in there..."

"Let you hit him?"

"Tempting, very tempting. But it would become part of his story with you. Feel free to jump in and force me to take a breath. That bastard pushes all the wrong buttons for me."

"Me, too. Let's keep each other from losing it in there."

Gemma opened the door to the room she'd only recently left, but this time instead of two jumpy boys, Coulter sat in one of the far chairs, in front of a monitor displaying a frozen image as he furiously typed something into his phone. He looked up at the sound of the door opening, his expression morphing from curious to magnanimous. "Garcia, Capello, good to see you."

"Cut the bullshit, Coulter." Garcia pulled out the chair furthest from him and sat down. "You gave us no choice and now we're here. Let's see it."

Cool and unruffled, Coulter cocked a single eyebrow. "You're all manners, Garcia."

"He has a job to do, and so do I." Gemma jumped in before Garcia snapped back at Coulter. "Lieutenant Morin made an agreement with you, so it's time to put your cards on the table."

"That's it, no discussion?"

"I have kids inside the school who could die at any moment." There was ice in Gemma's tone, the kind of chill that would have had her own brothers taking a step backward in self-defense, but she suspected Coulter wasn't sharp enough to recognize it. "Show us what they sent and then I have to get back before he calls. How long is the video?"

"About fifteen minutes. They took the time to edit it."

"How lovely of them. And how did you get it?"

"They sent the link to me through my Twitter account. And the password through Instagram. Not the station's account. Mine."

The way he pulled himself up and puffed out his chest set Gemma's nerves on edge. But she pushed her anger at his arrogance aside. He had something and they needed it, so she had to play along. "Let's see it then."

Coulter stared at her for a moment, his left eyelid twitching ever so slightly—*Good. He's not getting what he wants from us either*—then tossed a thumb over his shoulder toward the monitor. "It's right there."

"Roll it."

"You don't want to hear more about what they said in the message?"

"Does any of it pertain to what those boys did earlier today, or what we're about to see?"

"Well, not specifically—"

"Great, then you can make notes on it for us later," Garcia snapped. "Lives are at stake. This isn't a moment for you to shine. This is a moment for you to get out of the way."

Coulter's face went entirely blank, but he couldn't keep the rage simmering in his eyes from bubbling to the surface.

He wants to be the white knight sailing in to save the day, and he's not getting that from us.

"Move." Gemma leaned past him, grabbed the mouse, repositioned the cursor while Coulter spluttered and shifted his chair back, and played the video.

She and Garcia slid in closer, staring at the monitor.

In a woodland area, the two boys, one blond, one brunette, in T-shirts and jeans, stood together in the foreground, their backs to the camera. One held a shotgun, the other a rifle. In the distance, fresh paper targets hung between trees.

The light-haired boy turned to glance over his shoulder at the camera, as if confirming it was still capturing him.

The first thing that struck Gemma was the coldness in Hank Richter's eyes. Then she read anticipation and excitement. *He's enjoying this.*

It turned her stomach.

"You go first," Hank said, his voice tinny with the distance from the microphone. "Show me how you'd do it."

"You sure you don't want to go first?" Even slightly indistinct, Russ's voice carried a hint of insecurity. "Show me how it's done?"

"I can't correct what I can't see. Do it."

"Sure."

Russ settled the rifle securely against his shoulder and advanced on the target, pulling the trigger in rapid succession. He stopped partway, ejected the spent magazine onto the grass, slammed a new one home, and kept shooting. Then reloaded again when the second magazine was empty.

Gemma kept up the count in her head until he stopped shooting, standing about ten feet away from the tattered target, the torso covered by a ragged eight-inch hole from the repeated piercings.

Russ turned, a big grin on his face. "Got him! He didn't stand a chance." His smile slowly slipped as he looked at Hank, who again stood with his back to the camera so Gemma couldn't judge his expression. "Right?" Uncertainty filled his tone now.

"I guess if you want to give them time to get out of your way, especially with those reloads. Who's gonna run that school?"

"Us."

"Because we have...?"

"The power."

"What power?" Each question came fast on the heels of Russ's answers, not giving him time to think.

Russ held up his rifle. "This power."

Hank answered by holding up his shotgun. When he turned to look at the firearm held triumphantly high in the air, he was smiling. "Yeah. Want me to show you how I'd do it?"

Russ nodded and stepped out of the way.

"Pause it there," Gemma ordered and then waited as Coulter stopped the video. "Roll it back to where Russ started shooting."

"Why?"

"Because I don't know what you were looking at, but I was watching Russ and I need to know what Hank was doing while Russ was... failing, as far as Hank was concerned."

She waited while Coulter rolled the video back forty-five seconds and then kept her eyes on Hank as he said, "I can't correct what I can't see. Do it." She took in his stance—feet braced wide, one hand on his hip, one holding his shotgun under his arm, shaking his head as he watched Russ's first attempt. "He was disapproving right from the beginning. I get the impression he felt no one and nothing could live up to his standards."

Coulter paused the video when Russ finished and turned around. "Seen enough?"

"Yes. Play it forward."

Onscreen, Russ moved to stand in line with his own target as Hank stepped forward, grabbing shells two at a time from the pouch at his waist and loading them into the shotgun. He raised the shotgun to his shoulder, sighted down the barrel, paused, then took about six steps back until his head almost entirely blocked the camera. He took his left hand off the barrel to brusquely wave Russ farther off the course. Russ sent him an inquisitive look, but came to stand closer to him.

Hank took off like a cork coming out of a bottle, running toward his target. *Click clack BOOM! Click clack BOOM!* His paper target exploded in successive sprays of confetti as he fired into it three times, then four. Then he swerved, laying waste to Russ's target with three more shots. He stopped just before Russ's target, turned, and looked straight at Russ. "Now that's how you do it!" Then he threw back his head, laughing exultantly.

"Third time I've seen that," Coulter muttered, his tone subdued and his usual cockiness gone, "and it's still spooky as hell."

"Yeah," Gemma's voice was a little raspy as her mouth had gone absolutely dry at the sight of Hank's performance. "Imagine being fourteen and that coming at you and knowing you were going to die. Pause it for a second."

Coulter's hand trembled slightly as he clicked the mouse to pause the video, and the laughter cut dead.

"Thank you." In the silence, Gemma finally felt like she could take a breath. Turning, she looked at Garcia. His face was a neutral mask, but Gemma knew him well enough and had worked enough cases with him to recognize the equal parts fury and horror he was tamping down. The destruction of the paper targets was bad enough, but Garcia had seen what those kinds of weapons could do to a human body and could translate that to the nightmare of what lay inside the school, even though he had yet to set foot in it. He might let his emotions slip a little with his team—they all did; sometimes it was impossible in high stress situations not to—but he would never allow it with an outsider present, especially when that outsider was a member of the media. "Three seven-round magazines in the rifle. Seven shells in the shotgun."

"That was my count, too," agreed Garcia.

"Logan said Russ is carrying a Ruger Mini-14. He was practicing on that same rifle. And that's the same shotgun Richter used today, too. Logan's team recovered it—a Mossberg 590 pump-action with a tube magazine that would allow those seven shots." She studied the paper targets in the background behind Richter. "Logan also said Hank was using triple aught buckshot. Which would easily do the damage we just saw. Here and in the school. But you know what this is."

Garcia nodded. "Attack-related behavior. They're prepping for the event."

"Prepping. Practicing. Desensitizing themselves to what they're about to do, at least for Russ's sake. Hank likely never needed it. Keep it rolling."

They watched for another ten minutes as the boys ripped down the paper targets, Hank further ripping his into shreds as if the destruction there wasn't already enough, and running it again and again. With Hank's encouragement, Russ got more and more into it with each trial run, each subsequent attempt bringing more and more praise from Hank, that praise puffing Russ with pride.

Each turn made Gemma feel more and more ill as they racked up "kills," Hank playfully keeping score.

Finally, as Russ stood next to his decimated target, admiring the destruction he had wrought, Hank stalked toward the camera, his face alight with a victorious grin. He raised a hand, which disappeared from view, as he looked directly into the lens and flashed a wide, excited grin. "And that's how we're going to kill them all."

The screen went dark.

Gemma sat back in her chair, feeling drained.

"Does that help?" Garcia's shield had slipped and his face looked as haggard as hers felt.

"A lot, actually." Gemma looked sideways at Coulter, who watched them both with a sharp eye, even though he also seemed affected by what he'd seen, though less so with repeated viewing. She wanted to discuss the video with Garcia, but no way was she going to feed the media monster sitting beside her. She stood and opened the door, then looked pointedly at Coulter. "Thank you. Get in touch when you want your interview."

Coulter stiffened, his posture going mulish as if preparing to dig in. "That's it? Here's your hat, what's your hurry?"

"For now, yes. We've seen the video, and the interview will come later. Right now, I need to get back in there. Do I need to call an officer to escort you out?"

Coulter rose to his feet, yanking his electric blue jacket and a messenger bag off the adjacent chair with considerably more force than required. "For someone who's about to be interviewed, you apparently don't care if the story makes you look bad."

"I know you wouldn't dare risk the wrath of Lieutenant Morin by taking advantage of his generous offer of my time." As Coulter passed through the door, he tried to squeeze her over, but she held her ground, forcing him to brush against her. "That could make your life as a reporter wanting access to crime scenes extremely difficult. Now, you have a nice day." She snapped the door shut behind him before turning and leaning back against it.

"He's going to grill you like a freshly caught fish," Garcia said dryly.

"He can try. Now, I'm going to forget about him. I have much more important issues to deal with." Gemma returned to her chair, sank down in it, and stared at the dark monitor. "We knew it was a dyad with Hank as the dominant partner. Now I'm beginning to see exactly how much. Hank maintained his dominance at all times. Brought Russ down low, criticized his performance, and then built him back up again so that by the end, Russ was simply grateful for his praise."

"Like an overeager puppy. Couldn't miss the message reinforcement as well. Their power comes through violence."

"Because society holds up violence as an indicator of masculinity. Just watch any summer blockbuster. The women are few and far between. The men have the muscles and do most of the killing. We're looking at two kids here of middling social status, who likely consider themselves even lower than that in their own heads, which may have decimated their own self-respect. They felt weak and unwanted."

"What better way to counter what you feel is your own insignificance than to make yourself powerful? You know what they say, every villain is the hero of his own story. Heroes, that's how they may have seen themselves."

"It's going to take weeks or months of investigating these boys, and doing interviews with the people who knew them, before professionals with real knowledge about neuropsychiatric disorders can tell us definitively about the personalities involved. But I know a fair bit about some of those disorders and when I look at Hank, I see a narcissistic psychopath. The manipulation, the clear lack of empathy, the grandiose ego. The way he was polite and respectful for those in authority over him, while he was controlling and bad-tempered with those in his control. It's classic. For him, here, it's not about the people who are about to die, or how that will affect their loved ones, it's all about how it makes him look, and how it will make him feel."

"Some of that is bleeding over to Russ," said Garcia. "I don't get psychopath from him, more the mirror of it. But the same low self-worth could be playing out in the same grab for power. In their minds, they'll be remembered as the ones in control, who had the power to decide who lived and who died, and who had the strength and courage to carry out that killing."

Gemma's laugh was derisive as Logan's description of the boy on the front walk, and of his own reaction—as someone who had the strength and courage to carry out a killing if it was required of him in the defense of others—came back to her. "It doesn't take courage to gun down unarmed children."

"We know that, but I bet that's not how they saw it."

"I'm sure it wasn't. And did you notice that Hank declared himself the winner of their little contest? Because the shotgun loads shells instead of a seven-round magazine, it's the slower weapon. But he really enjoyed the destruction you get from buckshot, so he considered himself the victor."

"Not that it looked like Russ would argue the point."

"Definitely not." Gemma glanced at her watch. "I need to get back now. Shelby is manning the phone, but I'm not sure if another voice will sit well." Another glance at the blank monitor. "Let's see how I can translate what we've learned here into a stronger connection with Russ."

CHAPTER 25

Gemma scanned the busy area in front of the command center, searching through students, teachers, and officers, until she spotted Baker's sandy hair. He still wore his suit jacket to fend off the November chill, but his tie was now gone, leaving his collar open. "Principal Baker," she called. He looked around to find who had called his name, and she waved her arm in the air to attract his attention. He waved in return and wove through the crowd toward her.

Gemma waited as Baker met her near the bottom of the stairs. "I was hoping to find you."

"Can I help?"

"I think you can. I need some information about Russ and his history in that room."

"In room 317?"

"Yes. I think there's a reason he went there specifically. And there's a reason he's essentially glued to a single desk. I need to know what that is. Did he have classes in that room? If so, was that his desk? Who was the teacher? Does he or she remember anything significant about his time in that room?"

"I can't give you all of that personally, but I can go through his records and his schedules and tell you if he had a class in that room. And, if so, who the teacher was. Then hopefully we could get more information from that teacher."

"That's all I can ask. I assume you need access to the office again for that?"

"Yes. I can come with you if you're headed there now."

"I am."

They started down the sidewalk at a brisk pace. Gemma stayed silent, reviewing the footage she'd just seen in her head again, and the information provided by Morin from the investigations of the shooters' homes, building a line of questioning in her head. Baker fell into step wordlessly beside her, as if intuiting her need for silence.

Gemma was so deep in thought, at first she didn't register her name being called. Then some part of her subconscious latched onto a sound out of place at this scene—*Frankie?*—and she looked up and over the boulevard.

Her family clustered in the street, inside the police line, but staying to the outskirts. Their NYPD badges got them and their non-NYPD family inside the line, but they knew to stay out of the operation. Joe was there, as well as her brothers Mark, Teo, and Alex, along with Francesca Russo, better known as Frankie, Gemma's best friend and, essentially, one of the family from their childhood years onward. They'd all come to support Joe, to give him strength, and be additional eyes and ears.

Joe looked haggard, even from a distance; the uncertainty had to be killing him. But Gemma assured herself that she was doing the best she could for both Joe and Sam, simply in trying to end the standoff and bring all the kids out safely to their frantic families.

She wished she could give them more, but there was no way to update them at this distance, and no time, so all she could do was raise a single hand in greeting, then turn away and continue her hurried walk down the sidewalk.

Ninety seconds later, they were at the office door. "Capello and Baker, coming in." She opened the door, holding it for Baker, then snapped it shut behind her.

Baker made a beeline to the admin assistant's computer and immediately got to work.

Gemma circled the desk, pulled out her chair, and sat down.

Shelby's eyes had stayed locked on Gemma's face from the moment she entered the office. "How bad was the video?"

"Bad. But useful. I wish we had time to show it to you. Hank was a maniac and he manipulated Russ into every aspect of this attack."

"You don't mean you think Russ is innocent in what happened today?"

"God, no. He's one hundred percent responsible. While he might not have had the strength of will needed to blow the whistle on the attack beforehand, he could have refrained from taking part. Without Hank, I don't think Russ would be a school shooter. He might have been suicidal and taken himself out, but I don't think he'd have planned an attack like this on his own. I'm not sure it ever would have occurred to him. But Hank... what I saw further cemented my idea that he's a narcissistic psychopath." Gemma met Shelby's eyes. "He murdered his parents last night, then ordered pizza delivery and ate it while their bodies lay in the next room."

Shelby's eyes flared wide with horror. Even after a day like today, this extra layer of cruelty still packed the punch of shock. "Brutal."

Gemma's gaze flicked from Perez to Logan. Both had their eyes locked on her as she updated Shelby, and she could see that Hank's actions surprised even these two experienced officers. Her gaze dropped to Shelby. "Yeah. There was no saving him. He never intended to come home today. They both left suicide notes, but, interestingly, while Hank's was handwritten, Russ's was printed off a computer with only his signature in his own hand."

"Meaning he may not have penned it himself."

"That's my theory. Hank was such a control freak that he made sure Russ's final words weren't even his own." Gemma glanced at the time, deciding it was worth taking another minute to fill Shelby in so she could coach more effectively. "The short version of what was in their journals set the tone though. Hank hated the world and thought everyone should die. He felt that no one liked him and he was never responsible if and when anything went wrong. But while his writings were full of rage, Russ's writings were full of anguish. He considers himself a failure, and it sounds like he may be suffering from clinical depression. He considers himself unlovable, and everything that goes wrong is his own fault."

"Sounds like they were both suffering from self-esteem issues."

"That's what it looks like from here. And then they took those self-esteem issues and pumped themselves up on bravado and violence. There's no time for it now, but we definitely need mental health professionals to look at these boys to deduce what went wrong. In the meantime, we now have a better idea of what we may be looking at."

Gemma turned her attention to the monitor, studying the image onscreen. Not much had changed since she left. Russ still sat on the same desk, his sneakers on the seat and the rifle across his knees. The crumpled remains of his lunch sat at his hip. The students appeared to be in roughly the same positions, except now there was more movement. *Getting restless. That could be a problem soon unless he terrifies them into immobility.* Mrs. Fowler sat in the same place in the group, with the same two boys beside her, though she no longer held them immobile. ASL-signing Goth Girl sat in the same area, her eyes always moving, her hands clasped in her lap for now. "Any messages from our signer?"

"No. And I've been watching. It's been mostly quiet since you've left, though there's been a little more whispering and low communication. Russ doesn't seem to mind it happening, so there's been more of it as time goes on."

"They need to be careful with that. He may go from not caring about it to caring a lot in a flash." She dialed the phone and put it on speaker.

Russ picked up after the fourth ring. "Yeah."

"Hi, Russ. Has everyone had a chance to eat?"

"Yeah."

"Good. Thank you for the exchange. That goes a long way toward showing the NYPD that you're being reasonable. Now, let's keep going. Did you know that Hank shared a video of the two of you with local media?"

"What?" The surprise in Russ's voice paired with the jerk of the hand gripping the stock of his rifle convinced Gemma that he was genuinely surprised.

"The video is about fifteen minutes long. The two of you are in a wooded area where the trees are in full leaf. You're both wearing jeans and T-shirts, so perhaps late summer or early fall? You're carrying the rifle; Hank has the shotgun. In the distance are paper targets, and you two are practicing. Or, rather, you're practicing and he's correcting almost every last thing you do. Do you remember that time?"

"Yeah." The single word carried an edge that bordered on fury.

Remembering the put-downs.

"Hank sent that to a reporter this morning before you came to the school. I watched it. I'd like to know what you remember of that day."

"Not much to remember. We shot some targets for fun."

"That's what you started off doing. You, not Hank. For Hank, it was always two things. War and competition. Do you want to know what I saw?"

Russ stayed silent, which Gemma took for assent. "I saw someone who was belittled by a boy he thought was his friend, and then manipulated into doing what that boy wanted. He didn't give you a choice, Russ. Not if you wanted his approval. Wanted his friendship."

"Hank is…" He jerked to a halt. "Was… my brother."

"I have brothers. Four of them, in fact. And they can be a pain in my ass sometimes, but I know they love me. Someone who loves you doesn't convince you to die."

"We were going to go out in a blaze of glory."

"That was his justification for taking out as many people as he could. He didn't care if he died, and he certainly didn't care if you did. That's not brotherly love."

"No." It was nearly a snarl. "We had a bond."

Beside her, Shelby wrote a single word on the pad of paper—*Parents.*

Gemma gave her a nod of acknowledgment. She had him slightly off-balance. Time to put him a little more off-balance. "Have you ever met Hank's parents?"

"Yeah."

"Nice people?"

"They were okay to me. Hank says they weren't too nice to him."

"So much so you think Hank was justified in murdering them last night?"

Russ jolted and dropped one foot to the floor, half-rising off the desk. His mouth worked, but it took him a moment to put words behind it. "You're lying. We couldn't start this morning until after his dad had gone to work because we're using his guns."

"I'm not lying. Remember, Russ, I promised I wouldn't lie. And why would I lie about an easily provable fact? We haven't released it to the media yet, but will in the next few hours. If it's a lie, the Richters will step forward to disprove it. They're not going to do that. He shot them last night with a suppressed handgun out of his father's collection, then he ordered in pizza and ate it in the same house as his parents' corpses." She used intentionally harsh language to jar Russ further. "He lied to you, Russ. He lied in the video I saw, where he purposely shot you down so you'd be forever grateful for his subsequent praise. And this morning, he lied to you when he made you wait when his father was already dead and you could have started anytime." She went in for the kill, trying to sever the bonds in hope of saving not only this boy, but all the kids trapped with him in that room. "Brothers trust each other with the truth. They trust each other with love. He was no brother."

As Russ's harsh breathing came down the line, Shelby gave her a thumbs-up.

"The road he led you down wasn't yours, Russ." Gemma's voice was quieter, calmer, missing any hint of an accusatory tone. "And you still have the choice to stand on your own and to make your own decisions. Yours, not his. What brought you here doesn't have to be what brings you out."

"It's too late."

"It's never too late. Hank is gone. The person you thought Hank was may have never existed. This was never your plan, never your quest. It was always Hank's. But he needed help, so he convinced you to be his wingman. It was pure selfishness. He took advantage of you, but now you're free of him. You can make your own call."

Gemma jerked when Shelby's hand clamped down on her arm. Her head whipped sideways, but Shelby's gaze was locked on something on the monitor as her index finger jabbed in the direction of Goth Girl. Gemma muted the call. "What's going on?"

"She's giving us a warning. That kid is getting closer to Russ, who isn't wearing the rifle, just has it across his thighs. You have him so distracted he hasn't noticed the sling strap is drooping nearly to the floor. That kid's going to try for it."

Onscreen, Russ was oblivious to the teenage boy who was scooting slowly closer an inch at a time. Gemma had been concentrating so hard on Russ—and making progress, in her opinion—she'd only been watching him. Trying to gauge his mood, when to push and when to lighten up. So much so, she'd missed what the student was doing.

There was about to be a showdown in that classroom and she was two floors away.

Worse, Sanders, Sims, and ten other officers were immediately outside the door and they'd be through it in a heartbeat.

Gemma whipped around in her chair to look up at Logan. "This is maybe about to go to hell. Get up there and do your best to keep Sanders from going in."

Logan didn't question her request; he simply strode to the door. "Put your radio on. I may need to talk to you."

"Affirmative."

Then Logan was gone, only the quiet *click* of the door reseating and the echo of his footsteps pounding up the main staircase marking his exit.

Gemma took the phone off mute as she reached for the coiled throat mic and earpiece she'd left on the desk. "Russ, you're very quiet. Talk to me." She donned the radio set as she talked. "What matters now is what you think. Not Hank. You. Tell me what you think."

Onscreen, the girl's signing was becoming more frantic and Shelby was desperately trying to keep up in a frenetic scrawl on her pad of paper:

He's going to get us all killed.

Do something. Get Russ to move. If they struggle over the gun, someone's going to die.

Call through the door. Knock. Anything.

"Russ, do me a favor," Gemma said. "You've been in there a long time. Stagnating. Get up, take a walk. Get your bearings. With what you've learned, it's like a whole new world and you need to figure out where you stand in this. Get up, shake it off. And—"

"*What are you doing?*" Russ's bellow of rage was so loud the phone speaker buzzed. "*Who are you signaling?*" The phone dropped from his hand to the floor with a clatter.

Gemma hit the mute button even though the phone wasn't near him now—she couldn't take the chance he'd overhear anything—and activated her radio. "Capello to Sanders. It's going to hell in there, but I need you to stay out for now. Let me try to talk him down. You go through that door and we're finished."

Baker appeared beside her, bracing both arms on the desk and leaning in, his breath a rapid cadence.

Onscreen, Russ was on his feet, his rifle sling now out of reach of the boy who'd been inching closer and who now shrunk back as if he'd never made the attempt. Russ jammed the rifle against his shoulder and stalked toward Goth Girl, his face flushing and eyes bulging with the fire of his rage. "Who are you signaling?" He whipped a glance over his shoulder, then back again. "Is someone able to see through the blinds?" He braced the rifle and aimed right for her head.

88

The girl screamed and hunched into a ball, curling her forearms over her head. "I'm not signaling anyone. I'm nervous and fidgeting. Don't kill me."

Gemma's fear that the girl would point out the camera and everyone in the room would feel Russ's wrath eased slightly, but not her terror for the girl. However, she couldn't let on that she could see what was happening in the classroom. She hit the intercom button on the PA system so her voice could reach him. "Russ? Russ! Listen to me. Whatever is going on, you have to calm down. I heard what you said about the blinds. Trust me, no one is there. Go look for yourself. There are no ladders. You'd hear a drone if one was in the air. You're terrifying a girl who's doing nothing more than getting restless from sitting in the same position for hours. Russ? Do you hear me? Step back and take a breath."

Onscreen, Russ was frozen in place, the rifle still braced, but hesitating.

They had a chance.

Red light or not, Gemma had no choice but to cut the PA connection before she hit the mic on her radio. "Capello to Logan. Hold outside the door. He's hesitating. You hear gunfire, you have a go to breach. Until then, I need you to hold."

"Ten-four."

Gemma clicked the mic off. "Bet Sanders would like both our heads on a platter right now going around him like this," she muttered, and hit the intercom button again. "Russ? Talk to me, please. Tell me what you're thinking."

"This bitch needs to do as she's told." He was still talking to her like he was on the phone, and she had to strain to hear his words, not wanting to miss a single syllable or any of his inflection that could tell her more about his mindset than words ever could.

"She's learned her lesson, Russ. She won't fidget anymore." Double meaning there for sure; one for Russ, and one for Goth Girl. *No more communications. He'll be watching you now.*

"I won't. I won't, I promise." The girl's words were muffled behind her forearms.

"No, you won't." Russ pulled the rifle in closer and bent toward the girl.

He was going to kill her and then there would be nothing Gemma would be able to do but watch.

"Leave her alone!"

With a roar, the boy who'd been on the floor inching toward the rifle strap now launched himself at Russ from a crouched position. He aimed low, going for his knees, aiming to take him over and down. Russ had a fraction of a second to respond, but it wasn't enough time to swing the rifle all the way over, and instead took the hit, staggering sideways. But luck was on his side and his hip caught a desk, keeping him upright.

"That's Jake Terret," Baker hissed.

Jake Terret—the troublemaker Baker wanted out, who Russ deceptively hadn't released, and who was now going after Russ.

Jake was on his knees now, one hand clutching the desk beside him, having failed in taking his mark all the way down. Around him students screamed and cried, and Mrs. Fowler's voice could be heard pleading with Russ for peace. Russ wobbled but regained his balance, his rifle trained on Jake. Gemma braced for the gunshot, dreading it as the sound of her failure, but it didn't come. Instead, Russ reversed the rifle, flipping it upside down, and brought the butt of the stock down on Jake's head, striking his temple with brutal force. Jake let out a guttural cry of pain and went down to lie still on the tile floor at Russ's feet.

Russ flipped the rifle around, but stepped between the desks, putting more space between himself and the other students.

Not opening fire.

"Sanders to Capello," the voice in her radio earpiece snapped. "You're losing control. We're going to breach."

Intercom off. Radio on. "Sir, don't. Not yet. I have visuals, you don't. I swear if it truly is out of my control, I'll hand it straight to you. The suspect isn't shooting and is backing away from the hostages. Stand by."

Radio off. Intercom on. *Mess up communications and this is all going to be over.* "Russ, what's going on? Talk to me, Russ. The officers want to come in. Convince me to keep them out."

"Keep 'em out."

"I'm trying, but you have to give me something better than that. What happened?"

"Someone went after me. It was self-defense."

"What was self-defense?"

Silence.

"Russ? What was self-defense? I can't keep them out unless you're straight with me. Remember how I won't lie to you? You need to be straight with me too. And lying by omission is still a lie."

"Guy attacked me. Had to hit him."

"What guy?"

"Jake Terret."

"Is he hurt?"

"Dunno."

Gemma kept her eyes locked on the monitor where Russ backed closer and closer to the bank of windows, until all that was in her field of view was his boots. *Checking behind the blinds.* Gemma knew he wouldn't find anything. Scaling the school was never part of the NYPD's plan—too noisy and risky with a jumpy teenage gunman. Satisfied no one was there, Russ sidestepped down the aisle, back toward the same desk.

Shelby pointed at the desk and gave Gemma two open palms and a look that unmistakably said, *Why there?*

Gemma looked up to find Baker still at her shoulder. She also pointed to the desk and mouthed, *That one.* Baker nodded, returned to his computer, and went back to work.

The classroom quieted down, and Gemma had time to take a breath and try to calm her pounding heart. Bending her head, she rubbed her fingertips over her forehead and the headache building behind her temples. Things were getting volatile and she was running out of time. Knowing Sanders, she had fifteen, maybe twenty minutes to get this worked out before he pushed back. She'd pressed her luck with his command, sending Logan up there to talk him out of going in to take Russ down, but the final call was his and he was going to make it if she didn't pull a rabbit out of a hat immediately. His going in could mean a lot of dead kids, which would be a community tragedy and a media nightmare for the NYPD.

Time to get things moving.

She hit the PA system button, ending the connection, and picked up her phone to terminate the still-ongoing call.

"We need to get that kid out," Shelby said. "We need to make a trade."

"At this point, the trade is his continued safety in exchange for getting Jake out of there. That's the only thing that will satisfy Sanders. I'm going to call Russ. His phone ringing should remind him it's on the floor. We need to get back to private communication. Adam, where are we on figuring this out?"

"Getting there." Baker didn't even look up; he just kept scanning the screen. "If I have to make calls, I'll make them from my office where I won't interrupt your process."

"I need this information now. Things are getting unstable in there. I can try to control Russ, but I have no control over a room full of terrified kids with too many hormones and not enough brain wiring to not potentially do something stupid because they'd see it as brave. I'm not talking to them so I can't influence them." Gemma met his eyes as he looked up. His face had lost color after the attack and stress carved deep lines around his mouth and eyes. "We're running out of time. Hurry."

"I will." Baker returned to his searching.

She needed a Hail Mary to make this work, a long-odds, shot in the dark she could run with, straight to the end zone.

Hail Mary.

Her mother's voice came to her in that instant.

She mostly remembered her mother's voice from video footage; in some ways she only remembered her that way, through the camera's eye, rather than her own. Much of that was likely a self-defense mechanism, a ten-year-old's brain managing trauma the only way it could. But now one of her own memories came back to her.

Kneeling in St. Patrick's Old Cathedral, at her mother's side as she bent her head and prayed. Not praying herself, but instead taking in the white altar, pale, soaring ceilings, brilliantly colored stained glass, and miles of dark, gleaming wood. Her eyes fell on her favorite window, depicting St. Anne, the mother of Mary, with the Virgin herself, when she was still a girl. Even as a child, Mary was depicted wearing blue, while her mother wore more somber tones of white and brown. The love expressed as mother and daughter gazed at each other in stained glass never failed to touch Gemma, because it felt like a personal reflection of herself and her own mother. Maria Capello loved her boys, but Gemma felt her connection to her mother, that special mother-daughter bond, was stronger. Just like Mary and

St. Anne. She glanced at her mother, still and straight on the kneeler beside her, her hands folded and her forehead bent to rest on her linked fingers as she recited the prayer Gemma had learned by heart at her mother's knee.

Hail Mary, full of grace, the Lord is with thee.

Blessed art thou amongst women, and blessed is the fruit of thy womb, Jesus.

Holy Mary, Mother of God, pray for us sinners, now and at the hour of our death.

Amen.

Gemma swiveled to look at the screen, at the boy, armed with death, and the children at his feet, in a perverse portrayal of another window at Old St. Pat's—Christ taking the little children on his knee. She wished she had the faith Maria Capello had in her God and the Virgin. Because a Hail Mary might be the only thing to save the situation.

She hit the mic button for the radio. "Capello to Sanders, stand by. I'm going to try to pull out the injured student. Will require tactical support."

"Affirmative," said Sanders. "Standing by."

Shelby's indrawn breath jerked Gemma's attention away from her upcoming task. "What?"

"She's still signing when Russ isn't looking at her," Shelby whispered. "She's not sure Jake's breathing."

"That girl has serious guts. But she needs to stop now. She's going to get herself killed." She dialed the phone and watched as Russ looked down as the phone rang through Gemma's speaker. He bent down and picked it up, his hand searching for a moment as he kept his eyes on the students, but then his fingers closed over it and he straightened. He didn't answer; the phone just rang and rang. Gemma let it ring twelve times, then ended the call.

"He's shaken," Shelby said. "He didn't kill Jake, but he knows he's made things more difficult for himself."

"Yeah. But I can't help him sort through it unless he answers." Gemma waited another fifteen seconds and then called again, listening to it ring. "I don't want to use the PA system again unless I have to. It's like airing his dirty laundry, and being in the spotlight won't help him make a rational decision." More ringing, then she cut it again.

"You can only do that one more time," Shelby suggested. "Then you'll have to go back to the PA. You can't let him be totally in charge."

"Agreed. One more time."

She placed the call, her heart rate ratcheting with each additional ring as she felt her tenuous grasp on this boy slip through her fingers. Then, just before she was going to end the call one last time, he raised the phone to his ear and answered.

"Yeah." Russ's voice was flat, dispassionate.

"Russ, it's Gemma. We need to talk."

"Not much left to say."

"I disagree. But you've crossed a line in our discussion. Now, you can correct it, but we have to work together. I need you to release Jake Terret. You wouldn't before, but this time I need you to do it. You don't want his death on your hands."

"What do I get in exchange?"

"The officers outside your door will remain in the hallway."

"I'm not moving him. And he's not moving himself."

"Then I'll send someone in to get him. We can't leave him there like that, Russ. He could be seriously injured. He could die."

"Who's going to risk their life coming in here? Nothing to stop me from shooting them in the head."

Logan's voice interrupted her next words, carrying clearly through her earpiece. "Logan to Capello. I'll do it."

CHAPTER 26

It might not have been her intention, but Gemma had left her radio on so everyone had been able to hear her conversation with the shooter.

They all knew the injured kid might not be breathing.

The solution was simple—go in and get the boy out before he died of his injuries. The problem was more complicated—they were in the dark about the severity of his injuries. Had his skull been shattered? Was he bleeding, the pressure building up in his brain, as the organ slowly died? Head injuries were tricky. This boy needed a medical facility and possibly a surgeon. Stat.

He might have been taking too much on himself, but Logan felt he still owed Gemma. Back in that grimy, dim room at Rikers, she'd told him she felt betrayed by him when he hadn't trusted her enough to not take the shot that killed Boyle. He'd made her understand that between trust in her and her brother's life, he had to err on the side of life. That had meant taking Boyle's. He'd always felt the kill was justified to save Alex, but part of it continued to drag at him, even past the weight that any death left on his soul.

He could do this for her. Take the risk, get the kid, take that weight off *her* soul.

There was no time; he had to do it now. There was no choice but to convince her over the radio. He'd have had a better chance if he was standing in front of her. He'd once known her so well, known all her little tells, both verbal and physical. Now he had to depend on her words and tone only to make this work. "Detective Capello. Mute your call."

There was a brief pause. "I'm here, Logan. Make it fast."

"We can't leave Jake like that. I'll go in and get him." He looked across to Sanders, who could hear every word, saw the calculation, and knew he could convince his lieutenant. Gemma would be the harder party to persuade, and he had to have her onboard or they'd never convince Russ to let him get through the door alive.

"You can't do that."

"Why not? I'm the only person besides you he knows."

"Because he knows you're tactical. And he just threatened to shoot anyone who entered in the head."

"That wasn't a threat. That was teenage bravado. I recognize it because I used to have it. I did the previous exchange and I didn't screw him over, so that will give me a better chance than anyone else up here."

"You think you're going to walk in there with your weapons and he's just going to hand you the kid?"

"No. I'll be unarmed."

Sanders straightened abruptly and the clench in his jaw told Logan he was losing his lieutenant's approval. He partially turned away to concentrate on Gemma.

Several seconds ticked by and Logan could feel Gemma's shock filling the silence before she finally spoke. "You can't do that. It's too dangerous."

"I'll have my vest on."

"Wearing a vest won't help when you take a rifle round between the eyes." Her words cut through the low background buzz of radio static as a sharp snap.

Logan wondered if anyone else could hear the fear behind her words.

Gemma's tone was rising, her control slipping for the first time during official communications today. They were both aware it wasn't a private channel, and that every A-Team officer and likely Morin and her own father were listening during this crisis. "That's not going to happen." He wanted to appeal to her personally, but couldn't on this overcongested line. "I don't need your permission—Sanders or Morin will grant that—but I can't do it without you. Only you can talk my way in." He paused, then went for the emotional blow. "Jake needs us. We can't let a child die in there if we can stop it."

He could picture her—her body rigid, her fisted hands pressing into the desk, her narrowed eyes fixed unseeingly on something immaterial in the distance, her jaw locked and lips pressed tight. She'd be running every scenario in her head, weighing risks, calculating options.

He knew he'd won from the sigh that reached him. "You have command approval?"

"Approved." Morin's voice came over the line.

It was probably just as well that Morin was listening, because Logan had a feeling Sanders wasn't about to give his approval for what he'd see as a suicide mission for one of his officers. Morin, on the other hand, had the overall view of the situation. Morin and Sanders both wanted it finished, but each had a different risk calculation.

"And get it moving," Morin continued. "Or we're going to lose the boy. There won't be time or access to bring in a med team to move him properly, so we're going to have to hope there are no spine issues. I'll have EMTs come to the floor with a backboard to transport him out of the building."

"Thank you, sir," Gemma said. "Taking the phone off mute. Russ, we need to get Jake out of there."

"No."

"He's only causing trouble for you. You'll be safer without him in there."

"He's not causing trouble now." Russ's sneer carried straight through the phone.

"Then he needs medical assistance."

"Or he can die right here."

In the background, there were gasps and the sound of someone crying. The students could hear Russ's every word, so Gemma needed to keep things calm before one of them tried to take matters into their own hands again.

"Russ, things are going to start getting bumpy in there for you," Gemma continued. "You know you're in charge, but some of those students, they don't know that. And if they all rush you, sure, you'll kill some of them, but you won't be able to fight them all off. You want to keep things calm, and that means letting us get Jake the care he needs."

Silence.

"You remember Sean? He brought you lunch. He's willing to go in and bring Jake out."

Russ's laugh was derisive. "So he can shoot me?"

"No, he'll be unarmed."

"So I can shoot him."

"*No*. If you think things are bad now, it will be astronomically worse if you shoot a cop. Then there will be no stopping tactical from coming in. It's game over at that point. This is your chance to pull it out of the fire, Russ. You're in control; you're making the decisions. We're taking our cues from you, unless you force us to do otherwise. What do you say?"

For a few moments, there was nothing across the line but the gentle hum of low static.

"Russ?"

"Send him in. But just him. And no guns. No rifle or handgun."

"No guns. He'll knock and call out his name in a minute. Thank you, Russ." There was a pause, then her voice came back on the radio. "Call terminated. Detective Logan, you are cleared for entry."

"Ten-four." He put the safety on his rifle, then slipped off the sling and handed the weapon to Wilson, following it with his sidearm. "I'm ready. No rifle, no pistol."

"What about your knife? I promised him no guns, but..."

Logan's hand fell to pat the side pocket of his uniform pants to ensure the folded tactical knife he standardly carried—and had come in so handy at Rikers, as Gemma knew—was in place. "That's coming in with me."

"Good. You're ready, then. We'll be following along via radio. Sean... head up."

She used the catchphrase recited daily by Sergeant Thomson to his cadets, using repetition to reinforce sensible caution in a dangerous world. But he could hear what she was really saying.

Be careful.

"Eyes open." He completed the phrase. *I will.* "Going in." He tossed a look at Sanders to find his hard-eyed expression locked on him.

Sanders was a good cop, even if, in Sean's opinion, he leaned on force a little more often than necessary. But he was an excellent commander who trusted his officers and earned their trust in return. His reticence to do this rescue came more out of concern for his team than it did from giving a hostage taker too much leeway.

Logan gave Sanders a single nod and then walked to the door and called, "It's Sean. I'm coming in." He turned the handle and slowly opened the door.

Russ stood fifteen feet inside the door, his back to the nearby windows, far enough toward the front of the classroom that he was hidden from the A-Team behind the partially open door. He held the barrel of the rifle pointed directly at Sean's chest. Upon seeing Sean's Kevlar vest, the barrel angled up, aiming for his unprotected neck.

This situation was just as dangerous as Logan thought it would be.

Logan raised both hands into the air where they were fully visible. "Russ, I'm here for Jake. That's all. Let me get him and get out. He's all I want."

Russ jerked his head toward the boy on the floor but kept the rifle trained on Sean.

"I'm going to move forward slowly, hands in the air, so you can see exactly what I'm doing." Logan's words were equal parts to keep Russ calm, to let the students know what was happening if they couldn't see him clearly, and to keep the HNT and A-Team units in the loop as to his progress if the camera couldn't catch everything. He took one cautious step forward, then another. "Just slow steps. Nothing fast."

He dragged his gaze away from the dark, deadly hole at the end of the barrel—because watching for a bullet that moved too quickly for the human eye to see was a waste of time—instead scanning the floor for the downed student. He had to take several steps into the room before he could see the collapsed form of the boy in the aisle.

"Russ, I need to carry him out, so I'm going to bend down to pick him up. My hands will be out of sight, but they'll be busy with Jake."

"Don't try anything funny, or you'll die, and then they will."

Logan didn't need a clarification of "they." He knew Russ meant every kid in the classroom, and the teacher, as well. "Understood."

He made his way down the aisle and finally got an open view of the hostages. They'd huddled into the far corner of the classroom against the hallway wall, having pushed some desks into a barrier wall to give them some protection from anyone coming through the door. Or so they'd likely thought at the time, since that failure was now apparent. Most of the kids sat on the floor in a huddle with their teacher toward the front of the group. One boy stood leaning against the wall, tapping his hand rhythmically against his thigh. Goth Girl sat in a cluster of students, her hands now quiet in her lap.

Jake Terret's limp body lay stretched out on the floor along a row of desks, his feet facing Logan, his head hidden from view. Logan had to get four steps closer before he saw the blood running down the kid's face and matting his fair hair.

"I'm with Jake now. Head injury on the right temple, bleeding is significant." He stepped over Jake's legs. Instead of crouching, which would be more comfortable for him, as well as more efficient, he bent so he stayed in Russ's sight at all times, decreasing the chance of him panicking. Cupping one hand behind the boy's head and one at his shoulder, he carefully rolled him onto his back. A quick check of heartbeat and respiration told him he was in time. He scanned the bloody pulp of the head wound and weighed what he could judge of the injury against the ticking time bomb behind him holding the rifle. He was going to have to go for quick and efficient instead of gentle, as it would not only be faster, but more importantly, it would keep his right hand free. The cradle hold he'd used on the comatose girl earlier was simply too dangerous because it required both arms.

Fireman's carry it was, then.

"What's taking so long?" Russ's words were full of suspicion.

Logan straightened enough to make eye contact with the boy, who kept looking from him to the open door. *Worried about an incursion while he's distracted.* "I had to check him out before I could move him." He turned to Jake and made quick work of rearranging his body. He got Jake flat on his back, pulled up his knees, and planted his feet flat on the floor, then held those feet in place with his own left boot. "I'm going to pick him up now," Logan called.

He reached across Jake's slack body to pick up his left wrist with his own right hand. He pulled Jake forward as he partially straightened, his boot on Jake's feet forcing him into an upright folded position. Transferring his own weight to his right leg, he pulled Jake's left arm over his shoulders as he stayed bent, shooting his left arm straight between Jake's legs. Curling that arm around Jake's thigh, he caught Jake's left hand in his and then straightened using his legs, easily balancing Jake's torso over his shoulders and leaving his right hand free. Jake's head lolled against the back of Logan's shoulder, then lay still, his body secure in the fireman's carry.

Logan turned to find the rifle barrel still locked on him and raised his right hand into the air. "Almost done. Jake is secure, I just need to move him out. Hold steady, Russ. I'm not going to try anything with an injured kid on my shoulders."

His argument must have made sense to Russ, because he relaxed minutely, his white-knuckled grip on the rifle loosening slightly, color seeping back into his fingers.

Logan took slow, careful steps toward the door, conscious of how every second could mean life and death to the boy he carried, and balancing it against the slow process of not spooking a jumpy gunman. He kept his eyes on Russ's instead of the rifle. He knew the eyes would tell him first if the boy was going to squeeze the trigger. Five steps... six. Another four or five and he'd be out the door and meeting the EMTs in the hallway.

A crash of wood and metal behind him, followed by several shrieks, had Logan gripping Jake tighter even as his right hand fell out of habit to the empty holster strapped to his upper thigh.

Unarmed.

He whipped around just in time to see the kid who'd been standing against the wall scramble over the barricade of desks in a desperate attempt to bolt out the open door. Logan didn't even think, but simply put himself between Russ and the student, turning sideways to give the kid as much cover as possible and making himself as large a target as he could. "*Russ, stop! Kid, get behind me!*" Jake's shoulders and hips kept Logan from seeing anything that wasn't directly in front of him, so he could only hope that the escapee was behind him. He had no idea.

But he realized who would. "Gem, head up."

Eyes open.

Be my eyes.

"Sean, the boy's directly behind you." Gemma's voice carried calmly through his earpiece. Then the PA crackled to life. "Russ, I'm hearing from the officers in the hallway that one of the other students is trying to get out. But we had an agreement. You need to let Sean and Jake through the door safely."

"I didn't say the other one could go."

"That's true. That wasn't anything we planned. But you need to let him go. No bloodshed, Russ. Or officers will come through that open door and their only priority will be saving their officer and the hostages. You'll be collateral damage. That's not what you want."

"How do you know?" Russ's tone was bordering on belligerent.

"Because if you'd wanted suicide by cop, you'd have done it hours ago. You want to live."

"For what? Jail time? What's the point in that?"

"Because living means working toward redemption. We all make mistakes. We can't reverse them, but we can try to atone for them. Give yourself that chance. You're so young and there are so many years ahead of you. Let them go."

Logan could read the indecision on Russ's face. Gemma was slowly getting to him. Whatever his original purpose had been, coming to the school, even coming into this room, she was making him question it.

He took a single sideways step to the right, his eyes locked on Russ, one student a dead weight over his shoulders, the other, hopefully his shadow.

"He's following you." Gemma's voice now only came through the radio. "Take another step. Good. Now another. Wait!"

Logan froze, keeping his face neutral, not letting Russ know he was receiving any kind of intel.

"It's hard to tell from this angle, but I think the boy needs to get over one row of desks for a clear shot to the door because furniture's been moved around. It looks like he's trying to squeeze in behind you."

At that moment, a hand rested on Logan's lower back.

"Do you have him?" Gemma asked.

Logan nodded subtly—chin down minutely, then back up.

"Good. Now keep going, but you may want to move a little closer to the desks in front of you. There can't be much room for him behind you with Jake on your shoulders."

On his next sideways step, Logan angled forward slightly.

"Good, he's with you. Keep going."

Slow step after slow step, his eyes locked on Russ's, using his peripheral vision to judge his progress to the door. Then they were there, his right arm and shoulder hidden by the door, and he reached behind him, grabbed for the kid at his back, caught clothing, and dragged him into the hallway. He hesitated for a moment in the doorway, Jake still dead weight over his shoulders, knowing he could do some good here with a kid who'd made deadly choices, but could now choose life.

"Russ, think about what Gemma said about redemption. This doesn't have to be the end." Then he took the final steps into the hallway, closing the door behind him.

He turned to find Redding and Turner grouped around the boy who had made his escape. Jogging footsteps heralded a pair of EMTs with a backboard between them as they rounded the corner into the west wing, making their way toward them. They lay the backboard on the floor, then helped Logan lower himself to his knees, facing away from the board. He slowly released Jake and hands caught the boy from behind, cradling him and lowering his body to the board. The EMTs strapped him down, then padded his head with two rolled towels before they secured a large piece of medical tape over his forehead and around the top of the board. On the count of three, they picked him up and jogged down the hallway.

A hand slapped down on his shoulder. He turned to meet Lin's eyes.

"Good job, Logan. You're a crazy bastard, but you pulled that off and brought out an extra kid for your trouble."

"Thanks." Logan's gaze shot past Lin's shoulder to Sanders, who gave him a nod. High praise indeed from his über serious lieutenant.

Two more kids out.

Eighteen kids and one teacher to go.

CHAPTER 27

Gemma peeked around the open door into the office. Baker sat behind his desk working the keyboard of his own PC, his phone pulled close at his elbow. His room was comfortably furnished with a wide wooden desk and a tall bookshelf. Twin burgundy padded armchairs faced his desk, and the opposite wall was covered with framed degrees and certificates. The slat blinds covering the wide window were closed, ensuring no curious onlooker—or worse, media type—could peek in for a candid view.

Gemma rapped her knuckles on the doorjamb. "Hey."

Baker looked up from his computer, and one side of his mouth quirked in an exhausted smile. "Hey."

Gemma came in and dropped into one of the armchairs. "We're taking a breather. Everyone needs it. You coming back here to work was a good excuse for me to leave the front desk for an update."

"Happy to help."

"What have you been able to find out about Russ's history in room 317?"

"I can place him in the class in his freshman year. He had math there with Ms. Melissa Jane Carter. Ms. Carter still teaches here with us, so I called her on her cell. She'd been evacuated and was seeing her students onto the buses. I asked her to go to the command center and request an escort to here rather than us going to her. I assumed you need to stay in the office at this point."

"I do, thanks."

"She should be here any minute. Hopefully she can shed some light on Russ's motivation."

As if on cue, Perez's shout came from the front of the office. "Capello! Visitor for you. A Ms. Carter."

"Now that's timing." Gemma stood from her chair and stepped out into the corridor that ran between the admin offices. "Send her back here, please, Detective."

A few seconds later, a woman Gemma judged to be in her late twenties appeared at the end of the hallway. She wore her blond hair tied into a high, bouncy ponytail, and sported the same minimal makeup as Gemma—eyeliner and a little mascara. She dressed up black leggings with knee-high, riding-style, polished black leather boots, and a soft, cream-colored, asymmetrical, envelope-necked sweater. She clutched a cell phone in her hand as she hurried toward Gemma.

"Ms. Carter, thank you for coming in to assist."

"It's MJ, and how could I not? With what's happened today?" She looked to Baker, who stood behind his desk. "You're sure it's Russ?"

"Without a doubt. He was ID'd by multiple students early on, but since then we've made contact and confirmed it's him." He extended a hand to the chairs opposite his desk. "Take a seat." He waited while the two women sat. "First of all, MJ, are you okay? Your class?"

She melted into the chair, a picture of stress and exhaustion. "Terrified, but otherwise fine. We were in 209 when the shooting started. Two girls were murdered outside our room. I'd have let them in to take cover with us if I'd known." Dropping her phone in her lap, she twisted her fingers together, the tissues blanching under the pressure.

Gemma laid a hand on the young woman's arm. "You couldn't have known. And if you'd opened the door, you could have risked your whole class if the gunmen had forced themselves in as well. You followed protocol and safeguarded the children in your care. It was what you had to do."

MJ tipped her head back to stare up at the ceiling for a moment. "Part of me knows that, but part of me is already struggling with survivor's guilt and what I could have done to have stopped them. Or if there was something I could have done, could have said before today that would have set them on a different path."

"That's something we're all feeling now, and likely will for a while," said Baker. "And we need to look at what went wrong. How could we have had two kids in crisis like this and not known? Where did we go wrong?" He gave his head a little shake. "But that's a tomorrow problem. We need to deal with today first."

"You said I could help. I'm not sure how."

Baker simply looked at Gemma, letting her take the lead so she could explain exactly what she needed.

"Russ is in room 317. I think he chose that room on purpose, but I'm not sure why. And he seems attached to a certain desk in the room. Sits there for a while, gets up, moves around, comes back to the same desk. I'm looking for information about why that room, that desk, might be significant to him."

"Let me look." MJ opened the browser on her phone. "I have a website for my classes. Lists all their assignments and homework. When tests and exams are. When my office hours are. And there's a forum where the students can chat with each other or ask me questions." She looked to Gemma. "It's an electronic world, so I try to meet the kids where they are. But in this case, this will be useful for you because I keep all my notes on the back end of the site, which only I can access. Class lists, marks, teaching notes, student notes, parent teacher interview notes. Seating charts."

Gemma sat bolt upright. "You have actual seating charts from three years ago?"

MJ bent over her phone. "I should. Give me a minute."

Gemma and Baker waited patiently as she mumbled to herself as she paged through different screens checking information. Then she narrowed in on some specific information. "I found the class. Yes, Russ Shea was a part of my freshman math class that year. He did okay, too. Not a straight A student—he struggled with some of the harder concepts—but he was a solid B+ student."

"Did you ever teach his brother, David?"

"Not me personally, but I knew of him. He was a senior when Russ was a freshman. Really popular kid, excelled at all kinds of sports. And smart."

"Hard to be in a shadow like that."

"Oh, yeah. A kid like that has always been held to a higher standard. Often one they have no chance of approaching. I have my seating chart. What desk is it?"

"Can I show you?"

"How?"

"We have a fiber optic camera in the room, under the electric heater. Russ doesn't know, but we've had eyes on him the whole time. Which is how we were able to track his movements." Gemma looked down the deserted corridor. "It's back at the admin desk. Can you come take a look?"

"Of course."

The two women headed down the hallway, Baker trailing behind them.

Shelby looked up from the monitor as they approached.

"Shelby, this is MJ Carter. MJ, this is Detective Gina Shelby, another of our negotiators. All calm?"

Shelby rolled her chair back to make room. "Yes. He's been sitting quietly since Logan pulled out. He looks beaten down."

"That may play to our advantage." Gemma patted her chair. "Have a seat, MJ, so you can have a good look. Now, keep in mind the camera is coming from down low, making it not as clear-cut exactly what row he's sitting in."

"Let me see what I can figure out." MJ sat down and leaned into stare at the boy onscreen. "Am I a horrible person for wanting to hate this boy for what he's done? And yet, look at him. He looks... lost."

"Not horrible, just human. He's killed today. It was his choice to take a loaded gun into the school, but this was never his plan. He got sucked in by Hank Richter and didn't have the strength or the will to take his own road. He's responsible for the lives he's taken, but I'm hoping to make contact with that lost kid to save the lives trapped with him in 317."

"Whatever I can do to help with that, you have me." She looked at her phone, then again at the monitor. "That's not where he sat. He was near the rear of the room."

"Which is now filled with hostages," Shelby said. "So is there a reason he's there? Who sat in that seat when he was in the class?"

MJ's gaze flicked between the monitor and her phone a few times. "You're right, it's kind of hard to say exactly what desk he's sitting on from this angle, but I think it's... *oh.*" The last word came out as a whisper.

"What?" Gemma asked. "Who sat there?"

"Faith did. Faith Terret."

Gemma and Shelby stared at each other. "Did you say Terret?" Shelby asked.

MJ looked up in alarm. "Yes. Why?"

"Because we just carried what is likely her unconscious brother out of there on a board. He tried to take Russ down and Russ knocked him out with the butt of his rifle. The interesting thing is, we wanted to get Jake out earlier and Russ sent someone else out instead. Why would he do that?"

"It might have something to do with Faith. Faith was hit by a drunk driver in her freshman year in the weeks leading up to Christmas. She was killed instantly. The kids were devastated by her death, but I don't remember anything specific about Russ that stands out. So many of them were upset."

"He keeps returning to her desk. It certainly looks like there's a connection there. Think back to that time. After Faith died, did anyone sit in that spot in that class?"

"I don't need to think back. I remember it clearly. No one would sit there. I told the kids at the back if they wanted a better seat to come forward; not one of them did. That was Faith's seat—they wouldn't sit in it."

"So it sat like a shrine for the last six months of class. That might have had an impact on him if she meant something to him before her death."

Gemma pulled her phone out of her pocket and dialed her lieutenant. "Sir, we may have a connection. Can you get in touch with the investigator at the Shea house? We need to go back three years to look for the name Faith Terret in his journals."

"Terret? Isn't that the last name of the kid Logan pulled out of 317?" asked Garcia.

"Yes. I think that's the connection to the room. It at least seems to be the connection to the desk. Jake's sister Faith was killed by a drunk driver just before Christmas three years ago. It's her desk he keeps coming back to. I need to know if he knew her, considered her a friend. Maybe her death was the start of a spiral for him."

"Good work, Capello. Let me get back to you ASAP. Are you going to talk to him in the next few minutes?"

"Not unless I have to. I'd like to have the full story before I talk to him again. Hopefully one last time."

"Hang tight. I'll be back as soon as I can." Garcia hung up.

Gemma laid her phone on the desk and turned to MJ. "Is there anything else you can think of that would be important? I know it's a long time ago."

"Nothing else comes to mind right now. Could I get your number though, in case I remember something else?"

"Absolutely." Gemma grabbed a pad of sticky notes and a pen, wrote her number on the top sheet, and then tore it off. "Here's mine. We have yours, so we'll be in touch as well if we have any other questions. Officer?"

The patrol officer who had been standing with Perez came to attention.

"Please escort Ms. Carter out of the building." She held out her hand to MJ. "Thank you. You may have given us the final clue we needed to get Russ to stand down."

"What will… what will happen to him?"

"If he surrenders peacefully, he'll be taken in to custody."

"And if he doesn't surrender peacefully?"

"Then our officers will do what's needed to protect the lives of the innocent hostages. Hopefully, you've given us what we need to ensure it won't come to that." Gemma sat down as MJ and the officer disappeared through the door.

"You know, some things are making more sense now," Shelby said. "We wanted Jake out because Adam thought he might be a loose cannon. Maybe some of that behavior was seated in the trauma of losing his sister."

"Possibly. But Russ didn't release him."

"Because of Faith? Because that was his last physical link to her, except for that desk? Jake was once hers, so Russ kept him close?"

Gemma sat back in her chair and studied the boy onscreen. He seemed smaller now, less threatening, though the rifle in his lap was just as deadly as it had been an hour before. "And then he had no choice but to hurt him in self-defense."

"But that may be the key. He hurt him. He didn't kill him. He could have taken him down more efficiently if he'd simply pulled the trigger."

"If he had, every A-Team officer in the hallway would have been on top of him."

"Well, sure. But what if that wasn't the calculation? What if he did it to honor Faith? If the connection was strong for Russ, would he do something she would have hated him for?"

"That feels right to me. You know, something else makes sense now."

"What?"

"He's been sitting on that desk, apparently talking to no one for hours. Except he *is* talking to someone."

Realization lit Shelby's eyes. "He's talking to Faith."

"I think so." Gemma studied the blank screen of her phone. "Come on, Garcia, we need answers."

"There could be a few journals to look through, give them time."

"I have time to give." She pointed at the image onscreen. "It's Russ who may not."

For the next ten minutes, they could do nothing but wait. Gemma checked in by text to Garcia twice, but he had nothing. Shelby doodled on the sticky note pad, not out of boredom, Gemma could tell, but out of simply needing to do something, and pacing the office would have meant weaving around Perez. They both kept their eye on Russ, who remained fixed in place like a statue, and the rest of the class, who seemed terrified into immobility once again, including—thank God—Goth Girl.

Gemma wished they weren't so scared, but, in this case, it only helped the situation. One more cocky teen attempting to take Russ down, or making a run for it, and the whole situation would implode.

Her phone rang, Garcia's name lighting up the screen. Gemma answered, putting the call on speaker. "Did you get anything?"

"Yes. I think you hit the jackpot."

Shelby's eyes held the same relief coursing through Gemma.

"Faith is mentioned a number of times in his freshman year, starting in September when he meets her."

"Did he have a crush on her?" Gemma asked.

"Maybe, or it might have gone deeper than that. He talks about her as someone who gets him. Who understands who he is. They shared interests, and were in the same manga club—that's where they met. And they hit it off. Lots of common interests, the same worldview. Several times over the fall he states that she can 'see' him."

"Meaning he didn't think anyone else could," Shelby suggested.

"That's how I'd take it. He was a loner, a square peg in a round hole, awkward, and a little geeky. But he found his tribe in the manga club. Found Faith."

"It sounds like she was his tribe."

"A few other kids are mentioned, but nowhere near as frequently as Faith. He really depended on her, and saw a lot of his self-worth through her eyes."

"Remember, too, that while Hank wanted sex, Russ wanted intimacy with a girl. What he's still looking for is what he felt he had with Faith," said Gemma. "She died, leaving him with no meaningful connection, no support system. And when someone that age dies, especially in an accident as was the case here, there would be overwhelming feelings that her loss was immensely unfair."

"He was devastated and enraged at a world that would take away someone like Faith."

"Leaving him vulnerable to someone like Hank. Hank took Faith's place to fill the void in Russ's self-worth."

"So he goes to 317," said Shelby. "To kill himself? Was that the plan?"

"They left suicide notes, though they both may have been written by Hank. It was always Hank's plan not to survive this incident, either by their own hands or someone else's. And I think Russ may have thought it was the only way out. Perhaps once they split up, Russ decided that if he was going to take his own life, he was going to do it in the place where he felt closest to someone who made him feel like he mattered. So he went to 317, a room he'd spent time in with her, a room where her desk had become a sacred space no one else would occupy."

"Where he intended to join her in death." Shelby flipped her pen over and over in her fingers as she worked out the issue. "He gets as far as sitting on her desk. And then... can't do it?"

"Possibly because he knows Faith wouldn't have approved," Garcia said. "And he got stuck between his need to be near her, and that presence contradicting what he felt he had to do. He may be literally stuck in limbo up there."

"And that may be our chance," Gemma said. "We need to find a way for him to extract himself with enough dignity intact that he doesn't pull the trigger on himself or anyone else in the room."

"It's all going to be in the delivery."

"I know."

She thought of the loss of Boyle and the incursion at Rikers. This was her chance to close this negotiation her way—peacefully, with the hostage taker being taken into custody and the hostages being brought out safely. It was time to end this.

Now the only question was—could she pull it off?

CHAPTER 28

"Everyone ready?" Gemma asked.

"Affirmative." Sanders's voice, through her earpiece.

"Affirmative." Morin's voice, from the command center.

"Ready." Shelby at her side, pen in hand and pad of paper pulled close.

"Calling in now. I'm leaving the radio open so everyone can follow along."

The camera showed Russ still sitting on Faith's desk, rocking back and forth ever so slightly, so the overall effect was one of vibration. *Showing signs of stress.*

This needed to be wrapped up quickly for everyone involved. That classroom was becoming a pressure cooker and a single spark could set off an explosion.

She dialed the phone and put it on speaker, the ringtone echoing in the still room.

Click. "Yeah." Matching his physical stature, his tone seemed small. Hopeless.

Which could be extremely dangerous. A suspect who lost hope might be the kind to pull the trigger, on the hostages, on himself. *Come to the point quickly.* "Hi, Russ, it's Gemma. We had some excitement there for a few minutes. How are you doing?"

"Okay."

"Thank you for letting us pull Jake out. That means a lot. Especially to his parents." She purposely waited a beat. Two. "Nice people, the Terrets. Have you ever met them?"

"No." Short. Sharp.

Emotion. Better than the flat affect of the beginning of the call. "They're so relieved and thankful you released their son. They only had two children and one died three years ago in a tragic accident. Her name was Faith."

No sound came down the phone line, but, onscreen, Russ froze.

"She was around your age. Did you know her?"

No response.

"You know, Russ, we have your journals. You left them for us to find, after all. With your note. We know you didn't plan on going home again. But just because that was your plan, doesn't mean it has to be."

Still no answer, but the rocking started again.

"And we know you talked about Faith in your journal back when you were a junior. You knew Faith Terret, didn't you?"

"Yeah." The single word was low and scratchy, as if it was forced out past an obstruction in his throat.

"It sounds like she was a special girl."

"The best."

"You know, I have a friend like that." A vision of Frankie rose in Gemma's mind. So many memories—from cooking together in Gemma's grandmother's kitchen in Little Italy, to commiserations over breakups as teenagers, to late nights in Frankie's father's café, *La Cassetella*, to joint visits at Frankie's mother's bedside as they all weathered her journey with Alzheimer's together. "Sometimes it just clicks. You find someone who gets you. Who *sees* you. Was that what it was like between you and Faith?"

"Mmm-hmm."

"It must have been terrible for you when she died. All that life, all the promise. Gone."

"Yes." Just the thread of a whisper.

"Do you know what I think, Russ?" When no answer was forthcoming, Gemma continued. "I think you got in over your head today. And I think you realize it, too. And knowing that, and knowing you never intended to come home, you went to the one place you'd feel closest to Faith. At a crucial time in your teenage years, you met someone who could be the rock you'd build your foundation on. And then that rock disappeared, leaving you without the one person who really understood you. You loved her, not in a teenage crush kind of way, but in an elemental way. Like she was family. Am I right?" Russ nodded his head, but Gemma stayed silent, not letting on she could see him. "Am I right?"

"Yeah."

"You went to 317 to be close to Faith. Close to her memory. But once you got there, you realized what you had in mind was the last thing she'd want you to do. And you've been sitting there since, asking her spirit what to do next. Yes?"

"Yeah."

"And that's why you didn't release Jake when we asked for him. He's part of her, so you wanted to keep him there in the classroom with you. But then he rushed you."

"Gave me no choice."

"For Faith's sake, in her memory, when you could have shot him, could have killed him, you knocked him out instead."

Russ's fingers fluttered on the rifle barrel. "I couldn't shoot, for her sake."

"Which was the right decision. Russ, do you remember when we talked about reasons to live and redemption? That's what Faith would have wanted for you. Another chance at life. At trying to fix what you've done. At not walking farther along the wrong path. Faith would want you to put down your rifle and walk out of there."

The rocking became harder, and, at the other end of the classroom, Russ was attracting the students' attention and alarm.

Russ was breaking down. Things were going to go one way or another pretty much right now.

"Russ?"

"I don't know what to do." His words came out as a low wail. It was a reminder that she was essentially dealing with a child. A sad, lost child, who'd made deadly decisions and now didn't know how to end the downward slide.

Gemma muted the phone. "Capello to Logan. What's your position?"

"Directly outside 317."

"He doesn't know what to do, and he's starting to break down. These are the most crucial minutes of this negotiation. I don't think I can get him to walk into a hallway of officers. If I offer you going in, to relieve him of his weapon and escort him out, are you amenable?"

"Affirmative."

"This would be a transfer of power. Go in fully armed. If he changes his mind at the last second, I don't want you defenseless."

"I'm not defenseless, even when unarmed. But I take your meaning."

"Lieutenant Sanders, Lieutenant Morin, do I have your approval to offer Detective Logan's assistance? He's the one officer Russ might feel he can trust. Anyone else is an unknown commodity."

"Approved." The two lieutenants answered in unison.

Back to the phone call. "Russ, I'd like to make you an offer. Sean is still outside the door. He'd like to come in to help you. You say you don't know what to do, but I think that's not true. What would Faith tell you to do?"

"Turn myself in." There was no hesitation.

"I can help you with that, and so can Sean. He'll come in and escort you out. You'll walk out on your own two feet, under your own power. He'll make sure you're transferred safely into NYPD custody. Your parents are waiting for you, Russ. They want to help you. Remember the road of redemption Faith would want you to take, would walk with you in spirit. These are your first steps down that road."

"What about you?"

"What about me?"

"Would you come up?"

"I can't come into the room until everything is secured, but yes, I can come up. Give me two minutes. Is that okay?"

"Yeah."

"Two minutes, Russ. I'll be there." Gemma ended the call and jumped to her feet, pulling off her throat mic and earpiece. "Shelby, I need you on the radio, letting Logan know what Russ is doing that we won't be able to see from the hallway."

Shelby took the radio set and slipped it on. "You got it."

Gemma jammed her phone in her pocket and checked to make sure her Kevlar vest was secure. "Perez?"

"I'm with you."

They jogged from the office, then took the stairs two at a time to the second floor, and then up again to the third floor. Down the west wing, and straight into a hallway packed with black-clad, armored officers.

Logan stood in front of the door with his Glock in his thigh holster and his carbine back in place on its sling, watching for her from behind his safety glasses. "Ready when you are."

"Let's do this the old-fashioned way so he knows I'm here." Gemma stepped to the door and rapped her knuckles on it. "Russ? Russ, it's Gemma. I'm outside, just like you asked. Can I send Sean in?"

"Yes."

"Can Detective Shelby hear us?" Gemma kept her voice low.

"Affirmative," said Sanders. "She's reporting that Shea is still in the same position."

"Good. Logan, I can't hear her, so make changes as needed." She raised her voice to go through the door. "Russ, Sean is coming in now. And I'm here, in the hallway." She stepped back, out of Logan's way.

"Russ, it's Sean. I'm coming in." Logan turned the knob and opened the door an inch with his left hand, his right locked on the pistol grip of his rifle with his finger lying along the trigger guard. Ready to swing the weapon up, if needed. He pushed the door open halfway.

Beyond the doorway, Russ sat on Faith's desk, but now he was sideways, sitting where he could see both the students and the door. The rifle still lay across his lap, the sling draped over his knees, but his hands were limp on the barrel and receiver, not gripping it, not ready to fire.

Logan paused in the doorway. "Hi, Russ, I'm going to come in to help you, but the first thing I need you to do is to put the rifle on the floor, and then I need to see your hands in the air. Slow and easy. I'm here with you. You're not alone. And Gemma's here in the hallway, too."

Gemma stepped into Russ's sight line at Logan's shoulder, so he couldn't fail to see her. He wouldn't recognize her physically, but he'd recognize her voice. "Slow and easy, Russ. We're here with you. You're not alone." When he hesitated, she circled back to his emotional anchor. "Faith would want you to do this. End this peacefully. Remember who she was and what she'd want you to do. Do it for Faith."

"For Faith." Russ closed his eyes for a moment on a slow inhale, exhale, and then anchored himself with one hand on the desktop and wrapped his other around the barrel of the rifle and lowered it to the floor. Then he straightened and put both hands in the air.

Gemma could feel the collective breaths of Mrs. Fowler and her students whoosh free in relief at that moment. *Almost there. Hang on.*

"That's good, Russ." Logan entered the classroom and moved down the aisle to Russ. He pushed the rifle a few more inches away with his boot. "Stand up."

Gemma kept her eyes on Russ's face as Logan turned him around, fished his handcuffs out of the pouch on his belt and cuffed one hand, then the other. Russ's expression said it all—pain, loneliness, shame, self-recrimination.

New York State had no death penalty. Russ had made a mistake he would spend the next several decades of his life paying for, and he knew it.

It was a lot of time to redeem himself, but if he got help, he might start making inroads.

Keeping one hand on the cuffs, Logan bent, picked up the rifle, and engaged the safety. Lin moved into the room to relieve him of it and then got out of his way as Logan marched Russ out of the classroom. He stopped at the doorway when Gemma stepped into his path, but Russ kept his head down and wouldn't look up to meet her eyes.

"I'll make sure your parents know where you are." Gemma tried to see his expression, but he turned his face away, his cheeks flushed.

She stepped back. Her job here was done.

Logan gave her a nod and then led Russ into the hallway where Unit 1's officers converged around him in an ordered phalanx moving down the hall and then into the stairwell.

Gemma turned toward the cacophony that rose in the classroom. Students were hugging, fist-bumping, stretching. One girl sat at the end of the row, quietly weeping into her hands. Such emotion, but so much confusion as to how to even display it. Tears for the dead, relief for their own survival, guilt for the same.

Gemma took two steps into the classroom and was caught in a ferocious hug.

"Thank you, thank you, thank you."

She recognized the voice and rubbed her hand up and down Mrs. Fowler's back. "I'm glad I could help."

The older woman pulled away. "Help? You saved us." She half-turned toward her students. "All of us. I don't know how to repay you."

"You repay me by caring for these kids. Too many were lost today, and these kids and others will be scarred. You'll be scarred. You can help each other process the loss together."

"How…" Mrs. Fowler glanced sideways at her students, and lowered her voice. "How many did we lose?"

"I don't have a final count, but it's at least fourteen, likely more." The older woman gasped quietly, and covered her mouth with her hand. "I'm sorry, I don't have an official number, but what we know will be announced soon."

"Of course you don't. You've been trying to save us. But thank you for your honesty." Mrs. Fowler wiped away a tear, took a breath, and straightened her shoulders. "My last task for the day is getting these kids to safety."

Gemma looked over to where Sims and Sanders with Unit 2 and Unit 6 were helping students gather their belongings and line up to leave the classroom. "These officers will escort you out and to the buses that will take the students to the Barclays Center and their parents." Goth Girl caught her eye near the back of the group. "Now, if you'll excuse me, I need to thank someone."

As Gemma made her way toward the rear of the classroom, she passed the desk where Faith Terret had once learned math and where a boy in crisis had decided he wasn't ready to die. She paused, resting her fingertips on the scarred wooden surface.

Thank you, Faith. Because of you, we were able to end this without additional bloodshed.

You really are an angel.

CHAPTER 29

"Redding, Lin, take that classroom. Perez and Lewis, the one across the hall. Turner, with me."

The team split into pairs, each taking a locked classroom, getting them to open up or call someone with a master key to assist, as they didn't want to damage anything else now that the crisis was past. The door Logan found himself before was covered in maps with the window covered by yet another map, blocking the classroom from view. The grid lines of the map were at an angle, telling Logan it went up in a rush, probably right after the door was slammed shut and locked after the lockdown alert went out. He knocked on the door. "NYPD! Please unlock the door. We're here to escort you out."

"Prove it." The voice on the other side of the door was female and carried the overtones of a she-wolf protecting her young.

Logan glanced at Turner to find her eyebrow arched in surprise. "Prove we're NYPD, ma'am?"

"Yes. Slide your badge under the door."

Logan understood the distrust. After a day of terror, a responsible adult wouldn't be out of line asking for proof to avoid putting her students at risk. Unfortunately, this one had just asked for something he couldn't provide. "I'm sorry, ma'am, I'm from the Emergency Services Unit. We don't carry badges when we're suited up for tactical. Our names and badge numbers are stitched on our uniforms under our vests. Can you pull the map off the door? I'm Detective Sean Logan. You'll find myself and Detective Casey Turner outside your door. You'll be able to identify us from our uniforms."

There was mumbling from behind the door, then, slightly louder, "I said get back. You're not getting near the door until I can assure your safety."

With the snap of paper being yanked away, the map fell from the door to reveal the pale, suspicious face of a woman so young, it could easily be her first year teaching. Her gaze raked the two officers outside her door before she visibly relaxed, her tense shoulders dropping and her head bowing in relief. She opened the door and pulled it wide, allowing Logan and Turner to step inside. "Thank you. I'm sorry."

Logan looked past her to the group of students huddled together at the far end of the classroom. They clung to each other, clearly terrified, but there was no sign of injury. "No need to apologize. After today, your caution is warranted. Everyone okay?"

"Yes. It's myself and twenty-seven students. All accounted for. All fine, as long as you don't take our mental health into account."

"Our goal is to get you out of the school safely, but there are counselors at the rendezvous site to start to help you process what happened today."

The woman opened her mouth as if to question what had happened that day, then glanced sideways and shut it again. "Getting us out sounds like a plan. Class, grab your bags and line up."

Logan and Turner delivered the class to the officers stationed at the stairwell door, who then directed them down the stairwell to the exit. They then returned to the next area down the hallway, a pair of boys' and girls' bathrooms. Logan stepped to the closed door marked with a male symbol as Turner approached the girls' bathroom ten feet down the hallway to his right, pressed her palm to the door, and stepped inside as the door swung open. While still on alert, they no longer believed there were any shooters in the building, and instead of treating every area as a hot zone, entering with rifles at the ready to protect and defend, the A-Team officers had their weapons easily to hand, but lowered in an effort not to further terrorize the students. The injured had been removed by the EMTs, and the dead lay quiet behind closed doors until the living could be reunited with their loved ones. Then, once the school was empty, the crime scene techs would come, the morgue techs following to do what needed to be done.

He pushed on the door, his gaze dropping to the keyed lock just over the flat steel push panel when the door didn't budge. His gaze flicked to where the girls' bathroom door quietly thumped closed behind Turner, and knew there had to be someone inside.

Raising a fist, he knocked sharply. "NYPD! It's safe to open up now. Unlock the door and let us help you."

Silence came from behind the door.

Logan knocked louder. "Is there anyone there? I'm an NYPD officer and I'm here to bring you out of the school and get you to your parents. There aren't any more shooters. It's safe."

The seconds dragged on further with no noise from behind the door. Turner came out of the girls' bathroom and mouthed, *Empty.* Logan pointed to the classroom opposite them where the door was open and Lewis was lining up students for evacuation. She nodded and jogged over to help.

Unless the janitorial staff had locked the door because it was out of order, someone was in there. Logan raised his fist to knock again when quiet words filtered from behind the wooden panel. "Who's the Chief of Special Operations?"

Logan froze, his fist an inch from the door. "Chief Tony Capello," he replied automatically, without taking the time to consider his answer.

The lock shot back with a *snick* and the door opened. A gangly teenage boy stood in the doorway, wearing blue jeans, sneakers, and a bright blue sweatshirt emblazoned with the Italian football club crest. With a jolt, Logan realized the brown eyes peering up at him from under a shock of messy brown curls were pure Capello. And if he was a Capello, then he'd been raised into law enforcement, and would certainly know his grandfather's role in the NYPD.

"I had to be sure you weren't the shooter trying to fool me. You gave me the right answer too fast to be anything but a real officer."

After a day of tragedy and anguish, this small moment of triumph brought a grin to Logan's lips. "Smart reasoning. I'm Detective Sean Logan. You're Sam, aren't you? Chief Capello's your grandfather?"

"Yes, sir."

"You know, there are a bunch of people outside who are anxiously waiting to hear from you."

His face crumpled with worry. "When the shooting started, I locked the door and stayed out of sight."

"Also smart."

"But my cell phone was in my backpack." His eyes shot to a deserted classroom a distance down the hall. "We're not allowed to have them out in class, so I didn't have it with me, even in the bathroom. I couldn't let anyone know where I was. But I knew what to do. My dad made sure I knew what to do." He met Logan's gaze. "Run. Hide. Fight." His gaze shifted down the hallway, where more ESU officers were opening doors and leading students down the hallway and toward the west staircase. "So I hid."

"I've met your dad before. Lieutenant Capello is a solid cop. And he'd be proud of your presence of mind. You did the right thing, even if it cut you off from communications for a while."

His lips tight, Sam looked down. "I don't know he'd be proud."

"Why not?"

"I was pretty scared in there. Too scared to come out, even when things got quiet."

"And you think your dad won't be proud of you because you were scared?"

"Well… yeah."

"Wrong. Your dad is a smart guy. And smart guys know that only stupid guys aren't scared when their lives are on the line. It's what you do with the fear that matters. You did what you needed to do and then waited for us to come help you." Logan studied the boy, reading indecision on his face still. "You know, I went to the academy with your aunt Gemma."

That got Sam's attention. "You did?"

"Yeah. So I know what happened to her when she was younger than you."

"The bank? Where Nonna was shot?"

"Yes. If you want to talk to someone who went through what you did, and worse, you should talk to her. She knows exactly what you went through."

He nodded and stood a little straighter. "Is my dad outside?"

"Yes. So is your grandfather, and uncles, and your aunt Gemma." He caught Lewis's eye in the doorway of the classroom across the hall. "I'm going to take Sam Capello out to his family."

Lewis grinned down at the boy. "Chief is gonna be lit."

"The whole family is going to be lit." Logan laid a hand on Sam's shoulder and grinned down at him. "Come on, Sam. Let's go find your dad."

He led Sam away from the bloodshed and the scenes of terror, and down the stairs toward the light.

CHAPTER 30

Gemma stood on the curb, watching students stream from the east wing exit.

An A-Team officer stood at the doorway, directing students toward the lines of school buses, each loading to capacity and then pulling away from the curb, another immediately taking its place, as they moved the remaining students to the rendezvous location. The crisis was over. Any remaining interviews could come tomorrow.

Come on, Sam. Where are *you?*

So many students had come through that door, and she'd tried to keep her eye on every one of them. A few times, she'd seen a figure appear that looked like Sam, only to have the face turn toward her, or a few steps taken, and she knew it wasn't her nephew. Joe had wanted to run into the school, but Tony had stopped him, reminding him it was a crime scene and they had good men inside bringing the kids out. There were hundreds of kids still unaccounted for, and just getting down the external stairwells was going to take time, because the front foyer was still blocked off as a crime scene.

As much as Joe was listening to his father, Lieutenant Capello also recognized an order from his chief. Every dead child and teacher deserved an investigation free of technicalities, and that meant a grieving father, even if he was a police officer, had to stay out.

Gemma knew Joe was too wrapped up in his own misery to catch it, but she'd seen the pain flickering over her father's face as he'd commanded his son to stand down. It was agony not knowing where Sam was, and, as the minutes dragged by with no word and no sign of him, every one of them was getting more and more terrified they'd lost him.

A hand wrapped around hers to grip tightly. Gemma broke off her search of the students exiting the building to look to her left to find that Frankie had slipped in between her and Alex to take both their hands. Gemma squeezed back fiercely.

"Have faith," Frankie whispered.

"Trying…" But she held on, even as her gaze returned to the students pouring from the school. They walked through the doors and past the A-Team officer, but then most of them got three or four steps and then broke into a run, trying to put as much distance between themselves and the horror of the day behind them.

She couldn't blame any of them.

A dark-haired boy came through the door with another A-Team officer, but instead of heading straight for the buses, they cut across the lawn toward them. The boy broke into a half trot to keep up with the long legs of the officer who walked with his hand securely on the teen's shoulder. In a flash, she recognized the way the boy moved. More than that, even under all the equipment, she recognized the man.

"Joe! There's Sam! Logan has him!"

Joe followed the index finger she pointed toward the crowd and then leaped into the street, breaking into a flat-out sprint. Sam, spotting his father, ripped away from Logan and tore across the grass. They crashed together hard enough to knock the wind from both as they wrapped their arms around each other, clutching tight with desperation. The pain wouldn't have even registered; the relief of seeing each other, of holding on to each other, blotted out all else.

Gemma, Alex, Mark, Teo, Tony, and Frankie raced across the grass, everyone grouping around Joe and his son in a huge family huddle. Gemma threw one arm around Sam and the other around Joe and just held on. In his father's arms, Sam's breathing was ragged, as if he was fighting tears, and Joe kept repeating, "I've got you, I've got you…"

Gemma closed her eyes, for the first time in hours able to draw in a breath that wasn't strangled with fear.

It was over.

We have him, Mom. He's safe. Thank you for watching over us, today of all days.

Watching over us… Her head snapped up and she turned, searching for Logan. He stood only feet away, a smile curving his lips as he took in the reunion. She waited until he met her eyes to mouth, *Thank you.* He grinned and dipped his head in acknowledgment.

Under her arm, Sam wiggled and the group broke up to give him some air, though Joe stayed close and Sam didn't make any attempt to put any space between them.

Sam gave a watery sniff and looked up at his father. "I'm sorry I couldn't contact anyone."

"Where were you?" Joe asked.

"Trapped in the boy's bathroom on the third floor. My phone was in my backpack in the classroom, and I did what you said to do. I couldn't run, so I hid. But then I had no way to tell you where I was, and I knew not to come out until someone cleared the school."

Joe wrapped him in a one-armed hug and pressed a kiss to the top of his head as he dug his phone out of his pocket. "That was perfect. Even if you couldn't tell me where you were, you were safe. That's all that matters." He speed-dialed a number and handed the phone to his son. "Talk to Mom. Just be ready, she's going to cry."

Sam stood with the phone to his ear for a moment, then broke into a smile. "Hi, Mom. It's Sam." He listened to his mother's voice for a moment, then he blinked rapidly like he, too, was trying not to cry.

"Good work, Detective." Tony circled his family and extended a hand to Logan. "And not just finding our boy. That was solid work in there with the suspect."

"Thank you, sir." They shook hands. "We were watching out for Sam while we cleared the remainder of the school. The moment I saw him, I knew he was a Capello, so I wanted to make sure he came straight to you instead of losing more time on the buses."

"We're very grateful." Tony's smile slipped and his eyes went serious. "Everything I've heard says it's bad in there."

All animation left Logan's face. "Yes, sir." His voice was flat, but Gemma could hear the fury behind it. "Too many never had a chance. Some were only injured, but too many were… not that lucky." He flicked a glance in Joe's direction. "We need to work fast. Those parents, the ones who've lost their children… it's agony being kept in the dark."

"Agreed. We have every on-duty crime scene tech in the department coming in and more than a few who aren't on duty but want to help. They'll move quickly."

"Are you going to stay on-site?"

Tony looked over his shoulder to his children and his grandchild. "Normally, I would. And I'll continue to monitor. But tonight, now the crisis is over, I think I'd like to spend some time with my family. There will be lots of time to break down our response tomorrow."

Gemma slipped her arm through her father's. "That sounds good to me. Besides, there's a homemade *cassata* for you in my car."

"For me?"

Gemma tipped her head against his shoulder. "You knew everyone would be stopping by today. Now there's even more reason. We'll all have dinner together and then *cassata* for dessert."

"Did you say *cassata*?" Alex popped his head over her other shoulder. "All this stress has left me famished."

Gemma raised her head and fixed him with a pointed stare. "You're always famished. And you've been jonesing for that *cassata* since you watched me make it last night."

"Damn straight." Alex wiggled his eyebrows at her and returned to Frankie.

Tony headed toward incident command for one last check-in, and the group drifted away from the school.

Gemma watched her family for a moment, then turned to Logan. "I know Dad already said it, but I also wanted to thank you for bringing Sam out. We've been frantic all day, and it was such a relief to see him. Did he tell you who he was?"

"He didn't have to. He has the Capello eyes. I knew it was him right off. And the fact that he wouldn't open the door until I told him the name of the Chief of Special Operations was also a dead giveaway."

Gemma chuckled. "I guess there aren't too many fourteen-year-olds who know that information or would even think to ask that question."

"I seriously doubt it."

"Are you off shift soon?"

"Yeah, but we'll stick around until all the kids are out. Once we can turn it over to the techs, then we'll call it a day."

"It's certainly been a day." She gave him a crooked half smile. "You know, when we stop arguing and work together, we make a hell of a team."

"No doubt about it." He grinned back at her.

"But seriously, thank you for everything you did in there to help with Russ. You made a connection with him, and that paved the way to getting him to surrender with no more injuries or deaths. I know that wasn't easy, especially after all you've seen today. Another officer might have just wanted to take him out, end it quickly. It may be an unpopular opinion, and certainly Russ did some terrible things, but I think he's already regretting it. Hank's influence over him was suffocating and pervasively evil. On his own, he was just weak and lost."

"People died because of that weakness." A mixture of fury and disgust undergirded Logan's words.

"I know. And maybe if I'd seen the art room like you did, I'd be less torn. But I keep circling back to where the system went wrong for a kid like Russ. I don't think there was any saving Hank. But Russ... I can't help but wonder if he'd only gotten help, if someone besides Faith had really seen him, how different this might have been." She heaved out a sigh. "Something to struggle with in the coming days and weeks, I guess. Again, thanks for everything you did in there. I know it wasn't easy. Go home when you can, take a shower, have a beer, and watch something mindless on TV." She paused as a thought occurred. "Unless you'd rather have dinner with us?"

"Normally, I'd say yes. But I don't want to intrude. Not today." When she started to protest, he cut her off with a slice of his hand. "Not because of today, but because of twenty-five years ago. Today's a day for family, and you don't need an outsider in the mix. But why don't we catch dinner sometime in the next week or two when we're both off? If... if you're available."

He was giving her an out, not for her schedule, but in case she had a partner he didn't know about. *No worries there.* "I'd like that." She pulled out her phone. "What's your number?" She entered it as he rattled it off and sent him a text. "Now you have mine. Send me a couple of dates when you're free, and we'll make it work."

"Sounds good." He glanced toward the school and the smile left his eyes. "Back to it."

"Do what you need to do, then go home and disconnect from it. Don't let it eat at you."

"I'll do my best. Talk soon." He raised two fingers to his temple, gave her a little salute, and then turned and jogged toward the school, disappearing into the stairwell between students jogging out.

She stood for a moment, staring after him.

Her family had planned to be together that night in memory of Maria Capello, and while they'd now also celebrate the recovery of a much-loved member of the family, they were all too conscious of the families who were grieving much as they had twenty-five years before. The agony of the empty seat at their family table, now shared by so many other families, some of whom were still tormented in the dark of not knowing for sure their child was gone.

"Hey, earth to Gemma." Alex appeared, seemingly out of nowhere, and draped his arm over her shoulders. "Come back to us. No more work today. Just family."

She gave him a sly sideways look. "And *cassata*. That's why you want me to hurry up."

"I could eat."

"You can always eat."

Finally feeling light enough to laugh, she let him pull her away.

On the worst of days, out of nightmare and despair, hope had sustained them. And, unlike twenty-five years earlier, they were together at the end of the day.

In honor of Maria Capello, they would take that evening to celebrate family.

Hail Mary, indeed.

ACKNOWLEDGMENTS

In many ways, writing is a solitary pursuit. But along the way, it's the teamwork with colleagues and experts that truly make a book shine:

Shane Vandevalk, who spent hours with me studying state gun laws and selecting firearms and specific ammunition to make the attack as realistic as possible under current regulations. He took the time to walk me through his own collection of firearms and advised on which firearm modifications would be useful in the shooters' eyes. He was also responsible for devising the most covert and efficient way to get eyes into the hostage classroom, as well as for reminding someone who has been out of the classroom for far too long how school communications work. Shane, I seriously could not have written this one without you!

My editor, James Abbate, who willingly jumped into the fray to edit LOCKDOWN under extremely tight time constraints, which he handled like the total professional he is. As well, James was instrumental in working with the Kensington Books team in rebranding the NYPD Negotiators series from Jen J. Danna to Sara Driscoll. Most importantly, James advocated for this book as well as the greater series, allowing it to remain part of the Kensington family. James, as always, you make being an author in your care an extremely smooth and satisfying experience. So many thanks for really going above and beyond on this one.

My husband, Rick Newton, for all the time he spent formatting and preparing the manuscript when we thought it would be a self-published product. It had been a few years since the last time we'd done that dance, so there was a lot of relearning and referring to old notes and published works. Sincere thanks for all the extra work you willingly shouldered. Your hard work allowed the Kensington team to run with the ball on a short production schedule.

Alexandra Nicolajsen, Renee Rocco, and the Kensington team for all the work done rebranding the series and bringing it back into the fold on such short notice. It's always a pleasure to work with Kensington and this book was no exception.

My critique team, Jenny Lidstrom, Jessica Newton, Rick Newton, and Sharon Taylor. It seems like a miracle to me, but each time I reach out, you're always willing to share your time and incredible talents. I'm so very grateful to have you all by my side.

My agent, Nicole Resciniti, who embodies the ideal that an agent doesn't just represent a book, but an author through all the stages of their career. Thank you, Nicole, for staying with me through the long haul and for continuing to bring me new opportunities.

And, finally, to all my readers for your incredible patience as you waited for this book. You contacted me many times, asking for updates and telling me how much you wanted to read it. Many thanks for sticking with me and the series during the delay. I hope LOCKDOWN was worth the wait for you!

—Jen J. Danna, writing as Sara Driscoll